Gone

from

Lakewood Med

Book Five of the Lakewood Series

TJ Amberson

GONE FROM LAKEWOOD MED
Book 5 of the Lakewood Series
by TJ Amberson

Text by TJ Amberson 2022
Prior edition text by TJ Amberson 2020, 2021
Cover art, design, and layout by Maria Spada and TJ Amberson 2022

Paperback ISBN 978-1-7366513-2-2

For those in Pago Veiano
who so graciously welcomed me as part of the
family

Books by TJ Amberson

Love at Lakewood Med
Back to Lakewood Med
New in Lakewood Med
Change for Lakewood Med
Gone from Lakewood Med

Fusion
Between
The Kingdom of Nereth
The Council of Nereth
The Keeper of Nereth

One

It's going to be a long night.

With a sigh, I scoot my chair closer to my desk and begin scrolling through the long list of patient charts that have been piling up in my inbox over the course of my shift. My eyes widen when I realize just how many charts there are for me to finish. Twenty-six, to be exact. I've seen twenty-six patients today, and like always, my shift has been so busy that I haven't had a chance to start a single note. I sigh again, resigned to the daunting fate of having hours of documentation ahead of me. At least I wasn't supervising a medical student or resident today, too, otherwise I would need to review, addend, and co-sign those charts as well.

I try to get comfortable in my chair, and then I open the first chart so I can start working on my note. Before I can type a word, however, an announcement suddenly blasts out from the overhead speakers:

"Code Blue, ETA five minutes. Code Blue, ETA five minutes."

My body jolts, and I whip up my head to scan the mayhem of Lakewood Medical Center's gigantic emergency department. Through the fray, I catch a glimpse of the charge nurse, Laura. She's on the red landline phone that's designated for taking calls from incoming EMS crews. My heart rate ticks up another notch.

A coding patient is being brought in.

Moving fast, I click the computer mouse to exit out of the chart, push back from my desk, and spring to my feet. I yank off my long white doctor's coat and hang it over the back of my chair. I sling my stethoscope around my neck, cinch my ponytail tighter, and straighten my black scrubs top. With a familiar sense of adrenaline coursing through me, I leave my desk and charge toward the resuscitation bays.

As always, maneuvering through this gigantic, high-octane emergency department is like navigating an obstacle course. I dart and weave through the chaos while nurses rush from one exam room to the next, secretaries register patients, ED techs take ECG machines out to front triage, EMS crews wheel in patients on stretchers, radiology technicians steer the portable x-ray machines to patients' bedsides, social workers scurry by while talking on their phones, staff members clean the rooms . . . and all the while, med students, residents, and my fellow attending physicians are examining patients, performing procedures, taking calls, putting orders into the computers, running resuscitations, and trying in vain to keep up on charting.

Like I said, though, the wildness and coordinated chaos around here isn't anything new. Lakewood's emergency department is perpetually filled with critically sick and injured patients. Needless to say, it's a good thing Lakewood Medical Center opened this new humungous, state-of-the-art emergency department about five months ago. I consider myself immensely fortunate that I only had to work in Lakewood's old ED for a few months right after I was hired as an emergency medicine attending physician; that brief experience was more than enough for me to realize just how desperately this vastly larger, high-tech ED was needed.

I continue making my way toward the resuscitation bay where other members of the ED team are gathering. Around me, the typical Friday-night pandemonium persists, but I hardly notice the ruckus anymore. My mind is laser-locked on the task at-hand: someone in cardiac arrest—someone whose heart has stopped—someone who has technically died—is being brought in by an EMS crew, and it will be my responsibility to lead the effort to try to revive the patient.

I cross the threshold to enter the massive, brightly lit resuscitation bay, and I stop to survey the scene. An empty stretcher is positioned in the center of the room. The nurses, Pete and Tom, are preparing IV starts and readying bags of IV fluid. Another nurse, Carrie, is logging into the computer. One of the ED techs, Finn, is putting the code cart into position while a second tech, Penny, is setting up to do chest compressions. The pharmacist, Mona Queen, darts into the room and takes her position near the code cart. Brenna from respiratory therapy is setting out intubation supplies at the head of the stretcher. The secretary, Miriam, arrives; she's carrying a handheld device that she'll use to enter the patient's information once we have it. One of the ED's social workers, Cassandra Barlow, is waiting in a corner until her services are needed. A radiology technician is setting up the portable x-ray machine on the other side of the room.

Tom, who as usual is wearing a brightly colored t-shirt that contrasts with his generic, hospital-issue blue scrub pants, looks up from what he's doing and gives me a succinct nod. "Hi, Doctor Thatcher."

"Hi, Tom." I move to the foot of the empty stretcher. "What do we have coming in?"

"I haven't heard yet." Tom resumes working. "We're still waiting for Laura to give report."

As if on cue, Laura appears in the doorway. With her typical no-nonsense expression, Laura raises her voice and begins giving the preliminary report:

"Forty-one-year-old male. No known medical history. Witnessed collapse while watching TV at home. Pulseless v-tach on scene. Total downtime now somewhere between fifteen and twenty minutes."

It takes a moment for Laura's words to really sink in, and then a wave of shock and sadness washes over me. The incoming patient is only forty-one—just ten years older than me. Unlike most patients who go into cardiac arrest, this patient is relatively young and presumably otherwise healthy. While it's immensely tragic and difficult every time a patient codes, this gentleman's story shakes me to my core. He's only forty-one. He's too young to die. He has too much life still to live.

I have to help save him.

Adrienne Hayes, my friend and fellow emergency medicine attending physician, skirts around Laura to enter the room. Adrienne peels off the blood-splattered gloves she has on and snaps them into the biohazard bin. She then removes the procedure gown she has on over her scrubs. Still without breaking stride, Adrienne quickly waves to Cassandra, who happens to be her childhood best friend, and then she yanks up her dark blonde hair into a bun and joins the respiratory therapist at the head of the stretcher.

"Hey, Irene," Adrienne greets me above the commotion while she begins checking the intubation equipment. "I was suturing in Room Seventeen when I heard the announcement about the code. Since there aren't any residents available right now, I figured I could help by doing airway. Wes Kent and Ned Godfrey have the rest of the department under control." She pauses and then looks directly at me with her brown eyes. "Wait a second. Your shift is over in a few minutes, isn't it? Would you prefer to do airway and have me run the code? That way, you won't be in here for nearly as long."

I realize Adrienne is right: if I run this code, I'm going to be tied up in here for a long time. There's no telling when I'll be able to get back to working on my other charts. I'll be significantly delayed in leaving work this evening, which means I won't be able to meet my boyfriend for our date tonight. The date was my idea; I arranged for us to have dinner at one of my favorite restaurants because it's my birthday. I've really been looking forward to going out this evening—not because it's my birthday, per se, but because it has been such a long time since Stuart and I have done anything fun at all.

My eyes start shifting between the clock and the empty stretcher in front of me. Stepping down from running this code is the only way that I'll be able to leave work in time to go out with Stuart. Yet for reasons I don't entirely understand, something deep within me is compelling me to stay.

Exhaling a breath, I focus on Adrienne once more. "Thanks for offering, but it's all right. I'll run this."

Adrienne appears as though she's about to say more, but there's a loud noise in the doorway that causes both of us to spin toward it. My heart slams against my chest.

The patient is here.

Several Lakewood Fire and Rescue crew members race into the resuscitation bay while pushing a stretcher that has a man lying motionless upon it. One BLS provider is riding on the side of the stretcher, pumping on the patient's chest. Paramedic Jonathan Blackrock is bagging the patient to administer oxygen via the man's nose and mouth. Paramedic Steve Falco is running fluid through the patient's IV.

The resuscitation bay erupts as the ED team jumps into action. The techs help the EMS crews transfer the patient onto the ED stretcher. Penny assumes the exhausting task of performing chest compressions, allowing the BLS provider to step off the stretcher and wipe his brow. Finn begins hooking the patient to the defibrillator that's on top of the code cart. The nurses get to work placing another IV and drawing blood. Brenna steps in to bag the patient.

Paramedic Falco shouts to be heard over the din. "Forty-one-year-old male. No known past medical history. Watching television with his wife and two children when he slumped forward and became unresponsive. The wife called nine-one-one and began phone-assisted CPR. Upon our arrival, the patient was found to be in pulseless v-tach. Shock administered. He has remained in pulseless v-tach. In total, he's status-post three shocks and two rounds of epinephrine. One liter of saline infused. Total downtime now approximately twenty minutes."

I nod briskly to Paramedic Falco and then meet Adrienne's gaze across the chaos. Taking her cue, she picks up the laryngoscope from the tray beside her and says:

"Talk to me about the airway, Paramedic Blackrock."

"Difficult anatomy." Paramedic Blackrock is also raising his voice to be heard over all the noise. "Unable to intubate in the field. Bagged well, so further attempts at intubation were deferred until ED arrival."

"Copy that," Adrienne replies.

"Secure the airway, Doctor Hayes," I say to Adrienne.

Brenna stops bagging and steps back to give Adrienne room. While Penny continues performing chest compressions, Adrienne adjusts her stance, inserts the laryngoscope into the patient's mouth, and maneuvers the tool to get a view of his vocal cords. With her eyes glued to the patient's airway, Adrienne holds out her free hand. Brenna places the endotracheal tube onto Adrienne's palm. Adrienne slips the tube into the patient's airway and then removes the laryngoscope. Brenna steps closer again, connects the oxygen-delivery device to the end of the tube that's poking out of the patient's mouth, and starts squeezing the bag to administer oxygen.

"Good color change," Brenna announces to me as the colorimetric capnometer changes from purple to yellow.

Adrienne uses her stethoscope to ascultate the patient's lungs. "Good breath sounds bilaterally."

"Hold compressions," I loudly direct.

Penny freezes with her hands a couple inches above the patient's chest. The resuscitation bay goes completely silent as everyone snaps their eyes toward the monitor. My heart is drumming fast as thick tension swirls in the air. A second later, my stomach plummets when a rapidly repeating, arched waveform starts tracing across the screen.

"V-tach," I announce, keeping my voice steady. I look back at my team. "Do we have a pulse with that?"

Tom palpates the patient's neck, and Carrie reaches down to feel the patient's wrist. Both nurses shake their heads.

"No pulse," Tom tells me.

More dread rises up inside me. As I feared, this man remains in pulseless v-tach, a life-threatening heart rhythm that doesn't circulate the blood and oxygen he needs throughout his body. Every second this man's heart doesn't pump in a coordinated manner increases the risk that he'll sustain permanent hypoxic injury to his organs—and if we can't get this man back into a perfusing heart rhythm fast, we won't be able to revive him at all.

This man can't die, though. He has far too much life left to live.

I roll back my shoulders and look at Tom. "Prepare to defibrillate."

Tom promptly hits the button on the defibrillator. It lets out a shrill wail, which rises in pitch and then becomes a two-toned alarm to indicate it's charged.

"Everyone clear," I order above the noise. I look again at Tom. "Proceed with defibrillation."

Tom pushes another button on the machine. A loud buzzing sound cuts through the air, and the man's body shakes slightly as the burst of electricity is shot into his heart through his chest wall.

"Resume compressions," I tell Finn and Penny. I flick my eyes to Pete. "Administer one of epi and a dose of amiodarone."

The next two-minute interval of the code commences, with every passing second feeling like an eternity. Finn starts pounding on the man's chest while Penny rests her arms. Mona pulls a dose of amiodarone and epinephrine from the code cart and hands them over to Pete, who administers the medications through one of the patient's IVs. Tom hangs another bag of fluid. Carrie draws a tube of blood for more point-of-care lab testing. Brenna continues bagging the patient. The EMS crews pack up their supplies and exit the room. Laura appears in the doorway again, this time to announce that the patient's wife has arrived; Cassandra rushes out to meet with her.

I look to Adrienne, who remains at the head of the stretcher beside Brenna. With the patient's airway secured, Adrienne's role in here is done.

"Thanks for handling the airway," I tell her. "You're cleared to go."

Good luck, Adrienne mouths before she walks quickly out of the room to resume caring for her other patients.

I do another check of the clock and then drop my gaze to the man on the stretcher. Something sobering stirs inside me. I'm usually able to keep my feelings contained until a code is over, at least, but for some reason, this man's story is resonating within me too powerfully to ignore. This man was going about his routine and enjoying time with his family only hours— only minutes—ago. He's a husband. A father. He surely assumed he had lots of life still in front of him. He undoubtedly has a list of things he planned to get around to doing "one day." He must have so much more he wants to accomplish, do, and experience.

My heart thuds again as another thought hits me with staggering, perfect clarity: this man's story resonates because his situation reminds me a lot of . . . me.

Swallowing hard, I look again at the clock. The two-minute interval is almost over. I'm about to call for another rhythm check when a woman's distraught cry fills the resuscitation bay. My eyes leap toward the source of the sound. A woman is hovering outside the room, sobbing and clutching her hands to her chest, while Cassandra and Laura comfort her. The woman appears to be in her late thirties or early forties. She has her hair pulled up in a messy bun, and she's wearing mismatched slippers, suggesting she left her house in a rush.

I pull in a sharp breath. This woman must be the patient's wife.

The woman suddenly puts her eyes right on mine. Her gaze is terrified. Stunned. Pleading. In the split-second of silent communication we share, I understand what she's trying to tell me. This woman is begging me to save her husband's life. She's not ready for him to leave her.

My legs are shaking as I turn back to the team. "Hold compressions."

Finn takes his hands off the patient's chest. Once again, the resuscitation bay becomes totally still, and everyone turns toward the monitor. There's another excruciating moment of waiting, and then the silence is broken by the sound of a beep. And then another. And another. A new waveform begins tracing across the monitor—a waveform that looks like an organized heart rhythm going at a normal rate.

"Do we have a pulse with that?" I ask, barely breathing.

Tom palpates the patient's neck again. He puts his eyes on mine, and this time he shows a slight smile. "We have a pulse."

Relief overcomes me. It takes all I have to keep my voice even. "All right, everyone, we have return of spontaneous circulation. Let's initiate therapeutic hypothermia protocols."

"You got it!" Carrie flashes a thumbs-up before she dashes off to get the cooling machine. The device will keep the patient's body at a mildly hypothermic temperature to reduce the oxygen his body needs while he's recovering from his cardiac arrest.

I hear more crying from the doorway, and I check that direction once more. The patient's wife is brushing fresh tears from her face—this time, they're clearly tears of relief as Cassandra and Laura explain that her husband is alive. While I'm sure that's all the information the wife will process for now, I know Laura will also explain that the patient has several days in the ICU ahead of him, both to receive care and to undergo testing to determine what caused him to go into cardiac arrest in the first place. The patient has a long way to go, of course, but I'm optimistic he has a chance for a meaningful— even complete—recovery.

I scan the room. Brenna is getting the patient connected to the ventilator, which will be used to support the patient's respirations for as long as he needs. Pete and Mona are preparing medication that will keep the patient comfortably sedated while he's on the ventilator. The radiology tech has brought the portable x-ray machine to the bedside to obtain a chest film. Carrie and Tom are getting the cooling machine into place. Penny is readying to obtain and an ECG. Finn and someone from environmental services are starting to clean up the mess that was created during the resuscitation. Miriam has joined Cassandra, Laura, and the patient's wife.

Breathing easily for the first time since I heard the code was coming in, I step back from the stretcher and go to the high-tech, standing-desk workstation that's nearby. In a brilliant design move that was suggested by Dr. Kent, the leader of the movement to get this new ED built, the resuscitation bay workstations were positioned so that whoever is using them can still keep an eye on the clinical care that's happening in the center of the room. While standing behind the desk and watching the team's efforts playing out before me, I use the phone to call the hospital operator and request to have a STAT page sent to the on-call intensivist, the attending physician who manages patients in the medical ICU. After hanging up the phone, I log into the computer to review the patient's initial lab results, ECG, and chest x-ray. No more than another minute passes before the phone at my workstation rings. I answer and succinctly tell the intensivist about the patient. The intensivist states he'll have the ICU bed manager start working on preparing a room, and he'll be down to see the patient soon.

It turns out that when he said he would be down *soon*, the intensivist wasn't exaggerating. Shortly after I've hung up the phone, returned to the stretcher, and started examining the patient, the intensivist arrives. He first speaks with the patient's wife, who's still watching from the doorway. When the intensivist looks my way, I give him a nod. The intensivist turns back to the wife and says something else to her. He then leads her into the room.

The ED team falls respectfully quiet and makes room for the woman to get to her husband's side. With more tears cascading down her cheeks, the wife reaches over the stretcher railing to cradle one of her husband's hands in hers. Still holding his hand, she bends down and kisses her husband on the forehead.

"It's me, honey. I love you so much. You're going to be okay, and I'll be with you every step of the way," she whispers in her husband's ear. She unexpectedly raises her head to look at me. "Thank you for saving him."

My breathing hitches, and I have to fight back tears of my own. "You're welcome."

The intensivist gives me a smile before he begins examining the patient. With the patient officially transferred to the intensivist's care, I step away from the stretcher. Laura soon returns to the resuscitation bay to announce that an ICU bed is ready for the patient. Finn hooks the patient to the portable monitor while the rest of the ED team gets things ready to safely transport the patient from the ED to the ICU.

Watching again from the workstation, my eyes remain fixed on the man who's lying motionless on the stretcher. Incredibly, this man escaped the grasp of death. One day, he'll return to the life he knew . . . but something tells me that he'll never view life the same way again. This man and his wife won't ever take *living* for granted. They'll truly understand what's important. They'll cherish time with loved ones. They'll appreciate the little moments. They won't pass up opportunities, and they won't put off things they want to do or experience. They'll go forth with a deeper understanding of how precious and fleeting life is.

The adrenaline that has been pounding through my body finishes fading away, and as my mind calms, for some reason, I suddenly find myself recalling the final line of Mary Oliver's poem, "The Summer Day":

Tell me, what is it you plan to do with your one wild and precious life?

The poignant question hits me hard because, for the first time in my life, I realize that I don't know how I would answer it. Up until now, I've never doubted what I needed to do in life. After all, as anyone in the medical field will attest, my life was charted out for me by default almost from the moment I fell in love with medicine and decided to pursue it as a career. First, I had to ace the four fiercely competitive pre-med college years while also shadowing physicians, doing volunteer work, helping in labs, tutoring, and attending pre-med meetings and study sessions. After college, it was time to prepare for the grueling MCAT exam. Successfully passing the MCAT led to the lengthy process of applying to medical school. Next came the four rigorous, riveting, exhausting med school years. Upon graduating from med school, I moved away from the Lakewood area for the three incredible, career-forming years of my emergency medicine residency. About a year ago, I finished residency, and a few months later, I finally achieved my longtime dream of being hired as an attending physician here in Lakewood Medical Center's nationally renowned emergency department.

Now, though, as I replay the past eleven or twelve years through my mind, a profound and unexpected sense of aimlessness fills me. It's a sensation I don't understand. How is it possible that after all I've done, and after all I've seen and been through, that I feel . . . *lost*? I followed a plan, devotedly working toward my goal of becoming an attending physician in this high-acuity ED. Yet I'm stunned to find myself wondering: now that I'm here, what do I really want to do with my life?

The question is profoundly, dauntingly layered and complex. Unlike most people my age, I had to sacrifice my late teens and all of my twenties to the altar of my education and training. I basically had to put other aspects of my life on hold. Beloved hobbies were abandoned. Vacations needed to be skipped. Social events had to be missed. It never bothered me before, but in this moment, I cringe when I contemplate how much I've missed out on over the years.

With all that I had to give up, it's a miracle I've managed to maintain a relationship with my boyfriend, Stuart Morrison. Perhaps the reason our relationship has endured is because Stuart is totally wrapped up in his job, too. In a way, our demanding, merciless schedules allow us to relate to one another . . . but now I see that our schedules are also a reason why we've never noticed how much of life is passing us by.

The ED team wheels the patient out of the resuscitation bay, and I watch after them until they're gone from view. I've always believed there's something to be learned from every patient, and in this moment, I acknowledge that this man—this stranger—has perhaps taught me the most crucial lesson of all. While I love practicing medicine, I no longer want my job to be the only thing my life entails. I don't want to miss out on the other wonderful things life has to offer. Life is too short. Too fragile. Tomorrow isn't guaranteed. So I don't want to keep waiting to do the things I want to do. I need start living—really living—today.

My heart starts drumming with a sense of resolve that's both intimidating and empowering. Immersed in my thoughts, I step out of the resuscitation bay and return to my workstation. I sit down, reach under my desk, and fish around in my bag, which is at my feet. When I locate my phone, I type in my passcode. The phone opens in selfie mode, and I freeze when I find myself staring at my reflection. My long, thick, dark brown hair is hanging limply in a ponytail, missing any sign of the sheen it used to have. My green eyes appear sunken and tired. My complexion is pale. It's a harsh reminder that I can't even remember the last time I looked or felt rested.

Quickly exiting out of camera mode, I compose a text to Stuart, explaining the situation and apologizing that I have to cancel our date. As soon as I hit the *send* button, I feel a terrible jab of remorse. Missing my own birthday dinner isn't exactly living more fully, but I have no choice. All I can do is push aside my self-pity, reminding myself that uncertain and variable hours, disrupted sleep patterns, and working nights, holidays, weekends—and even birthdays—are part of what comes with a career in emergency medicine. I truly do love the specialty; in many ways, the unpredictable, high-stakes nature of emergency medicine is precisely why I chose it for my career. So missing a birthday dinner isn't that big of a deal.

Or is it?

Suddenly, I'm not sure.

I move my chair closer to my desk, attempting to focus on charting. Thankfully, if there's any time that I'll be able to summon the will to power through hours of documentation, it's tonight. Starting tomorrow, I have two weeks off. *Two weeks off.* Two. Weeks. Off. Though the break has been on my calendar for months, I still can hardly believe it's real. This will be the longest break I've had since . . . well, since before residency . . . no, actually, since before medical school . . .

I feel more gnawing regret, which I do my best to ignore. I remind myself that Stuart and I can celebrate my birthday later. Besides, I'm sure Stuart won't mind having to delay our date. Just this morning, in fact, when we were talking on the phone, Stuart mentioned that he's swamped at work, so I'm guessing he'll actually be relieved when he hears my birthday dinner has been postponed.

"How did it go in there, Irene?"

I look up to see Adrienne taking a seat at the workstation beside mine. Since I last saw her, she has donned her long white doctor's coat over her scrubs, and she has her hair hanging loosely around her shoulders. In striking contrast to my own appearance, Adrienne basically looks like a supermodel. She naturally always does, even when she's makeup-free, wearing scrubs, and working swing shifts. That being said, while Adrienne's looks may make her appear like a social media influencer, she's a confident, calm, brilliant physician, and a wise and loyal friend.

"I saw the intensivist down here," Adrienne goes on, "so I assume the code must have gone okay?"

I nod. "We managed to get return of spontaneous circulation, and I'm cautiously optimistic he'll have a good recovery."

"That's awesome." Adrienne smiles warmly. "Nice work in there."

"Thanks. It was definitely a team effort, though. Great job with the airway."

"I was happy to do it." Adrienne's fingers fly over her keyboard as she enters orders for one of her patients. "We new attendings have to have each other's backs, right?"

I laugh and reface my own computer. "Definitely. Though as hard as it is to believe, I suppose we're not really *new* here at Lakewood anymore, are we?"

Adrienne stops typing. "You're right. It's hard to fathom that it has been a year since we both finished our residencies, and that it has been about nine months now since we started working here." She shakes her head. "It's crazy how fast time flies. Makes me wish life would slow down, you know what I mean?"

I look toward the resuscitation bay and exhale a breath. "I think I know exactly what you mean."

Adrienne resumes typing, but then she stops again. "Oh, I almost forgot!" She reaches under her desk and grabs her bag. Reaching inside her bag, she pulls out a bright pink envelope and hands it over to me. "Happy birthday, Irene."

"Aw, thank you." I accept the envelope with an appreciative grin.

I open the envelope and slide out the beautiful card from inside it. As I do so, something falls out of the card and onto my lap. It's a gift card to my favorite ice cream parlor— the place where I took Adrienne after I met her at the new-attending orientation last year.

"This is perfect!" I pick up the gift card and show Adrienne another smile. "With this July heat wave, you and I should definitely go treat ourselves."

Adrienne laughs. "I won't complain. However, I was thinking you could use that to go out with Stuart. You know, make it part of your birthday celebration or something."

My smile falters, and I slip the gift card back into the envelope. "That's really thoughtful of you, but Stuart doesn't eat sugar. Ever. Not even on birthdays."

Adrienne's eyes momentarily go wide, and then she clears her throat. "I, um, applaud him for being so conscientious about his health." She gets to her feet and adjusts her stethoscope around her neck. "Here I was, thinking I was good about maintaining a healthy diet and exercise routine, but even I don't mind splurging once in a while."

"I don't mind, either," I reply. "Stuart, however, is adamantly opposed to anything remotely unhealthy, so on those occasions when I do indulge in a treat, I typically wind up doing so alone."

Adrienne observes me, and I'm pretty sure there's a hint of genuine pity in her gaze.

I make myself busy putting the birthday card into my bag. "Anyway, I suppose there's some good news: if Stuart won't join in, that means more ice cream for you and me."

Adrienne smiles and opens her mouth to reply, but she's cut off when a man's belligerent shouting starts echoing through the ED. Adrienne checks over her shoulder. I also look toward the noise. A BLS crew is wheeling a man into a nearby exam room. The man is yelling about how upset he is that his chest hair got singed off when he tried lighting leftover fireworks while hanging upside-down from his back deck. Clearly, this man is yet another latent Fourth-of-July casualty; they've been trickling in all week.

"I should go hear report from the EMS crew about this new guy." Adrienne shows me another smile as she backs up. "Happy birthday, Irene. I'll talk to you soon."

With a wave, Adrienne turns and heads toward the new patient's exam room. I resume working on charts, but soon I hear a ping from my phone. It's a text from Stuart. As I predicted, he's fine with the change of plans, noting the delay in celebrating my birthday works out better for him, anyway, since he wanted to stay late at the office tonight.

I stare at Stuart's text for a long second or two, and then I put away my phone. As if drawn there, my eyes drift back to the resuscitation bay. I next look across the department. I glance at the clock. Lastly, I look back at my computer and all the charts I still need to finish.

I love emergency medicine, but this can't be all my life entails any longer. It's time to start embracing life more fully. And I'm going to begin tonight.

Two

"Hi, hon. Thanks for coming." I push back from the little table in the corner of the ice cream parlor where I've been waiting for Stuart to arrive. Springing to my feet, I put on a smile and give Stuart a quick kiss. "I know meeting like this was a bit unexpected."

Stuart arches an eyebrow as he removes his jacket and carefully drapes it over the back of the cute chair that's on the other side of the table. He yawns as he takes the seat. "_Unexpected_ is an understatement. It's ten at night, Irene."

"I know, and I'm sorry it's so late." I sit down again, slide my chair closer to the table, and reinforce my smile. "It's Friday, though, and neither of us needs to work tomorrow, so after I finished charting, when I realized there were still a few more hours before my birthday was officially over, I thought it would be fun to do something to celebrate." I gesture around the ice cream parlor. "We've never done a late-night date before, and it's kind of exciting and spontaneous, isn't it?"

Stuart doesn't reply. Instead, his eyes slowly scan the ice cream shop's pink-and-white striped walls and turn-of-the-century décor. Adjusting his glasses, Stuart next lets his gaze drift over to the server's counter, behind which countless mouth-watering flavors of ice cream are on display. He wrinkles his nose slightly, the only demonstration of emotion I've seen from him so far tonight, and then he focuses on me once again. At last, he replies:

"Since there's nothing in here but sugar, I obviously won't be getting anything. I hope you don't mind."

My smile slips. I pull the gift card Adrienne gave me out of my bag. "Actually, they serve several sugar-free flavors here, too, so I think you'll be able to find something to enjoy. My treat."

"Thanks, but it's all right. I'm not hungry, anyway. You know I never eat after six." Stuart half-stifles another yawn and lifts his glasses to rub his eyes. He makes a motion with his hand, indicating I should put away the gift card. "Tell me what you would like, though, and I'll go order for you. I'm buying."

I look toward the counter. What I would *like* is a humungous waffle cone filled with three scoops of ice cream, specifically one scoop of cookies and cream, one of chocolate chip mint, and one scoop of straight chocolate. Because this is a celebration. For several reasons. For one thing, it's my thirty-first birthday. For another, I'm kicking off the longest vacation I've had in years. Also, I got Stuart to do something spontaneous, which alone is cause for a party. Most importantly, though, and little does Stuart yet know, this moment marks the beginning of a wonderful change I hope to implement in our lives. I want to strive to find ways, both through the small things and through the big things, for us to live to the fullest. I don't want us to wish we had seized the moment when we had the chance. I don't want to look back with regret . . . even when choosing ice cream.

Yet when I open my mouth to give Stuart my order, I hear myself say, "I'll take a single scoop of low-sugar vanilla in a cup, please."

Stuart nods with approval and gets to his feet. "I'll be right back."

Stuart walks off toward the counter. I blink as I watch him go, still processing what I said. Though it's only ice cream, I sense something inside me wilt. What happened to my resolve to embrace every moment? To live life to its fullest? To have no regrets? Clearly, I have a long way to go. With a sigh, I slouch in my chair, vowing that the next time I'm out on a spur-of-the-moment date at an ice cream shop, I won't be too self-conscious to order the three scoops I really want.

I catch a delicious whiff of the fresh waffle cones that I won't be enjoying tonight while I continue observing Stuart as he waits in line at the counter. Despite the late hour, Stuart is still dressed in the crisply pressed slacks and button-up shirt he undoubtedly wore to work today. His dark red hair is combed with precision. Also like always, Stuart has his watch-slash-smart-phone-slash-fitness-gadget-slash-computer thing strapped on his wrist, and as the gal behind the counter rings up my pathetic order, I see Stuart check the time on the device and heave a sigh.

I sigh, too. Stuart wasn't always this . . . uptight. When we met through a dating app six years ago, while I was a busy third-year medical student and he was starting a new job at an IT company, he was much more relaxed. His organized-yet-laid-back demeanor balanced the regimented, brutal schedule my medical education required, and I think that was part of the reason why Stuart and I hit it off well. We dated exclusively while I completed my hectic last two years of med school, and Stuart supported me when I made the choice to move away for residency. I knew putting us through a long-distance relationship would be hard, but Stuart understood and respected my desire to get a broader scope of experience by doing residency training in a different part of the country from where I had done med school.

Stuart and I successfully adjusted to a long-distance relationship for the three years I was in residency. Last year, about the same time I returned to the Lakewood area and got hired as an ED attending, Stuart was promoted to the position of a project manager. So all of a sudden, it felt like everything clicked into place for Stuart and me. We had reached our career goals. We had proven we were a solid team, having withstood the curveballs and challenges life had thrown at us. We were settling into a groove with our jobs. So as we advanced into the next stage of our adult lives, I actually began thinking

Stuart and I might start discussing the possibility of settling down together officially, to marry and perhaps eventually start a family.

However, things haven't played out like I anticipated. There has been zero talk of marriage; Stuart clearly prefers to avoid the topic altogether, and I'm certainly not interested in pushing the issue if he's not ready. Even more significantly, though, Stuart has changed since I first met him, and the change has been happening at an accelerated pace over these past few years. The relaxed man I fell in love with has become guarded, particular, and regimented. He's consumed by his work. His sense of humor has been displaced by relentless work-related duty, devotion, and discipline. He's still Stuart, but he's a different Stuart.

That's not to say I don't still love him. Of course I still love him. Besides, I realize I've changed over the years, too, in various ways. In fact, I give Stuart credit for sticking with me all this time; being in a relationship with a med-student-then-resident couldn't have been easy.

"Here you go."

I snap out of my thoughts when Stuart returns to our table, sits down, and slides a tiny cup of low-sugar ice cream over to me. I grab a napkin and a couple of plastic spoons from the dispenser on the table, pick up the miniscule cup, and show Stuart a smile.

"Thanks." I offer him one of the spoons. "Are you sure you don't want to try some of this?"

Stuart makes a sound almost like a scoff. "I'm sure."

Saying no more, I concentrate on my birthday ice cream, trying to decide how much I should put on the spoon to trick my mind into thinking I got more dessert than I really did. I then take my first bite. I have to suppress a grimace. Now I'm glad I only got a single scoop. Low-sugar ice cream is a disaster.

"You mentioned both of us having tomorrow off." Stuart crosses one leg over the other, propping his ankle on top of the opposite knee. "However, I need to go into the office tomorrow and probably again on Sunday. I hope you didn't have anything planned. If so, I'm really sorry."

I set the sad excuse for ice cream on the table. "Your office isn't even officially open on Saturdays. Why do you have to go in?"

Stuart exhales, sounding weary, and the darkness under his eyes reminds me of the excessively long hours he has been working for months now.

"My team has to give our presentation soon, but it's nowhere near ready," Stuart replies.

I don't hide my surprise. "But you and your team have been working on that presentation for weeks, and a few days ago, you told me it was finalized."

Stuart sighs again. "I was wrong. I went through the presentation again today, and I realized it's still not good enough. That's why I must work on it this weekend." He uncrosses his legs and leans forward slightly in his chair. "As

I've told you before, there's a lot riding on this presentation, so it has to be perfect."

I pause to inhale and exhale. "But you're not the one who's supposed to have to work on the presentation," I point out calmly, aware that Stuart does better when we converse like we're in a business meeting rather than when emotion is brought into the equation. "You're the project manager. You have several people on your team—people you supervise—who are specifically hired to do the work. Can't you delegate to them?"

Stuart snorts a laugh. "No. They're precisely the reason why the presentation still isn't good enough. The only way to get this presentation where it needs to be is for me to do the work myself."

I lower my eyes. I see my ice cream starting to melt, forming a pool of vanilla in the bottom of the cup. It kind of fits my mood.

"Gee, Irene," I hear Stuart say, "I didn't realize this would cause you to get so upset."

I raise my eyes to him again.

Stuart tips his head slightly to one side as he observes me. "Did you have something planned for us to do tomorrow? Did you want to celebrate your birthday again?" He checks the gadget on his wrist, taps the screen a couple of times, and reviews what appears to be a mini calendar. "If you insist, I could *try* to cram in all the work I need to do on Sunday, leaving me open to do something tomorrow."

I resume staring at the puddle of ice cream. Do I dare tell Stuart the crazy idea I schemed up while I was waiting for him to arrive here? If he thinks a late-night ice cream run is a bit much, he's going to think my next idea is ludicrous. It's probably not worth even mentioning.

Yet I can't deny how potently the patient encounter I had during my shift is still resonating inside of me. Stuart and I need to start *living*, not merely existing. While we've been swamped with our education and careers, the rest of life has been passing us by. We need to start experiencing this beautiful life, and we need to start doing so now. After all, tomorrow isn't promised.

I clear my throat and put my eyes squarely on Stuart. "Yes, I did have something planned for us to do."

Stuart frowns briefly and makes a few emphatic last taps on his wrist gizmo. "All right. I'll plan to go into the office only on Sunday."

"Actually," I go on, my hand playing with the plastic ice cream spoon, "for what I have planned, you'll need to take off at least a week."

Stuart freezes. He pins a horrified-appearing gaze on me. "What?"

"I was hoping you would take the next week or so off from work," I tell him.

Long pause.

"Irene." Stuart emits an awkward-sounding laugh. "You're kidding, right?"

I shake my head. "I'm not kidding."

Stuart opens and closes his mouth a few times, but no sound comes out.

"Let me explain a little bit more." I break into a smile, my excitement about my plan returning. "I was thinking we should take a trip and leave tomorrow. What do you say to something spontaneous like that?"

Stuart is going pale. "Irene, come on. We can't both just leave for a week. We have responsibilities. We have things we need to do. We—"

"We can make it work," I interject evenly, knowing it's best to interrupt Stuart before he goes too far down the negative road. I begin counting off points on my fingers. "We have the funds. I have over two weeks off from work. You have tons of vacation time accrued. Your team knows exactly what to do to perfect your presentation, and you'd still be back in plenty of time before you have to present it." My smile widens. "So let's not over-think it. Let's just do it. Let's leave on vacation tomorrow."

Stuart starts rubbing his chin with one hand, which he always does when he's stressed. Frankly, I'm surprised there isn't a permanent indentation there.

"Let me guess," Stuart finally utters, "you already have somewhere in mind for us to go?"

"Absolutely." I sit up taller, beaming. "Rome."

Stuart does a double take. "Rome?" he squeaks. "As in, the Rome in Italy?"

"Of course, the Rome in Italy." I laugh. "You know how I've always dreamed of going to Italy, right? Well, this evening I had the crazy idea that we should throw caution to the wind, get on the first-available flight to Rome tomorrow, and just *go*."

Stuart resumes rubbing his chin. "We don't have plane tickets, or hotel reservations, or an itinerary, or—"

"I know, and that's precisely the point." My smile fades, and my brows draw together. "Stuart, we've been so meticulous about every aspect of our lives that we've never noticed how *life*—real life—has been passing us by." I pause to swallow. "At work this evening, I was reminded of how important it is to embrace life while you have it. Life can't be taken for granted." My hand is trembling as I motion between Stuart and me. "I realized that you and I can't continue on like we've been doing. We're not really living. We're just . . . *existing*. I want to make changes to our routine and our priorities so we can start experiencing, exploring, and enjoying life. I don't want us to look back one day with regret about all we didn't do."

Stuart blinks. "Changes. Changes in our priorities."

"Yes." I nod. "Changes to our priorities, our routine, everything."

Stuart searches my face for what feels like a long time. "Is this how you really feel?"

"This is how a really feel." I break into another smile as anticipation about awaiting adventure courses through me again. "So what do you say? Do you want to go to Rome with me?"

Stuart is quiet for another second or two. He then reaches across the table and takes my hands in his. "No, Irene. I don't want to go to Rome with you."

My heart screeches to a stop. "Wait . . . what?"

Stuart releases my hands and sits back in his chair. "I don't know what happened during your shift today, but I do know that what you suddenly proclaim to want isn't remotely close to what I want."

I restlessly tuck my hair behind my ears, trying to process what I'm hearing. "But how can you truly be happy with the way things are now? Our lives are so mundane and almost entirely consumed by work."

Stuart's brows pull lower. "That may be your perspective, but I'm doing precisely what I want to be doing. My job is my life, and that's how I want things to stay."

His remark sinks in, and then my chest gets heavy, and it starts hurting to breathe. "Y-your job is your life?" I echo, stunned. "Stuart, is that . . . the truth? Do you value your job over . . . me? Over us? Over our relationship?"

"You know it's impossible to answer that question." Stuart's affect is strangely aloof now. "What I'm saying is that while you may have all sorts of ideas about how you want to change our lives, I have no desire to change. My life is exactly how I want it, and I won't let anyone force or guilt me into living differently."

I'm clutching my hands in my lap while desperately searching Stuart's face for signs of the man I used to know, but it's like staring into the face of a stranger.

"I'm glad you're happy, Stuart, but my life isn't how I want it to be at all." My voice catches. "I don't want to continue living this way. I *can't* continue living this way."

Stuart studies me for a long time. He then sits up taller, and he adopts the demeanor he uses whenever he gives one of his boring, slightly condescending work presentations. It's a demeanor I know extremely well, since I've let him practice giving presentations to me countless times over the years.

"Well, Irene, it's clear we want very different things out of our relationship and out of life." Stuart is now speaking with exaggerated patience. "That means you're going to have to make a choice: are you going to stay with me, or are you going to abandon our relationship to start chasing some sort of fantasy life you've suddenly become obsessed with?"

I stare at him, feeling totally numb. "The choice you're giving me is no choice at all. I need to change, Stuart. I have to start embracing life." Hot tears are stinging my eyes. "But I'm not going to beg you to follow."

"I see." Stuart exhales a breath. "Then I think the decision has been made. We're breaking up." He shows a platonic smile. "I recognize this isn't the optimal place or time to break up, of course, but I suppose there's never an ideal way to end a romantic relationship."

The floor seems to drop out from underneath me. My stomach lurches. My head gets light. I'm still struggling to breathe. This cannot be happening. This can't be real. This wasn't how things were supposed to go. Stuart and I are a team. We've been together for six years. We were supposed to take a gloriously spontaneous trip together, not break up. Things can't be over between us. We can't end our relationship without attempting to work through our differences.

Yet I know Stuart means what he said. I meant what I said, too. I can't turn back. I cannot remain in this high-stress, work-controlled rut that I call a life. I cannot continue living without passion. I need joy. I need fulfillment. I can't keep putting off things that I want to do. I have to start embracing life while I have the chance.

I grip the edge of the table for support, and when I speak again, it's barely above a whisper. "I agree there's no good way to end a relationship. However, if work is what's most important to you, I certainly don't want to get in your way."

Stuart nods again. He's acting as though we're talking about something as trivial as the weather. "I think that's a reasonable perspective, Irene. I appreciate the years we spent together. I think we both learned a lot from the experience." He pushes back from the table and gets to his feet. "I wish you the best in all you do."

I stare at the man I thought I knew. "You, too," I eke out.

Stuart puts on his coat. He checks the gadget on his wrist and starts heading for the door, but he stops to look back at me.

"Happy birthday, by the way."

Three

I stagger into my condo and weakly shut the door. With a sob, I drop my car keys, collapse against the wall of the entryway, and slide down to the floor. I bury my face in my hands and continue ugly-crying like I've been doing ever since I rushed out of the ice cream parlor. It still hurts to breathe. I think I might throw up. The last few minutes don't seem real. Everything feels like a horrible nightmare I can't wake up from.

Stuart and I broke up.

Memories of my life with Stuart are flying through my mind, each one more bittersweet than the last. It's impossible to calculate all the time and emotion I devoted to Stuart over these past six years. I did so because I loved Stuart, and I believed he loved me. Only now do I realize I was wrong. Only now do I understand the horrible, gut-wrenching truth: Stuart didn't even value and prioritize our relationship enough to take a trip with me.

I lift my head, flinching as my eyes flick across the front room of my condo. Everything in this place—the photos on the walls, the knick-knacks on the shelves, the Blu-rays sitting by the television—reminds me of Stuart. Only this morning, these things symbolized something in my life that I thought was solid and secure. Now, however, each and every item is like a knife to the heart—a humiliating, devastating memorial to a relationship that I never truly understood.

A surge of restlessness rises up inside me fast. With a loud hiccup, I scramble to my feet. My respirations quicken, and my heart clatters in my chest. I have to get out of here. I cannot remain in a place where everything I see makes me think of Stuart . . . not while the pain of our break up is so acute, at least.

I need to get away. Far away. And I need to leave now.

I stumble into my bedroom. In a frantic, surreal daze, I peel off my scrubs, bolt into the bathroom, and take a shower. With my hair still dripping wet, I rush back to the bedroom and change into a lightweight shirt and jeans. Barely able to see through my tears, I drop down onto the chair at my desk, turn on my laptop, and get on the Internet. I navigate to a website I can use to search for airline tickets. And then I pause.

Where, exactly, am I going to go?

Las Vegas? No. Too many memories of a sad excuse for a vacation that Stuart took me on years ago. D.C.? Los Angeles? I heave a sigh while more ideas swirl and collide in my mind. The daunting truth is that I could go anywhere. It doesn't matter. I just have to get away from here. I . . .

I grow still as my thoughts suddenly come into focus, and an idea takes on perfect clarity in my mind. My heart starts beating hard.

I know exactly where I should go.

I get up from my desk, cross the room, and tug open the bottom drawer of my dresser. Reaching underneath a pile of t-shirts, I carefully pull out something that I've had for years but never used: my passport. I slowly stand up straight, and for several seconds, I stare down at the passport that's in my hand, almost awed by its navy blue cover with the gold emblem upon it. Renewed resolve rises up from my core. Stuart may not have wanted to go to Italy, but I've been dreaming about going there for as long as I can remember. And tonight, I'm going to do it.

Whipping around, I return to my desk and resume my Internet hunt. Using the search engine, I click on the tab to book a new flight. I type in *Rome* as the destination. When I realize it's practically midnight, I select tomorrow's date for my departure. I'm soon asked to enter a return date, and I pause. I don't know when I'll be ready to return, so all I can do is click the button to buy a one-way ticket.

My hands are shaking as I finish filling out the required information and press the *enter* key. A few seconds later, the screen reloads, and the search results appear before me. I gasp when I see there's a flight to Rome that's departing in a few hours, and it still has a seat available. Granted, it's a middle seat in row thirty-four, and it's next to the lavatory, but I don't care. All that matters is going to Rome.

I use my phone to access my bank account and put a travel notice on my credit card. I want to make sure my transaction isn't declined; after all, the bank isn't used to seeing charges for international flights accrued by me. This realization triggers another pang of remorse to reverberate through my soul. I've always longed to travel internationally, but I've never done so, even when I could have squeezed in a brief overseas trip between rotations in medical school or residency. Why? Because Stuart never wanted to go with me.

I'm not going to miss out on travel opportunities anymore, though. I'm not going to let *life* pass me by any longer.

Refocusing on my laptop, I resume the process of purchasing my plane ticket. I select the one remaining seat on the flight. I go through the process of entering the rest of the required info. Finally—emphatically—I hit the *purchase* button. After a pause, my phone lights up with a text that lets me know my boarding pass has been emailed to me. I open the email in a state of wonder and amazement. I am going to Rome. *Rome.* I'm actually going to fulfill my lifelong dream—

I notice the time, and my body jolts.

I have a plane to catch.

Leaping up from my chair, I dash across the bedroom, slide open the closet door, unbury the one suitcase that I own, and heave the luggage onto my bed. When I unzip the suitcase, my eyes fall upon an old baggage tag that's crumpled up inside. The tag is from the trip that Stuart and I took to Las Vegas a few years ago. I remember Stuart insisting that the Venice-themed hotel there would be "good enough" to satisfy my dream of going to Italy. At the time, I convinced myself I was okay with the plan, but deep down, I knew Stuart just didn't want to be away from work for more than a couple of days. I heave a sigh, realizing that was one of countless instances when I turned a blind eye to Stuart's real priorities.

I snatch up the bag tag, rip it into tiny pieces, and throw the shards into the trash can. Then I get to work.

Sprinting across the room, I pull open my dresser drawers, scoop out a bunch of underwear and socks, and haphazardly dump everything into the suitcase. Without breaking stride, I charge back over to my closet and start tugging shirts off the hangers, wildly flinging them over my shoulders so they land somewhere in the vicinity of my luggage. I next grab a jacket and a few pairs of jeans. I scoop up a couple pairs of sturdy shoes. Arms full, I spin around to face the suitcase once more.

After pausing only long enough to take a much-needed breath, I dive forward and smash the clothing and shoes into the suitcase along with everything else. I next rush into the bathroom and gather up hair elastics, a hairbrush, toothpaste, floss, a toothbrush, deodorant, a small shampoo bottle, and whatever other toiletries I can get my hands on. I also grab ibuprofen. A lot of ibuprofen.

Scampering back to the main bedroom, I toss the toiletries on top of the growing pile of stuff that's filling my suitcase. The bag isn't large, and it's well beyond capacity now, but like those people who develop super-human strength when their adrenaline is pumping, I manage to close the suitcase and press down on it hard enough to zip it shut.

I pull my still-wet hair into a ponytail and throw on my jacket. I move back to my desk. I slide my laptop into my computer bag, and I toss my phone and its charging cable into the bag, too. Slinging the computer bag over one shoulder, I return to the bed, lift my bulging suitcase down to the floor, and wheel it behind me as I escape the bedroom. Reaching the entryway, I collect my keys and wallet from where I dropped them on the floor. I then stop and look behind me, surveying the condo to make sure there's nothing I'm forgetting to do or pack. Once I'm ready, I draw in a fortifying breath, open the door, and step outside.

It's time for me to seize the moment.

Four

I lock my condo's door and position myself underneath the nearest streetlamp. I check the time on my phone—it's about two in the morning now—and then use an app to arrange a ride to the airport. Within minutes, a little white car pulls up on the other side of the street. Even from where I'm standing, I can hear the thudding bass line of the electronica music that the driver is playing.

Confirming the car's license plate matches the ride I'm waiting for, I hurry toward the vehicle, pulling my suitcase behind me. I open the back door of the car, and I slide inside with my suitcase and computer bag securely in my grip. Once I've buckled my seatbelt, the driver pulls away from the curb. In a rush, it hits me all over again: I'm on my way to the airport.

The driver still doesn't say anything, and I don't mind. I'm not exactly in the mood for talking. Instead, with the music pounding in my ears, I just stare out the window at the passing scenery. At times, tears sting my eyes. Other times, I'm filled with determination. More than once, though, I have to tell myself that Stuart and I really broke up. Our six-year relationship is over. A huge part of my adult existence, and something I structured a significant part of my life and identity around, is suddenly gone. The man I loved, and the man who I thought loved me, chose to prioritize his job over me—over *us*. The pain is unspeakably acute. The void is devastating. I'm hurt and humiliated. Yet much like the patient I cared for during my last shift, there is one tiny silver lining: I have a new lease on life, and I'm determined to make the most of it.

"What airline?"

I snap out of my thoughts when I hear my driver speak for the first time. He's peering expectantly at me through the rearview mirror. I glance out the windshield, and my eyes widen with surprise. We're already pulling into the airport.

"Miss?" The driver is still studying me through the rearview mirror, and I'm starting to get nervous about how much time is passing while he's not watching the road. "What airline?"

I clear my throat. "Journey Airlines."

The driver pulls up to the curb where there's a hanging sign displaying the logo for my airline. I push open my door, slide out of the backseat, and pull my bags along with me.

"Thanks," I tell the driver before shutting the door.

The driver gives me a nod, adjusts his wireless earpiece, and zooms away, his music fading fast as he disappears from view.

Suddenly, I'm standing alone on the curb. I look around, the reality of my situation sinking in fully. It's in the middle of the night. I'm by myself at the airport. I'm dragging around my suitcase, but I don't even remember what I packed. My boyfriend and I just broke up. I'm trying to re-invent my life. I'm about to leave the country without having any sort of plan whatsoever.

Perhaps this impulsive, liberating, seize-the-moment plan of mine might not have been such a good idea.

I sigh despondently. What am I really doing? What possessed me to think that rushing off on an overseas trip would be helpful? I should go back home and start working on sorting out the utter mess my entire life has suddenly become.

I wince. I can't go home. I refuse to go home. My life may be a complete disaster, but it's the only life I have, and it's time for me to start living it.

Gripping my suitcase more tightly, I hike my computer bag up onto the other shoulder and march through one of the large sliding doors that lead inside. The airport is busier than I expected it would be at this time of night. Lines and crowds are everywhere. Sappy instrumental music is playing overhead, interrupted frequently by loud safety announcements that echo throughout the terminal. The air is tinged with the aromas of newspaper, gummy candies, and exhaust fumes that rush in from outside every time the doors slide open. An airport employee zips by me driving something that looks like an elongated golf cart, nearly running me over.

Per the email I received when I bought my ticket, even though I have a boarding pass, I'm still required to do an in-person check-in for my international flight. Scanning the ticketing area, I spot a lone customer service agent standing behind a Journey Airlines desk, and I hurry in her direction. The check-in process goes fast, especially since I'm not checking a bag, and the agent issues me a freshly printed paper boarding pass.

"You'll be departing from gate fifty-six," the agent informs me with a yawn.

"Thanks."

I back up from the counter and glance down at the new boarding pass, which is already becoming wrinkled in my grip. I feel a punch of urgency when I read that I only have an hour before my flight starts to board. I need to get moving.

I shrug my computer bag higher up onto my shoulder, grab my suitcase by its handle once more, and run to the closest security checkpoint. Once through security, I pause only to check the giant monitor on the wall in order to confirm my departure gate. I then resume scampering through the airport, following the signs that lead me down an escalator and onto an underground train, which takes me on a short ride to the terminal that I need. As soon as the train stops and its doors open, I rush off, but then I'm forced to an abrupt halt. In front of me is a plethora of barricade tape and orange construction cones, and there's a sign that says the *up* escalator is broken. With a groan, I pick up my suitcase, trudge over to the long staircase, and begin the climb.

Flushed and breathing hard, I summit the staircase to reemerge at ground level. I drop my suitcase back on the ground, wiggle my sore fingers, and peer around. There's one store that's still open, and I bolt toward it. Scouring the store's shelves, I grab water bottles, a few bags of trail mix, a cheap outlet converter, and some home-decor magazines to read on the flight. I pay for my items, exit the store, and charge for my gate. By the time I reach my destination, my head is pounding, I'm panting, and my shoulder is aching from hauling my computer bag for so long. The good news is that the monitor at the gate confirms I'm in the right place, and my flight is departing on time. I'll take that as a win.

I hear an ominous chirp from my phone, which is buried in my computer bag. The phone's battery is almost dead. I look around, hoping to locate a place where I can sit down, catch my breath, and charge my phone, but the whole area is packed with people. Exhaling hard, I start wheeling my suitcase through the crowd, attempting to find a vacant seat while not rolling over anyone's feet with my suitcase in the process. I finally spot two available chairs by a large window that overlooks the tarmac, and to my relief, there's an outlet between the seats.

I practically collapse onto one of the open chairs. With a sigh, I slide the computer bag off my shoulder, drop the plastic bag that contains my purchases from the shop, shake out my arms, and roll my suitcase off to one side. I then start staring at nothing while attempting to collect my thoughts.

Another chirp from my dying phone brings me back to the moment. I bend down and begin digging around in my computer bag to locate the phone's charging cable. As I do so, out of the corner of my eye, I see someone take the open seat beside me and promptly plug a huge laptop power cable into the single outlet that's between our chairs . . . the outlet I was going to use to charge my phone.

I pause, still bent down over my bag. I realize I'm grinding my teeth. Any other day, I wouldn't care about the outlet getting used. Any other day, I would assure myself that I'll be able to charge my phone on the flight, and if not, it won't matter since I can't get reception in the air, anyway.

This, however, isn't any other day. This is the day when my whole world went off the rails. This is the day I realized that I need to overhaul my life. This is the day my boyfriend and I broke up. This is the day when I need to take control of something, and this little outlet is going to be it.

I sit up fast, phone charger in my grip, and spin toward the person in the chair beside me. "Excuse me, but I was going to use that outlet. I . . ."

I freeze when I find myself staring at the most handsome guy I've ever seen in my life.

I gulp.

The handsome guy with the laptop appears to be about my age. He has thick brown hair, mesmerizingly dark brown eyes, and an olive complexion. His strikingly handsome features and jaw line are perfectly well-defined, and even though he's seated, it's clear he has a muscular build. He's wearing a crew-neck shirt, a jacket, and dark jeans. He has a professional-appearing suitcase and computer bag at his feet.

"I'm sorry?" The guy has his laptop resting on his thighs, and he's studying me with his eyebrows slightly raised.

Mentally slapping myself out of my mesmerized stupor, I sit up taller and use my free hand to tuck a loose strand of hair behind one ear. "I said I was planning to use that outlet."

The guy's eyes track my movements while I work on my hair, and then he puts his gaze back on mine. "I see. I didn't realize this outlet was reserved."

"Well, it . . . was," I sputter, growing flustered under the guy's steady gaze. I try again. "I mean, it is . . . I mean, I'm trying to charge my phone."

The guy's hypnotically dark eyes begin glistening with something that looks suspiciously like amusement. "And I'm trying to charge my laptop."

I do a double take, and my mouth falls open. Is this guy actually going to *fight* me over this?

"But I need it." I glance down at the outlet like it's the last source of water in the desert.

The guy breaks into a breathtakingly handsome grin. "So do I."

My phone chirps again.

With a huff, I lean closer to the guy to steal a glimpse of his monitor. "How much battery life does your laptop have left?"

Still grinning, the guy leans toward me in return. "How much battery life does your phone have left?"

I look up at him, and our eyes lock. Under his dark-eyed gaze, a fire ignites inside my chest, and a tingle zips down my spine. I draw in a shaky breath and promptly refocus on his computer.

"You've got twenty-four percent battery life left," I point out. "My phone only has . . ."

I trail off when I process what the guy has up on his computer screen. He's surfing a website of vacation rentals, and currently he's looking at an apartment in Rome. There are only a few pictures of the apartment on the website, but it's evident the place is gorgeous. With increasing curiosity, I skim the rest of the information. The apartment is described as being located in a quiet neighborhood near the Colosseum, and it's managed by someone named Donato Conti. I see Mr. Conti's profile photo in the corner of the screen, and I nearly smile. He's an adorable, elderly Italian man with a warm twinkle in his eye. He . . .

I suddenly remember that I'm leaning into the sexy guy while blatantly staring at his computer screen. In a rush, I become acutely aware of the heat of his nearness and the incredible scent of his cologne. My face flushes, and I quickly sit up straight and lean as far back from the guy as I can.

"Wow," I blurt out clumsily. "That apartment looks amazing."

"I think so," the guy replies in a steady tone, though another grin is tugging at his lips.

My phone chirps once more, gasping its final breath. The sound snaps me out of the spell that this guy has cast upon me. Readopting a serious tone, I clear my throat and go on:

"Well, anyway, my phone is about to die, and I specifically sat down in this chair because I intended to use the outlet to charge my phone before my flight."

The guy's lips curve upward in an aggravatingly alluring way. "And I specifically sat in *this* chair with the intention of using the outlet to charge my laptop before the flight."

I flare my nostrils. "Fine." I gather my things, stand up, and turn the other direction. "You stay here and charge away. I'll go let my phone die somewhere else."

"Wait," I hear the guy say, "I was only joking with you. There's—"

"Don't worry about it," I cut him off.

I take a step to leave but halt when I notice that there's another outlet on the other side of my chair . . . the outlet that's actually intended for the occupant of my chair to use.

"Oh." I blush hard and sheepishly look over my shoulder at the guy. "There's another outlet . . . right here."

"Yeah." The guy appears to be trying really hard not to resume grinning. "That's what I was going to tell you. I—"

An announcement blares out from overhead speakers. Spinning around, I see an airline employee standing behind the desk at the gate; she's using the PA system to address the crowd. The employee begins with a greeting. She then states that general boarding will begin in a few minutes, but those who are traveling in Premium Class are invited to board now. I don't know what Premium Class entails, exactly, but I'm guessing it involves more leg room, less noise, decent food, and maybe even one of those hot towels to put on your face.

There's a rumbling of activity throughout the area as the lucky souls who will be enjoying the luxuries of Premium Class during the flight start lining up to board. They're mostly somber-appearing business types who are dressed in suits and in possession of fancy luggage.

I remove my own boarding pass from my pocket and look it over again. I've been assigned to Boarding Zone Eight. I can't say for sure, but I have a sneaking suspicion this means I'll be stuck waiting to board for quite a while.

I stuff my boarding pass back into my pocket while my thoughts return to the guy with the laptop. He had no business messing with me, but technically I was the one who was wrong about the outlet, so I suppose I owe him an apology. I turn to face him once more.

"Hey, I'm sorry about . . ."

I trail off. The guy is gone. I peer around, and my eyes come to a hard stop when I spot the guy standing in line with the other Premium Class passengers. He has his laptop bag secured to his carry-on suitcase, and he's carrying himself with an air of someone who travels a lot. Now that he's on his feet, I also have a full view of his height and muscular build, and the sight causes my insides to quiver.

The guy hands over his boarding pass and passport to the airline employee, receives the documents back from her with a polite tip of his head, and steps forward to pass through the gate. Unexpectedly, though, he pauses, and he turns and peers across the crowd at me. He actually has the audacity to break into a roguish smile and wink. I don't have a chance to react before the guy steps through the doorway and disappears from view.

Five

I'm jarred awake when the child in the row behind me kicks the back of my seat . . . again. With a weary groan, I open my heavy, burning eyes. It takes a few seconds to remember where I am and why I'm on an airplane. Once my thoughts come into focus, I sigh and flop my head back on the tiny excuse-for-a-pillow that the flight attendant handed me before takeoff. In a rush, the emotions and exhaustion of the past several hours overwhelm me again, and a few tears drift down my cheeks. I don't bother to wipe them away.

The cabin lights have been turned back on, and the sky outside the airplane windows is bright. It's daytime in this part of the world, though most of the passengers are still dozing. Flight attendants are passing through the aisles, offering folks little bottles of water. The loud hum of the airplane's engines is occasionally accented by the pinging sound of someone hitting a call button. I smell cheese, that generic airplane odor, and the never-failing aroma of the nearby lavatory.

Lifting my head again, I confirm my seat's entertainment console is still stuck on the *Welcome!* screen. It froze about ten minutes after takeoff, and the flight attendant explained there was no way to fix it. Everyone else's consoles seem to be working fine, though, so I've been stealing glances at the movies the other people in my row are watching. (The lady in the window seat to my right has started watching the same rom-com for the third time, and the man in the aisle seat who likes to hog the arm rest is clearly a fan of end-of-the-world-total-destruction-everything-gets-blown-up shows.)

I shift in my chair and uncross my stiffened legs, which is no small feat, even though I'm not particularly tall, because I only have about one millimeter of leg room between my knees and the seat in front of me, which its occupant has kept reclined during the entire flight. Reaching into the seatback pocket, I pull out my phone to check what the time is back at home. Thankfully, the USB port at my seat is working, at least, so I've been able to charge my phone while we've been in the air. Based on what time it is, I calculate there are about two more hours before we'll touchdown in Rome. Suppressing a yawn, I drowsily play a couple rounds of a mind-numbing game on my phone, and then I tuck my phone back into the seat pocket, drop my chin to my chest, and shut my stinging eyes in an attempt to will myself to fall to sleep.

"Ladies and Gentlemen," a flight attendant says over the PA system, shattering the relative quiet. "One of our passengers is experiencing a medical emergency. Is there a doctor on the plane?"

I raise my head.

Everyone on the plane goes silent. There's an apprehensive pause, and then the flight attendant's voice carries over the speakers again:

"If there's a physician on the plane, please ring your call button."

There's another surprised beat of silence, and then passengers start talking to each other in hushed, excited tones. As the sounds of multiple conversations fill the cabin, I sit up taller, trying to get a better view of what's happening toward the front of the plane. However, everyone else is also trying to see what's going on, so all I'm able to see are the backs of the other people's heads.

"Ladies and Gentlemen, we have a passenger who's experiencing a medical emergency," the flight attendant repeats, sounding increasingly anxious. "If there's a doctor on the plane, we request that you ring your call button. We ask all other passengers to remain in their seats."

I glance around the cabin again. As my mind continues waking up, a familiar feeling of adrenaline starts clearing the rest of the weary haze from my mind.

"Ladies and gentlemen," the flight attendant begins another appeal, "if there's a—"

I reach up and hit the call button above my seat, the pinging sound barely audible above the din. The light over me turns on, shining down upon me like a spotlight.

The passenger to my left notices my light. He pauses his end-of-the-world movie and turns to me. "This isn't a good time to bother the flight attendants, sweetheart," he says, the odors of pretzels and tomato juice strong on his breath. "They're trying to find a doctor."

My expression goes deadpan. "They're in luck, then. I just happen to be a doctor." I get to my feet, slip my phone into my jeans pocket, and motion to the aisle. "So if you would please excuse me, I need to go help someone."

The passenger's mouth falls open. He clumsily brushes the sandwich crumbs off his lap, unplugs his earphones from his entertainment console, and squeezes out of his seat to give me room to pass. I slide into the aisle, paying no attention to the other passengers who are staring at me while whispering amongst themselves. I shift toward the front of the plane, making eye contact with a female flight attendant who's rapidly approaching.

"You're a doctor?" the flight attendant asks, her curly hair bobbing with each step she takes.

I nod.

"Wonderful. Please come with me." The curly-haired attendant turns toward the front of the plane and motions for me to follow.

I trail the attendant up the aisle, passing row after row of gawking passengers. When the attendant and I reach the front of the main cabin, she pulls aside a curtain, steps into the Premium Class section, and keeps the curtain held back so I can join her. Once I'm at her side, the attendant lets go of the curtain, which swings closed behind us.

I flick my eyes around. Premium Class is like an entirely different world. There are only eight rows of seats, each consisting of two huge recliner seats on each side of the aisle. Soft LED lighting creates a spacious, relaxing ambience. Passengers are watching movies on large-screen consoles, enjoying delicious-looking breakfast foods, and sleeping with their seats comfortably reclined nearly into a bed.

The glamour of Premium Class isn't what I'm concentrating on right now, however. I'm scanning the seats in a search for my patient. It only takes me a moment more to spot him: a middle-aged man who's seated on the aisle on the left side of the second row. He's leaning forward and appears to be breathing fast. There are two flight attendants, a blonde female and a slender male, standing in the aisle by his seat, and they both look over at me with concern etched in their features.

I make my way to the man, so laser-locked on my new patient that I'm barely aware of anything or anyone else around me. When I reach the man's seat, the two flight attendants step back to give room. I kneel in the aisle in front of the man's chair and do a rapid initial assessment.

He's a well-dressed man who appears to be somewhere in his fifties. His respirations are fast but otherwise unlabored. His eyes are big, and his gaze is panicked. The area immediately around his lips is pale, while the rest of his face is flushed. There's an unmistakable urticarial rash on his chin that extends down the front of his neck to the upper part of his chest, which is exposed between the open top buttons of his collared shirt.

"Sir, I'm Doctor Irene Thatcher," I say, keeping my tone calm and steady. "I'm a board-certified emergency medicine physician. What are you allergic to?"

Still breathing fast, the man shifts his wide eyes to mine. "What? Nothing. I'm not allergic to anything."

I look up at the flight attendants. "Do you have diphenhydramine and epinephrine on board?"

"I'll check." The male attendant tugs open a narrow closet door and begins rifling through it.

I refocus on my patient. "Are you having any difficulty swallowing?"

The man shakes his head.

"Do you feel as though your lips or tongue are swelling up?"

"No," the patient replies, still speaking without difficulty.

"Are you experiencing shortness of breath or chest pain?"

The patient huffs with unmasked annoyance. "No. I'm not feeling anything like that. I just broke out with this rash, and now my arms feel itchy, okay?"

I actually exhale with relief when I hear his retort. The man is moving air well, and he's not audibly wheezing. His rapid breathing appears secondary to his anxiousness, not because his lungs are tight or his throat is swelling shut. Considering we're about thirty-thousand feet in the air, I would definitely prefer to manage a panicked and irritated patient over someone who needs to be intubated because of anaphylaxis.

"Here's our medical kit." The male attendant places a suitcase-sized bag on the floor beside me.

I open the kit and scan its contents. I have to say, I'm impressed. There's a lot of great stuff in here: sphygmomanometer, stethoscope, oropharyngeal airways of various sizes, IV-start kits, bandages, adhesive tape, gloves, syringes, and several medications, some of which are in oral form and others that can be administered via an IV.

I locate diphenhydramine tablets and pop them out of the packaging. With my other hand, I pick up the cup of water that the patient has on his seatback tray. I hold out both the pills and the water for the patient to take.

"Sir, I do believe you're having an allergic reaction, and I recommend that you take these antihistamine pills."

The patient recoils slightly. "Are you joking?"

"No, I'm not joking." I continue calmly holding out the medicine. "It's important that you take this medication to both treat your current symptoms and hopefully prevent your allergic reaction from becoming more severe."

"I'm not having an allergic reaction, all right?" the man barks. "As I've already said, I don't even have allergies." He shakes his head and peers up at the flight attendants. "Is there a different doctor on the plane we could call for assistance? Someone more . . . *experienced*, perhaps?"

The flight attendants exchange a look. The blonde attendant then puts on a smile and tells the man:

"Sir, we made several requests for a doctor. No one else responded."

I adjust how I'm kneeling to prevent my legs from going numb. "Sir, you're welcome to ask anyone else on this plane for his or her opinion or advice. In the meantime, though, I strongly recommend that you take this medication. A straight-forward allergic reaction is one thing. Life-threatening anaphylaxis is an entirely different ballgame, and you should try to prevent it, especially since we're probably somewhere over the North Atlantic right now."

The patient pauses before he looks at me again. He heaves a sigh. "Fine."

The patient snatches the medication and water from my hands, tosses the pills into his mouth, and takes a fast swig of water to wash them down. I sit back on my haunches and continue evaluating him. Since I began speaking with him, he has already calmed down somewhat, and his breathing has slowed to a normal rate. Meanwhile, the rash on his skin hasn't spread. So far, so good.

Pulling my eyes from my patient, I take a moment to check what else is in the emergency kit. I grab the epinephrine injector to have it handy, just in case. I next remove the stethoscope. I then ask the attendants:

"Would you please ask if any passengers have prednisone or ranitidine with them?"

"Prednisone or raniti-what?" The blonde attendant bends down closer to me.

"Prednisone or ranitidine," I repeat before putting in the earpieces of the stethoscope.

While the blonde attendant uses the PA system to make the announcement, I turn back to the patient, hold up the drum of the stethoscope, and ask:

"May I listen to your lungs?"

The patient sets down his water. He rolls his eyes again, but he does lean forward to expose his back. "Suit yourself."

I hear the pinging sounds of call buttons starting to go off in response to the attendant's latest request, and out of the corner of my eye, I see her jog down the aisle and slip past the curtain to venture into the main cabin. I get to my feet and position myself so I'm standing behind the man. Using the stethoscope, I ascultate his lungs. Fortunately, they remain clear.

"Your lungs sound good," I tell the patient, removing the stethoscope from my ears.

"Of course they do. Because I'm not having an allergic reaction." The patient takes another drink of water, swallowing easily. "As I said, I don't have allergies."

I turn on the light above his seat and take another look at his skin. The rash is starting to fade, suggesting the dose of antihistamine is already starting to kick in. Satisfied things are going well thus far, I put the stethoscope around my neck. Keeping my voice low to give the patient as much privacy as possible, I move so I'm facing him again and inquire:

"What medical history do you have?"

The patient sits up and puffs out his chest. "I'm extremely healthy. Only a little high blood pressure, which is controlled with medication."

"What about any new exposures or ingestions? New medicines? New hygiene products? New foods?"

"No, for the last time there's absolutely nothing I'm allergic to, and I . . ." the patient trails off. He blinks a couple of times. His eyebrows rise, and he looks at me again, almost like he's seeing me for the first time. "Hang on, I take that back. A couple of days ago, I was started on amoxicillin for an ear infection. I forgot all about that."

I kneel back down. "And have you ever had penicillin products before?"

"No." The patient's harsh tone relents as he observes me in return. "Are you thinking I'm having an allergic reaction to the antibiotic?"

"I think it's a good possibility."

The blonde attendant reappears from the other side of the curtain and comes my way. She holds out her hands, showing me several travel-sized medication bottles. "A few passengers volunteered these. Hopefully, something will be what you're looking for."

"Thanks." I take the bottles, check the labels, and find the medications I need. I hand over a couple of the pills to the man. "I recommend you take these, too. One is another type of antihistamine, and the other is a dose of a steroid. They'll also help settle things down."

This time, the man takes the medicines without complaint. "Thank you."

Convinced a mid-flight airway crisis has been averted, I remove the stethoscope from around my neck and return it to the kit. I also tuck the epinephrine back where it belongs. I hand the pill bottles back to the attendant. As I work, I gradually start becoming aware of my surroundings. I hear the other passengers' conversations. I smell the foods people are eating. I notice the movie that's playing on the console of the passenger across the aisle.

Zipping the kit closed, I raise my eyes back to my patient, stopping short when I realize that the passenger who's seated next to him— and who happens to be watching me closely at this very moment—is the sexy guy with the laptop. The guy I sparred with about the outlet before we got on the plane. Currently, the guy has his laptop on his seatback table and noise-cancelling headphones down around his neck. Since I last saw him, he has developed facial scruff on his upper lip and chin, which only further enhances his strikingly handsome features.

The guy's dark eyes sparkle with amusement as he shows me an impish grin. "Well, hello again."

I don't have a chance to respond before the male attendant comes to my side. "Excuse me, the captain is wondering if you feel we should make an emergency medical landing before we reach Rome."

Everyone else in Premium Class whips their heads in my direction and goes silent, waiting for my reply. I can almost hear the wheels turning in everyone's heads as they contemplate what a delay will do to their schedules and itineraries.

I get to my feet while doing another rapid assessment of my patient. He's sitting up comfortably and watching a nature documentary on his entertainment console. He's taking sips of water without difficulty. He's breathing normally. His rash has nearly resolved.

"How are you feeling?" I ask the patient.

The patient puts down his cup. "I feel great. The itching is gone. No complaints at all."

I turn back to the attendant. "I think it's safe to continue to our destination."

There's a collective sigh of relief from the passengers who've been shamelessly eavesdropping on the conversation.

"Thank you. I shall inform the captain." The male attendant goes to a phone on the wall, lifts the receiver to his ear, and begins speaking into it quietly.

The blonde attendant returns the emergency kit to the closet and then steps toward me. "I've asked a passenger who was seated just behind the curtain to move to your row for the remainder of the flight. We would like to keep you close by until we land, if that's all right with you."

I shrug. "Sure. That's no problem."

"Wonderful." The attendant tips her head toward the curtain. "This way."

When I take a step to follow after her, I hear my patient say:

"Hey, thank you again, Doc."

I stop to give the patient a smile. "You're welcome. I think you're going to be fine, but allergic reactions can rebound, so please let me know immediately if you have any new or returned symptoms. I also recommend that you have extended monitoring in a medical facility once we land."

"Gotcha," the patient replies. "I can do that."

The blonde attendant chimes in, "My colleague is already notifying the airport in Rome about the situation." She shows the man a well-practiced smile. "Once we land, airport personnel will be standing by to assist with getting you to a local hospital for further evaluation."

"Sounds good," the man tells us both.

The blonde attendant resumes heading toward the curtain. I'm about to follow, but as if pulled there by an invisible force, my focus shifts back to the guy with the laptop. As soon as our eyes meet, he gives me another grin. My heart leaps and then starts beating vigorously within my chest, nearly taking my breath away. I'm so stunned by my own reaction that all I can do is stagger backward a step, quickly spin away from the guy, and chase after the attendant who's leading me to my new seat.

Immediately upon re-entering the main cabin, I find myself under the scrutiny of a few hundred people's inquisitive gazes. The blonde attendant gestures to a nearby aisle seat that has been vacated. I take the chair, and the attendant leans down closer to me and says:

"When we reach Rome, we'll have you and the patient get off the plane first."

"All right." I buckle my seatbelt and motion toward the back of the plane, where the poor, innocent person who had to give up this seat is undoubtedly now stuffed behind a reclined chair and surrounded by sappy movies, a man with pretzel breath, and a kicking child. "Should I go get my things and bring them up here?"

The blonde attendant shows me her dazzlingly white teeth. "My colleague is already retrieving them for you."

I turn and spot the attendant with the curly hair making her way down the aisle toward us. She has my suitcase, jacket, and computer bag in her hands. Summoning Herculean strength, she begins jamming my things into the already-stuffed baggage compartment above my row.

"Also," I hear the blonde attendant continue saying to me, "because medical assistance was rendered during the flight, our protocol is for you to speak with the medical personnel who will be waiting at the gate when we land. They'll want to get a brief report from you before they take the patient to the hospital."

"Certainly. I'm happy to do that." I peer up at the blonde attendant once more. "Out of curiosity, do you know how long that might take?"

"Not long at all," the blonde attendant assures me. "They'll just want a quick report about what happened. The process is brief."

"Great. Thanks."

I exhale and lean back in my seat. I can feel the adrenaline evaporating out of my system and the exhaustion kicking back in. I can't wait to get to a hotel and finally get some sleep.

Six

The process of giving medical report definitely wasn't brief.

My discussion with the medical personnel who were waiting at the gate wound up taking over an hour, mostly because I don't speak Italian, and the medics didn't speak English. After six attempts, I got my phone connected to the airport's spotty WiFi, and then I was able to open the language-translation app that I sometimes use when caring for patients in the ED. The medics and I proceeded to have our entire conversation using the app. I suppose the one upside to the situation was that the delay allowed me to keep an eye on my patient a while longer, ensuring he continued doing well.

Anyway, my patient is now on his way to a local hospital for further observation, and I've just made it through Customs. It's some time in the afternoon here in Rome, but my body certainly doesn't think I should be awake. Admittedly, in my jet-lagged state, the wonder of being halfway around the world for the first time in my life isn't currently forefront in my mind. Instead, I'm trekking through the arrivals hall of

Leonardo da Vinci-Fiumicino Airport in a physically and emotionally exhausted daze. Wetting my parched lips, I pass the luggage carousels while following illustrated signs that point the way to the Leonardo Express train station. From what I gleaned after doing some quick Internet research, the thirty-five minute train ride will take me from the airport directly to Rome's main metro station, Termini, which is in the heart of downtown. Once I reach Termini, it sounds like I can ride either the A or B metro lines to get pretty much anywhere I need to go in Rome.

I make my way outside, where I'm smacked with the sweltering summertime heat. Merging into a passing crowd, I keep following the signs for the train station. I'm starting to sweat as I haul my luggage down a staircase, across a busy road, and up another set of stairs to enter the station's stuffy, crowded central hall. The ceiling is high, and sunlight is pouring in through windows far above. The gray walls are accented by an array of colorful posters and advertisements. The odor of diesel fumes is thick in the air, and constant overhead announcements are ringing in my ears. Above the ambient din, I hear pigeons flying around inside the building.

Using my phone to again reference the information I found online, I reach one of the station's red self-serve kiosks, which is where I'm supposed to buy a train ticket. I'm relieved there's a button on the kiosk's touch screen that converts the instructions into English; after that,

I'm able to figure out how to purchase my ticket to Termini without too much difficulty.

Ticket in-hand, I ride down an escalator to the train platform, validate my ticket at a little green-and-white machine, board the Leonardo Express train, and collapse onto my seat with my luggage. The quiet, partly filled train soon pulls out of the station and begins rolling smoothly along the tracks, emerging into the sunshine to give me a view of graffiti-covered warehouses and apartment buildings with laundry drying from little balconies. The sunshine and the motion of the train start lulling me to sleep, but then one extremely important thought blasts through my mental haze, jarring me wide awake:

I have no idea where I'm going next. I don't even have a place to stay.

In a surge of extreme panic, I sit up fast and again concentrate on my phone. Cell service on the train is slow, but I finally manage to get a signal. Once I'm online, I navigate to a website for making hotel reservations. I enter the pertinent data and hit the *search* button. The results take eons to load, and when they finally do, my stomach crashes. According to the website, there are no available hotel rooms anywhere in the city. None. No vacancies at all.

I stare at the phone in stunned disbelief. This can't be right. Rome is humungous. It's a tourist mecca. There has to be an available place to stay.

Right?

Unease is prickling inside me as I switch to a different travel website and do another hotel search. To my relief, this website shows there is something available. My relief is short-lived, however, when I read that the vacancy is in a hostel where I would share the room with three strangers, and it's located in what reviewers describe as a "shady" part of town. Several other people comment on bed bugs.

With a groan, I drop the phone onto the empty seat next to me and hang my head in my hands, racking my brain in a desperate effort to figure out what to do. My mind is so fried right now, however, that I can hardly think at all.

What am I doing in Rome? Why did I come here without a plan? What possessed me to think that impulsively leaving the country was a good idea, or that charging off to Italy would suddenly let me start living life to its fullest?

Raising my head, I despondently peer out the window, watching the scenery pass. I suppose I could take a train to somewhere else in Italy. If I look long enough, I'm sure I'll find somewhere to stay. However, it's smack in the middle of summertime, which means hotel options will be limited wherever I go. Do I really want to start a hot, exhausting, stressful scavenger hunt across the country in order to find lodging? But do I have a choice?

I moan to myself again. Maybe I just need to admit that this trip was a huge, reckless mistake. Once I get to Termini, I should turn around, ride the next train back to the airport, buy another plane ticket, and return home.

Immediately, my body grows cold at the thought, despite the heat. I don't want to return home. I can't return home. Not yet.

I rest my head against the window, still attempting to think through my options, but my worn out mind wanders and starts replaying the events that led up to me getting in this mess: caring for the coding patient during my last shift, breaking up with Stuart, impulsively buying a plane ticket, sparring with the sexy guy with the laptop—

My heart slams hard. The guy with the laptop. When I was arguing with him at the airport, he was perusing a travel website and had managed to find an amazing apartment near the Colosseum. If I recall correctly, the apartment was owned by a sweet-appearing, elderly man whose name was Donato Conti.

A flash of hope shoots through me. If the guy with the laptop can find lodging in such a great neighborhood, so can I.

I grab my phone, get back online, and navigate to the same website I saw the guy using. I'm first required to create a user profile, and the process proves to be aggravatingly slow over the train's WiFi, which does nothing for my frayed nerves, but I eventually get an account set up.

My fingers fly over the phone as I fill in what I'm looking for: the city (*Roma*), the first day when I need lodging (today . . . gulp . . . cringe), and the last day I need lodging (I have no idea, so I say one week from now). When the website asks for any additional search filters I want to include, I type in "Colosseum" and "Donato Conti." I then tap the *enter* button.

I'm clinging to my phone as I wait for the results of my search to populate, and then I nearly let out a cheer. There are two rental apartments in Rome that are managed by Donato Conti, and one of them is available! Flooded with relief, I click on the available listing to read more about it.

I pause in surprise.

The apartment that's available is the same one the guy with the laptop was looking at when we were at the airport. Apparently, he didn't reserve it. As I noted previously, there aren't many photos of the apartment, but from what I can see, the lodging is lovely. It's described briefly as a "spacious apartment in the heart of Rome" that's within walking distance of the Colosseum.

I note an emblem of a four-leaf clover next to the listing, which apparently means the apartment is considered a lucky find because it's usually booked. Even better, Donato Conti is labeled as a "top-tier host." I don't know precisely what any of that means, but it seems good. Reinforcing my favorable impression are the sixty-three reviews from people who've previously stayed in the apartment; everyone has given the place a top rating. Upon further reading, I learn the apartment has two bedrooms and two bathrooms, it's near a metro station on the A line, it's only a fifteen-minute walk from the Colosseum, and the cost per night is reasonable.

I exhale a breath of relief as I take it all in. I have no idea why the guy with the laptop passed up this incredible place; he was clearly out of his mind. And he's going to be extremely disappointed if he tries to book it later because I'm going to reserve it right now.

Wasting no more time, I click the *reserve* button before the guy with the laptop or anyone else can steal the place out from underneath me. After entering my payment data, a confirmation screen states my reservation request is under review, and I'll receive an email indicating whether or not the host has accepted it.

The train conductor begins talking in Italian over the PA system, causing me to raise my head and look out the window. The train is slowing as it makes its approach into what must be Termini Station. Around me, the other passengers start getting up and collecting their belongings. Taking their cue, I jam my phone into my pocket, sling the strap of my computer bag over my shoulder, and ready my suitcase.

The train lets out a hiss as it comes to a stop at the platform. One of the passengers pushes a button on the door of our car, causing it to slide open, and then he steps off the train. The others begin to follow. Towing my luggage behind me, I hurry to do the same.

Stepping down onto the platform, I'm again doused by the suffocating summertime heat, and I become surrounded by throngs of people who are passing by me in all directions. I see tourists hauling oversized luggage, school-aged kids in matching shirts on some sort of field trip, and locals who are clearly well-adapted to ignoring the chaos. The smells of cigarettes and pastries are thick in the air. Loud announcements spoken in Italian are echoing over the PA system, accented by the shrill sounds of train conductors blowing their whistles.

I start following the throngs toward the doors that lead into the train station. People's rapid-paced conversations continue all around me; it's both intimidating and thrilling to realize I don't understand a word of what anyone is saying. As the crowds thicken, I recall warnings I read on the Internet about Termini being a major hangout for pickpockets, and so I tuck my computer bag close under my arm and tighten my hold on my suitcase. Lifting my chin, I adopt a no-nonsense air and try to appear as though I know what I'm doing while I walk briskly along the platform and enter the massive station.

The cyclone of activity only expands inside. The air in here remains thick with the odors of cigarettes, food, and exhaust. Announcements are still blasting out from overhead speakers. Digital reader boards are flashing with a dizzying array of information about train departures and arrivals. Armed police officers are strolling the premises, keeping a sharp eye on the mayhem.

Steering my suitcase through the fray, I reach a wall that's out of the way, and I stop to catch my breath and get my bearings. There are little shops throughout the station; some are selling food, and others are peddling purses, suitcases, scarves, and souvenirs. There are also several ATMs. Deciding I should have some cash on me, I grab my bags once more, dive back into madness, and head toward one of the banking machines. Thankfully, like when I bought my train ticket, there's a button on the ATM that switches the instructions to English. I withdraw some euros and discreetly stuff the money into my wallet. I can't help smiling. I'm carrying foreign currency. Somehow, it makes this whole crazy adventure feel a little more real.

My stomach growls, prompting me to go next into a tiny, jam-packed café. I grab a water bottle and a huge mozzarella sandwich from the refrigerator, and then I maneuver over to what I assume is the line to pay for my food. When I reach the front of the line, the man behind the counter punches a couple buttons on an ancient cash register and rattles off something to me that I don't understand. Luckily, the amount I owe is also displayed on the register. I fumblingly retrieve some euros from my wallet and hand them over. The man hands me change; I have no idea how much, but I'm not about to clog up the line while I try to count it. Instead, I push my way out of the shop, relishing the feeling of completing my first-ever overseas purchase. It's a small thing, but at the same time, it's not.

I head back to the shade, sit down with my back against the wall, draw in my bags close beside me, and pull out my phone. I have a new email. To my delight and relief, Donato Conti has accepted my payment and agreed for me to rent his apartment for the week. There's even a brief message from the sweet man himself, which is in perfect English. Mr. Conti welcomes me to Rome and provides directions for how to get from Termini Station to his apartment. He's included a map, too, and the route looks pretty simple: catch the A line, get off at the *San Giovanni* stop, and walk approximately fifteen minutes to the apartment. Mr. Conti concludes his message by providing his phone number and asking me to text him after I get off at *San Giovanni*. He'll meet me at the apartment, provide a key, and give me a tour of the place.

I put away my phone, relaxing for the first time in hours. I may have decided to overhaul my life, broken up with my boyfriend, and traveled halfway around the world to a place where I don't know a soul or understand the language, but at least I have a meal and a decent place to stay. With this little bit of comfort, I take a few minutes to eat while enjoying some fascinating people watching. Once I'm done, I pull myself back to my feet, prepared to tackle the last leg of this journey.

Following signs for the metro, I head to the center of Termini and ride an escalator underground. The wide corridor down here is as crowded and bustling as the train station above, and with shops and eateries lining both sides, it feels like an underground shopping mall. I slip into a passing throng, tracking the signs that are marked with a bright red A.

When I reach the turnstiles that lead into the metro station itself, I come to a halt, nearly

causing people to crash into me from behind.
Everyone is scanning tickets across the turnstiles'
electronic readers before proceeding to the
metro platforms. It looks like I'll need to buy
another ticket before I can go any farther.

I slip out of line and turn in a circle,
spotting a row of red-and-white machines
underneath a sign that reads, "*Biglietto Veloce*."
Checking my language-translation app, I confirm
the machines are what I need, and I pull my
luggage against the flow of pedestrian traffic to
reach them. There's an astounding number of
ticket options, and so I just make my best guess
for purchasing a single-ride ticket.

Reversing course with a ticket in my grip,
I return to the turnstiles. It takes me four tries to
scan my ticket, but I eventually make it through,
and I only bang the sides of the turnstile with my
luggage three times in the process. I find the
platform for the A train that's going in the
direction of *San Giovanni*, and I join the others
who are waiting for the train to arrive.

There's a rush of wind from the tunnel at
my left. A bright light appears in the darkness,
and then a train emerges with its brakes
squealing along the tracks. The train stops, and
all its doors open simultaneously. A few people
disembark, and then those who've been waiting
on the platform start shoving themselves into the
overcrowded train cars. I lower a shoulder and
jam myself and my luggage in with everyone else.
Since all the seats are occupied, I squeeze next to

a bunch of guys in business suits who are smashed together in the center of the car.

The train car's doors shut, and it immediately becomes apparent that there's no air circulating in here. At all. This train is muggy, hot, and stuffed with people. It's a good thing I don't get claustrophobic.

The train begins rolling forward, the sudden change in momentum causing me to stagger. I grip the nearest handrail, barely stopping myself from toppling into the guys in the suits. The train makes two stops before reaching *San Giovanni*. When the doors open, I push my way out of the car, dragging my luggage behind me. I'm mercifully met by a hint of fresh air, which is drifting through the station. Trailing the others who disembarked, I ride up an escalator and pass through a turnstile. I feel a stronger rush of wind, and I eagerly inhale another breath. I must be nearing the exit.

I round a corner, and I have to come to another stop. I've reached a junction where I need to choose one of five possible exits out of the station, and based on the signage, each exit leads to a different street. If I go the wrong way, I run the risk of getting lost. And I have a feeling that getting lost would be bad.

I blow a strand of hair out of my face and use my phone to review the message from Donato Conti. Thankfully, he indicated the exit I need. I venture that direction, carry my suitcase up a flight of steps, and emerge onto a busy street corner. Bathed in the blazingly hot sunshine once more, I squint hard to shield my eyes from the intense brightness. I realize I forgot to pack sunglasses, and I make a mental note to buy a pair as soon as I can.

I text Donato Conti's number, letting him know I've reached the station. A moment later, he replies with a thumbs-up emoji, which I take to mean that the sweet old man is on his way to the apartment to meet me.

Keeping my phone discreetly open to the map, I trek down the busy sidewalk. Turning a corner, I come across a row of quaint eateries at my left, where patrons seated at small outdoor tables are talking jovially, enjoying delicious-looking food, and smoking cigarettes. Across the road, perched majestically at the top of a hill, is a stunningly gorgeous white building, which must be the *Basilica di San Giovanni* itself, for which the metro station was named. It's a breathtaking reminder that I'm actually in Italy. Amidst the chaos, I had almost forgotten. I make another mental note, this one to come back later to visit the church. For now, though, I'm melting in this heat, achingly sore from carting luggage, and exhausted beyond description. With the thought of a cool, comfortable apartment almost within my reach, I trudge onward.

I pass a street market where knock-off bags, suitcases, jewelry, purses, and other items are being sold. I turn right onto the next road, which leads into a non-touristy area consisting mostly of tall apartment buildings. The buildings appear clean and well-maintained. Small cars are parked along the curbs, and trees line the sidewalks. I get the sense that this area is safe and quiet, which I'm grateful for. In fact, the only noise I hear is coming from a construction site far in the distance, and based on what I can decipher from some posted signs, the construction is being done on the metro system's C line.

A much-needed breeze stirs the trees. Despite the wind, however, sweat is rolling down my back, I'm certain my cheeks are bright red from the heat, and I'm equally certain my hair has become a frizzy, disheveled mess. Needless to say, I can't wait to get to take a cold shower and crash to sleep.

Staying on the shady side of the road, I continue referencing the map until I reach the final left turn, which brings me to a smaller street that's also lined by apartment buildings. I locate my building up ahead on my right. Like I saw on the website, there's a tall, dark green fence in front of the building with a gate that leads into a small courtyard.

I reach the gate and push it open, the sound of its squeaking hinges drifting through the air before fading away. Wheeling my suitcase behind me, I cross the courtyard and get to the double doors that lead into the building. To the right of the doors, there's a panel of buttons, one for each apartment with the tenant's last name listed underneath it. I find the button labeled "*Conti*," and I give it a push.

Waiting for my host to open the door, I draw in a steadying breath and close my tired eyes. In a few minutes, I'll have a place to rest, clean up, sort out my thoughts, and sleep. Finally, I'll have a chance to—

I jump when there's a loud buzz from the double doors, followed by a clicking sound that indicates the doors have been unlocked. Reopening my eyes, I see one of the doors is being pulled open. I begin getting a glimpse of the invitingly shady foyer inside. I put on my best attempt at an I'm-not-completely-exhausted-or-boiling-in-this-heat smile as I wait for my host to appear.

"You must be Irene," I hear a man say. He doesn't have a hint of an Italian accent. "It's nice to . . ."

The man trails off as he steps outside into the sunlight. I do a double take, blink, stare, and blink again.

This isn't the sweet elderly man whose photo was on the website. This is the hot guy who stole the outlet from me. The guy with the laptop. The handsome man with the mischievous gleam in his dark eyes.

My heart starts beating hard.

What in the world—literally—is he doing here?

Seven

There's another beat of stunned silence as the guy and I stare at each other. His lips then curve up into a grin.

"Well, hello again, Doctor." The guy's dark eyes are sparkling in the sunlight. "Fancy meeting you here."

I don't reply. I can't reply. All I can do is continue gawking at the guy while I take in the sight of him. He looks even more handsome now than the last time I saw him, which I wouldn't have thought could be possible. He's wearing a dark blue t-shirt and jeans, which happen to sit perfectly on his muscular frame. He's cleanly shaven, and his thick hair is slightly tousled. He's obviously well-rested and totally unaffected by the scorching temperatures or the jet lag. I, meanwhile, undoubtedly look like the apocalypse personified. The wind is blowing my frizzing hair into my face, my cheeks are probably a deep shade of crimson by now, sweat is still creeping down my back, and I'm gripping my luggage as if it's my lifeline to sanity.

I snap out of my trance when it abruptly dawns on me why the guy is here: he's attempting to steal the apartment out from underneath me. When he couldn't find lodging elsewhere, he went back to the online listing for this place to reserve it, and when he discovered it was no longer available, he rushed over here to sweet-talk the nice old man into giving him the apartment instead.

My jaw clenches. This guy's long-lashed eyes and captivating smile aren't enough to make me let down my guard this time. I may have conceded the outlet at the airport, but I am not—I am most definitely not—going to let him take this apartment. I will chain myself to the front doors of the building if I have to.

The guy is still grinning. "So you're Irene Thatcher?"

"I am," I reply coolly. "And let me just say right off the bat: don't think for a minute that you're going to take this apartment from me. I reserved it, fair and square, and I won't back down. There's a lot more at stake than a measly outlet this time, and I refuse to give up what's rightfully mine."

The guy's smile vanishes. His eyebrows rise. "Excuse me?"

I harpoon him with another suspicious glare. I have to say, his faux disbelief would be convincing if it weren't for the fact that I've witnessed his sneak-in-and-steal-what-someone-else-has-already-claimed technique before.

"Look." I exhale tiredly and rub my aching forehead. "I'm exhausted. I'm hot. I'm so hungry I could eat your shirt. I'm not in the mood for playing around, all right?"

The guy opens his mouth to say something, but I cut him off and go on:

"I really, really need some sleep. So please just let me go inside and claim the apartment that I rightfully rented."

The guy stares at me a moment longer. He then clears his throat, steps to one side of the doorway, and motions toward the foyer. "Please head on in."

So far, so good. The guy isn't going to fight me on this . . . at least, I don't think he is. Then again, his gesture of defeat may be another one of his tactics. I can't say for sure. Until I'm safely inside the apartment with the keys in my hand, I'm going to have to keep a close eye on this guy.

Not that I mind the view.

"Thank you," I reply curtly.

I tip up my chin and enter the building, wheeling my suitcase behind me. As I pass the guy, I catch a whiff of his amazing cologne, which sends goosebumps of delight up my arms. The aroma is something woodsy and spicy . . . and I like it a lot.

Once inside the foyer, I spin around to face the guy again. "I assume you already know where Donato Conti's apartment is?" I don't mask the accusatory tone in my voice.

The guy enters the building and closes the heavy door, shutting out the sunlight and casting the foyer into gloriously shady, dim coolness.

"Yes, as a matter of fact, I do," he replies evenly.

My eyes narrow again. I knew it.

The guy takes a step closer to me. His expression is serious now as he pulls a set of keys from a front pocket of his jeans. "I know you're exhausted and ready to get some rest, Irene, so I'll just give you a quick tour of the apartment and then clear out."

My barely working brain slowly processes what the guy just said. My eyes then start shifting between the guy's face and the keys he's holding in his hands.

"Hang on," I begin, my voice cracking, "are you . . . I mean, you can't be . . . I mean, you're obviously not Donato Conti."

The guy's serious expression gives way, and he's clearly on the verge of grinning once more. "I'm Paul Conti. I'm Donato's grandson. I'm here to let you into the apartment."

"You're . . . you're *what*? You're *who*?" My face reignites. I'm not sure whether to laugh or be infuriated. With a groan, I push my hair from my face. "You could have told me, you know."

"I could have." Paul shrugs. "It was more entertaining this way, though."

My mouth drops open.

Paul chuckles and extends a hand. "It's nice to officially meet you, Irene."

Doing my best to ignore the amused gleam in his eyes, I reach out in return and shake Paul's hand. As soon as we touch, an electrifying sensation shoots up my arm and fills my chest, causing me to pull in a sharp breath. I gaze at Paul without moving or speaking. Paul keeps his eyes on mine as he slowly releases my hand.

It takes another split-second for the electrifying sensation to fade from my body, and then I manage to collect myself. Okay, so yes, Paul is the hottest guy I've ever seen, and yes, there's some sort of fiery magnetic pull of attraction I feel toward him. However, none of that matters. None of it matters because I'm planning to sort out things with Stuart. During my journey halfway around the globe, I did a lot of thinking, and I realized it would be a mistake for Stuart and me to simply throw away the past six years of our lives without at least talking about what went wrong between us. So once I catch up on sleep, I'm going to call Stuart. I don't know if we'll be able to make things right, but I need to find out.

I grab hold of my suitcase handle, as if doing so will help me steady myself and my emotions. "So, Paul, are you actually the owner of the apartment?"

Paul shakes his head. "No. The apartment is owned by my grandparents. They live here in Italy. I live in the States, in the Lakewood area, but I come out here a few times a year to help my grandparents with the properties they manage."

"Oh." My heart flutters again. "Well, running into you again has certainly been . . . unexpected."

Paul peers right into my eyes. "Yes, it has."

The instinctive pull I feel toward Paul grows stronger. Quickly diverting the discussion,

I use my free hand to motion vaguely around the foyer while saying:

"This building is absolutely beautiful."

And it's true. Signs of skilled craftsmanship are everywhere, from the colorful tiles on the floor to the intricate woodworking of the high ceiling. One could easily confuse this place for a fancy museum, if it weren't for the fact that mailboxes for the building's tenants are mounted on the far wall. Adjacent to the mailboxes is a narrow, accordion-style door, which I think leads into an elevator. Far to my left is a wide staircase with ornate carvings in its dark wood banisters and railings. Tipping back my head, I count at least six switchbacks before the staircase finally reaches the apartment building's top floor.

"I'm guessing the thought of climbing several flights of stairs doesn't sound too appealing to you at the moment." Paul comes to my side and follows my upward gaze.

I actually laugh. "No, admittedly, it doesn't. I feel like I've already had my cardio for the month."

Paul laughs while pointing to the elevator. "That thing is barely big enough for one person. You take the elevator, and I'll take the stairs and meet you on the fourth floor."

"Thanks."

I take a step toward the elevator while pulling my luggage behind me. At the same time, Paul reaches down to take my suitcase for me. Our hands brush, and another thrilling sensation flies up my arm and spreads up to my head and down to my feet. I halt and slowly put my eyes back on Paul.

"Allow me," Paul says, his gaze searching mine as he lifts the suitcase with ease.

I don't reply. How can I reply? I'm spellbound by Paul's stare . . . and by his gigantic biceps, which currently happen to be flexed and on full display past the edge of his short sleeves while he holds my luggage.

A split-second later, I manage to cough and look the other way while saying, "Thank you again."

I scoot up my computer bag on my shoulder and beeline for the elevator. Paul goes to the other end of the foyer and starts climbing the stairs. With the sound of Paul's steady footsteps filling my ears, I attempt to focus on figuring out how to work what is unquestionably the tiniest, oldest, oddest elevator I've ever encountered.

There's an enormous circular button on the wall just to the right of the elevator's accordion door. When I press the button, it lights up green; I assume this means the elevator is on the ground floor and ready. So I pull open the door, which hinges outward to reveal the even punier door of the elevator itself right behind it. I push the door inward and slide into the elevator, barely able to fit with my computer bag on my shoulder. I'm now standing in what feels like a tall box. Once again, I'm grateful I don't get claustrophobic.

I have just enough room to turn around so I'm facing the panel with the buttons. I tap the button for the fourth floor, and with a jarring lurch that causes me to stumble into the wall, the rickety elevator starts to ascend. The elevator groans and creaks as it rises slowly . . . extremely slowly. At last, it comes to a jiggling stop on the fourth floor.

"You all right in there?" Paul calls from the other side of the doors. He sounds as though he's smiling.

I can't help giggling. "Hurry and help me get out of here before I run out of oxygen."

I hear Paul let out a rich laugh as he opens the outer door. I tug the inner door toward me, and then I press my body against the side wall to start squeezing past it. I'm about halfway to freedom when the strap of my computer bag catches on the door's handle. I stumble, letting out a yelp as I fall the rest of the way out of the elevator. The next thing I know, Paul has caught me in his arms.

Everything gets intensely quiet and still, and for another beat, neither Paul nor I move. Being held in Paul's arms is making my breathing get shallow and my heart race. I barely manage to steady myself on my shaking legs as I gather my footing and step back from him.

"Nice catch," I quip, pretending as though my skin isn't still hot from the memory of his touch. "I suppose it'll be safer if I stick to the stairs from here on out."

Paul breaks into another grin. "I thought you handled that quite gracefully . . . for a novice."

With a wink, Paul takes hold of my suitcase once more and wheels it alongside him as he goes down a short walkway to reach a tall wooden door at the end of the hall. He puts a key into the lock, pushes open the door, and enters the apartment, pulling my suitcase behind him. I catch up and follow him inside.

As soon as I cross the threshold, the tension I've been carrying for so many hours starts to disappear. For reasons I can't explain, I instinctively feel welcome and at home here. The effect is profound. Everything about the aura in this place makes me feel comfortable and safe. Like I belong.

I'm standing in a spacious entryway. There's a framed mirror hanging on the wall across from the front door. Positioned under the mirror is a lovely little table, which has a vase upon it that's filled with fresh hydrangeas. As charming as the sight is, however, I quickly look away. I don't watch to catch a glimpse of my reflection in the mirror at the moment; I can only imagine how terrifyingly sweaty and messy I appear.

"Let me show you around, and then I'll leave you to get settled in." Paul slides my suitcase against the wall.

Paul commences with his quick-but-informative tour, and it takes me only about one additional second to decide this apartment is even more enchanting than the photos on the website led me to believe. Leaving the entryway, Paul and I pass through an arched doorway on our right to step into the main room. The space is large and filled with natural light, which is pouring in through big windows and a set of double doors that lead out to a small balcony. A long dining table sits at the near end of the room. On the other end of the room, bookshelves line the walls, and an L-shaped couch is facing a flat-screen television. A chandelier hangs from the ceiling. Gorgeous watercolors adorn the walls. It's all stunning, but I think the most beautiful feature of all is the floor itself, which is done in a herringbone pattern.

"So are you really a doctor, or do you just pretend to be one whenever you're on an airplane?" Paul casts me a side-glance as he grins.

I snicker. "I'm for real. However, that was my first time practicing medicine in the air, and I have to say: I prefer treating patients on the ground."

Paul leans casually against the wall, his expression becoming more pensive. "You did a great job taking care of that man. I don't know if he understood how much you helped him."

"Thanks." I meet Paul's steady gaze. "His condition certainly could have worsened, so I was glad he agreed to let me assist."

Paul's lips form into a frown. "I'm sorry he was so disrespectful to you at first. It was all I could do not to say something to him."

"I appreciate that." I sigh. "For good or for bad, though, his behavior didn't throw me off too much. That kind of thing comes with the job."

Paul's eyebrows pop up. "Really?"

"Really."

Eyes narrowing with concentration, Paul turns his head to look out the window, which gives me a view of his stunningly handsome profile. Before I can look away, Paul faces me again and catches me staring at him. I clear my throat and promptly avert my eyes, pretending as though I'm admiring one of the pieces of artwork on the walls.

"I saw you talking with the medics when I deplaned," I hear Paul go on. "May I ask what happened after that?"

"The patient continued doing well, and he was taken to a hospital for routine observation and monitoring." I show Paul a wry smile. "However, it turns out that giving a medical report via a language-translation app is a tad time consuming, so I wound up being stuck there for quite a while."

Paul winces. "I'm sorry. Your day just kept getting better and better, didn't it?"

I exhale a breath. "You . . . have no idea."

Paul doesn't reply for a time. At last, he pushes off from the wall and says, "Let me show you the bedrooms."

I trail him into the first of the apartment's two bedrooms. The room is gorgeous. There's a queen-sized bed positioned against one wall, floor-to-ceiling cabinets lining the opposite wall, and a window in the back that's so tall it nearly reaches the vaulted ceiling. The room is decorated with floral-patterned wallpaper, framed art, an antique chair, and a nightstand on each side of the bed. This is definitely going to be my room for the duration of my stay.

"So is it just you staying here?" Paul puts his eyes on mine from across the room. "Or are you traveling with someone else?"

I pause before replying. "No, I'm not traveling with anyone else. It's . . . just me."

Paul is still for a second or two. He then strides across the room and opens the door that leads into the *en suite* bathroom. "And may I ask what brings an ER physician to Italy alone for a week?"

I have to swallow past the lump that's forming in my throat. "The decision to come was . . . kind of a spontaneous thing."

Paul stops and looks my way again. "Hence the reason you only made this reservation today."

"Correct." I blow a wayward strand of hair from my face. "I wasn't planning on coming."

Paul slowly blinks before he resumes where he left off with the tour, launching into an explanation of the quirks of the bathroom. I'm hardly paying attention to what he's saying anymore, however. My brain is growing increasingly weary, and I'm distracted by the fresh reminder of what happened between Stuart and me.

Still in a haze, I wander with Paul into the other bedroom, which I vaguely note has dark wood furniture and a rich blue hue painted on the walls. Lastly, Paul orients me to the galley kitchen, and though I'm still only half-listening, I'm generally aware that it's equipped with everything I could possibly need.

"There's a twenty-four-hour grocery store about a three-minute walk from here." Paul leads the way back to the main room. He picks up a black binder from off the table. "This binder is the last thing I want to show you. It contains information you might find useful: WiFi passwords, maps, recommendations for places to eat, emergency phone numbers, instructions on how to use the washing machine and air conditioner, tips for sightseeing, how to get a cab, and hopefully anything else you might want or need to know." He sets the binder back on the table. "That being said, if you have questions or something comes up, feel free to call or shoot me a text."

I snap to attention. "Do I have your number?"

Paul pulls his phone from the back pocket of his jeans. "You can use the local number I was texting you from earlier; it's also listed in the binder. If you would like to give me your number, I'll text you from my regular phone, too, so you'll have it as well."

I give Paul my number, and he enters it into his phone. A second later, I hear a ping from my own phone, which is buried somewhere in my computer bag.

Paul slips his phone back into the pocket of his jeans. "I think we've covered everything, so unless there's anything else I can help you with, I'll head out and let you get some rest."

"Actually, there is something," I say before I can stop myself. "I have a few questions for you."

Paul fixes a concentrated gaze upon me. "Fair enough. Ask away."

I slide my computer bag off my aching shoulder. "Why are you helping your grandparents run a rental apartment in Rome?"

Paul sits on the edge of the table and crosses his arms over his broad chest. "My grandparents do most of the work themselves, but they occasionally need assistance, especially with the legal mumbo-jumbo that comes with managing properties. So I visit every few months to help them out. I'm always happy to do it."

"Does this mean you're an attorney?"

"Yeah, but please don't hate me too much." Paul laughs and stands up again. "I do estate law. I don't mess with doctors."

I arch an eyebrow. "We'll see about that."

There's a pulse of palpable silence as my remark seems to linger in the air. Paul is watching me more intently now, and I sense my heart rate picking up again. I hurriedly break the stillness by asking:

"Do your grandparents own a lot of properties?"

Paul remains quiet for another second, and then he answers. "They own three in total: two apartments here in Rome—this one and the apartment where I'm staying, which is in the next building over—and their own home."

"And is your grandparents' home in Rome, too?"

A smile takes over Paul's face. "No, they've lived their entire lives in a small village called Pago Veiano. It's about a two-hour train ride away from here."

I smile, too. "I bet it's a lovely place."

"It is." Paul steps closer to me and lowers his voice. "Well, I should probably get out of here."

My body instantly awakens at the intoxicating sense of his nearness. "Y-yes," I stutter. "Okay. I mean, um, thanks again for the tour. This is a fantastic apartment."

"I'm glad you like it." Paul's eyes linger on mine a moment more, and then he heads for the entryway. "I'll leave your set of keys on the front table."

I stay rooted in place, listing as Paul steps out of the apartment, shuts the door behind him, and locks it. I hear his footsteps fade as he descends the staircase, and then everything is silent.

I exhale a stuttering breath, and I have to grab hold of the back of one of the chairs at the table to steady myself. A hundred thoughts are crashing around in my sleep-deprived, exhausted mind, and my heart is drumming with emotions I've never felt before. Eventually, I stagger over to the couch and flop down upon it. And I sigh. It feels so good to be off my feet.

For a few minutes, I do nothing but breathe in and out, listening to the silence while trying to process the whirlwind that has consumed my life since my last shift in the Lakewood emergency department. Strangely, out of everything that's colliding around in my head and competing for my attention, my thoughts settle again on Paul, the extremely handsome guy from the airport who just happens to be an intelligent, alluring, part-Italian man who lives in the Lakewood area, has a good job, and does nice things for his grandparents.

I let out a weird laugh, grab a couch pillow, and smash it over my face. I can't get swept off my feet by the spell Paul has cast upon me. I need to sort out things with Stuart. Stuart and I may have different needs and priorities, but that doesn't mean we shouldn't at least try to fix things. We need to talk.

But first, sleep.

Weariness is pulling hard at my eyelids as I push myself up off the couch and shuffle into the kitchen. I find a glass in one of the well-stocked cupboards, fill it at the sink, and gulp down the much-needed hydration. Setting the glass on the counter, I go into the bedroom, peel off my sweaty shirt, kick off my shoes, and flop down onto the bed.

Eight

I groggily open my eyes. I'm lying on a bed in an unfamiliar room. The air is stiflingly hot, and through the sheer drapes that are hanging over the window, I can see that it's dark outside.

I have no idea where I am.

Punched with panic, I sit bolt upright, frantically trying to figure out where I am and why—

My jumbled thoughts come into focus, and then I remember everything—every terrible, life-changing, jet-lagged detail. I'm alone. I'm in Rome. I came here because I realized that I needed to start living my life to the fullest, and I somehow wound up breaking up with my boyfriend in the process.

With a weary moan, I begin searching in the darkness for my phone, which I find buried underneath the folds of the bedspread. Squinting as the phone screen illuminates, I see that it's three in the morning. I also notice that I've received a new text, and the sight of it triggers a lurch of anticipation in my stomach. The text isn't from Stuart, though. It's a message from my cell phone carrier, informing me that I'm being charged ten dollars per day for international service. I scowl and toss the phone aside.

Pushing myself to my feet, I locate the light switch and turn on the chandelier that's hanging high above the bed. I head to the window, about to let in some cool air, but then I have a vague recollection of something Paul mentioned during the apartment tour. He explained how to use the air conditioner, and he said something about a remote control to turn it on. Spinning around, I rifle through the nightstands until I find the remote, which I point at the AC unit that's mounted high above the bedroom door. I set the temperature to eighteen degrees Celsius, which will have to do since I can't make it go any lower.

The AC unit comes to life and begins blowing refreshingly cool air around the room. I return the remote to the nightstand, sit down on the edge of the bed, and restlessly drum my fingers on my thighs. I'm too tired to think clearly, but I'm too awake to fall asleep. My confused circadian rhythms are telling me it's evening, and I—

Hang on: if it's in the evening back at home, that means Stuart is awake.

I should call Stuart. We need to talk.

Knots of nerves are forming in my stomach as I dive across the bed to retrieve my phone once more. My fingers are trembling as I tap the screen where it shows Stuart's name sitting at the top of my favorites list. I clear my throat and put the phone to my ear. After a long delay, it rings. It rings again. And again.

"Hello?" Stuart's voice suddenly reaches my ear.

"Hi, Stuart. It's . . . me."

"Hello, Irene."

Silence.

"So, um, how are you doing?" I prompt.

"I'm doing fine." Stuart sounds as though he's walking.

I frown. Stuart is *fine*? How can he be fine? We just broke up after being together for six years. He can't be fine.

Well, if Stuart is going to pretend to be fine, then I'll pretend, too.

I brighten my tone. "What are you up to right now?"

"I'm at the office."

I resist the urge to roll my eyes. Of course Stuart is at the office. He's always at the office.

"Well," I go on, playfully dragging out the word, "you'll never believe where I am right now."

There's another pause. I sit up taller, waiting for Stuart to reply. This is it. This is the moment when I'm going to tell Stuart that I'm in Rome. We'll then discuss what happened between us, and we'll talk about if—

"Hey, Irene, I'm sorry to have to cut short our conversation," Stuart says in his workplace voice, "but I need to get back to working on my team's presentation."

My knotted stomach crashes to the floor. "Oh. Okay. Would you . . . be interested in talking some other time?"

"I would be available for a call next Saturday night."

"You mean, a week from now?"

"Yes. Next Saturday night would be the most convenient time for me. I need to focus on my work until then."

"Oh. I—"

"I appreciate your understanding, Irene. I'll mark my calendar."

Stuart ends the call.

I slowly lower my phone to my lap. I have no idea what to think right now. I'm not sure whether to be disappointed, offended, heartbroken, or content. Considering Stuart and I just broke up, and we're both working through how we feel about it, I suppose a spur-of-the-moment conversation wasn't going to go perfectly. In fact, I suspect Stuart is burying himself in his work even more than usual, using it as his coping mechanism, much like impulsively hopping a plane to Italy was mine.

I heave a sigh. The more I think it over, the more I realize it's not a bad thing for Stuart and me to wait a week before hashing things out. This will give us both time to ponder how we truly feel and what we really want. Until then, I've got a great place to stay and some of the world's best sightseeing to keep me busy. The week will go by in a flash.

Feeling more satisfied, I decide to tackle the next item on my agenda: a much-needed shower. Then I'll unpack. After that, I'll catch up on work emails. Later, I'll hit that grocery store Paul told me about. Maybe I'll end the day by going to see the Colosseum.

I make my way into the bathroom and open the sliding glass door of the white-tiled shower. The shower is smaller than what I'm accustomed to at home, but it's nice and newly remodeled. I reach into the shower to turn on the water, and then I hesitate. There are three valves with fancy handles, but they're not labeled. I'm not sure which valve does what. Also, there's a long white string dangling from the ceiling that runs down the far corner of the shower until it stops about a foot or so from the ground. I have no idea what a string inside the shower is for, either.

After another moment's deliberation, I take a guess and give one of the valves a turn. Water starts jetting out from the showerhead. So far, so good. I turn another valve, and the water gets warmer. Perfect.

With the shower heating up, I head to the entryway to retrieve my suitcase from where Paul left it. I return to the bedroom, toss the suitcase onto the bed, open it up, and dig out the shampoo and shaving razor I thankfully remembered to pack. Heading back into the now steam-filled bathroom, I put the toiletries on the shelf in the shower, strip off my clothes, and step into the cascade of hot water.

Bliss.

I don't know how long I stand there letting the water run over my back and shoulders. I then wash, shave, and massage shampoo through my hair. It's like coming alive again. As I turn around to rinse off, my eyes drift over to the string that's hanging down the corner of the shower. Curiosity piqued, my gaze tracks up to where the string emerges from a tiny hole in the ceiling. There's a canned light in the ceiling right beside it, which is currently turned off. Ah-ha. The string is a pull cord for the shower light. I grab the string and give it a good yank.

A deafening alarm suddenly starts echoing through the apartment. I shriek in startled, terrified surprise, turn off the water, and leap out of the shower. Breathing fast, I scan the room, and I spot a small red light mounted on the wall that's flashing red in time with the alarm's horrendous sound. As steam starts clearing from the air, I gulp when I notice a little sign below the flashing red light that reads:

Allarme

My phone begins ringing in the bedroom. It's probably Stuart wanting to apologize for abruptly ending our previous call, but it's not like I can answer at the moment, considering I've set off an alarm that's probably waking up everyone in the entire building. Instead, I lunge for one of the fluffy white towels that are hanging on the shower rack and wrap it around myself, and then I bolt across the bathroom and commence slapping the flashing light with my hand in a desperate, manic attempt to turn off the alarm. The ear-piercing sound continues, however, and I swear it's getting even louder.

With a groan, I sprint out of the bathroom and begin charging from one room to the next, flipping every light switch and pulling open every cupboard in a mad hunt for an electrical panel or a control switch that will turn off the alarm. Finding nothing, I bolt back into the bathroom, slipping on the wet floor and nearly falling to the ground in the process. I push my sopping-wet hair from my face and spin around helplessly, racking my brain for what I should do.

Over the din, I hear a loud knock on the front door. I gasp. The other tenants are coming for me.

"I'm so sorry!" I shout toward the entryway, leaning out of the bathroom as I do so. I doubt my voice can be heard above the racket, and even if I can be heard, whoever is outside may not understand what I'm saying. Still, though, I keep shouting. "I'll have the alarm turned off in a moment!"

There's another firm knock on the door.

I rush out of the bedroom to get closer to the entryway. "I'm sorry! I'm working on it! I'll—"

The front door is flung open. I scream and stumble backward.

"Irene?" I hear a man bark above the ruckus.

I stop screaming, steady my footing, and lift my head. Paul is standing in the entryway.

"Are you okay?" Paul shuts the door and comes toward me. He's breathing fast, and his dark eyes are locked on mine.

"Y-yes. I'm f-fine." I put a hand to my chest, working to catch my breath. I cringe as the mortifying realization hits me. "Oh my gosh, you heard the alarm all the way over in your apartment building?" Good grief. I've woken the entire neighborhood. This is even worse than I thought.

Paul comes to a stop right in front of me. Surprisingly, the lines of concern in his face fade away. He focuses on his phone, which he has in his hand, and taps the screen a couple of times. The alarm shuts off. Everything is quiet.

"You pulled the alarm cord in the shower, which sent an alert to my phone." Paul calmly raises his head and puts his eyes back on mine.

I stare back at him, expressionless. "You have an alarm cord. In the shower."

Paul's lips twitch upward. "They're required here."

"They are?" My cheeks flame, and I moan again. "I thought that cord turned on the light."

"Don't worry. It's all right. You're not the first tourist who has set that thing off." Paul chuckles easily. "Most people don't set it off at four in the morning, though."

That's when I register the fact that Paul is wearing a black t-shirt that's slightly wrinkled, a pair of blue athletic shorts, and flip-flops. His hair is disheveled, and facial scruff is visible along his strong jaw line and upper lip. It's obvious the alarm woke him from sleep . . . but I also can't help noting that he looks as handsome as ever.

What a disaster.

I drop my head in my hands. "I'm so sorry you got woken up."

"Like I said, it's all right." Paul's tone is thick with amusement now. "I definitely don't mind."

"I must have disturbed all the neighbors."

"No, actually, you didn't. The alarm isn't loud in the other apartments. I promise. You have nothing to worry about."

"That's nice of you to say, but I most certainly do have something to worry about." I peer at Paul again. "I was taking a shower and . . ."

The rest of my words get stuck in my throat. The shower. I was just taking a shower. I'm wearing nothing but a towel right now.

My eyes get huge. "Um, please excuse me." I wrap my arms around myself, now acutely aware of the water that's dripping from my hair onto my bare shoulders and rolling down my arms. "I'll just, um, go put on some clothes."

Paul shrugs, still grinning. "Suit yourself."

I bolt into the bedroom and slam the door behind me. I collapse with my back against the door and exhale hard. My pulse is pounding, though whether from the chaos or Paul's arrival, I can't say for sure.

I stand up straighter. Okay, I need to get a grip. I'm scheduled to talk with Stuart. I can't get swept up in thoughts of Paul.

I take slow breaths, composing myself. I then push off from the door and change into a lightweight pink top and jeans. I grab an elastic from my suitcase and pull my wet hair into a bun. Once I'm ready, I return to the main room. I find Paul seated on the couch and looking at something on his phone. When I enter, he gets to his feet.

"You know," I begin wryly, "you could prevent this from happening if you put a label on that string to warn innocent tourists that it's connected *to an alarm*."

Paul scratches his chin. "It's funny you should mention that. I was going to do so yesterday, but someone made a last-minute reservation, and I wanted to let her get settled in." A playful gleam shines in his eyes. "That's why I made sure to clearly explain to her what the cord did when I gave her a tour of the bathroom."

"Oh." I cough. "Perhaps that particular someone may have been extremely tired during the apartment tour and didn't hear everything you said."

Paul breaks into laughter. The deep, rich sound makes me all giddy inside, and I start laughing, too. I can't explain why, but it feels so . . . *natural* and easy to be laughing with him. When our laughter eventually dies away, quiet again takes over the room. Our eyes meet, and something about Paul's searching gaze triggers a thrilling jolt inside my chest. I immediately deflect the feeling by remarking:

"Anyway, as a clueless tourist who didn't arrange for a place to stay here in Rome, I can't tell you how relieved I was to discover this apartment was available."

Paul crosses his arms. "I'm glad it worked out. Usually, a family from Spain vacations here in the summer, but they unfortunately had an emergency and needed to cancel without much warning."

"I hope everything is all right for them." I go to the far side of the dining table and plunk myself down on one of the chairs. "As I said, though, I'm grateful there was somewhere for this very out-of-sorts traveler to go."

Paul tips his head a little to one side, still observing me. "Yeah, you mentioned something about it being a last-minute decision to come here."

I don't respond. Instead, I look out the window. The sun is starting to come up, illuminating the sky with soft shades of pastel orange and yellow. After another couple of seconds, I hear Paul say in a more subdued tone:

"I'm sorry, Irene. I didn't mean to pry."

I sigh softly. "You're not prying." I pull my gaze from the window and rub my face with my hands. I guess there's no point in hiding the truth. I look at Paul once more. "Yes, it was an impulsive decision to come here. It was my birthday, and while my boyfriend and I were out on a sad excuse for a date, I told him about a patient encounter that inspired me to make some changes in life. I told Stuart that I wanted us to start embracing every moment we could." I laugh sadly and shake my head. "I thought he would be willing to take a spur-of-the-moment trip to Italy with me. Instead, we . . . broke up."

Paul's eyes widen momentarily, and then his brow furrows. "Your day was even worse than I realized. I'm sorry."

Paul's tone is genuine and without judgment, and his reaction causes a lump of emotion to form in my throat. It's cathartic to be speaking openly about my feelings, and it's nice to be really listened to. Stuart and I haven't had this kind of a heart-to-heart discussion in a long time.

Paul shifts his stance and more quietly asks, "How long do you think you'll stay?"

"I . . . don't know," I admit. "Stuart and I are taking a week to think things over, and then we're going to talk about . . . us. I don't know what's going to happen after that."

Paul studies me for several seconds. Unexpectedly, a gleam appears in his eyes. "Well, since your plans are fairly uncertain at the moment, I have a deal to propose."

Nine

"Deal?" I echo suspiciously, observing him. "What kind of deal?"

Paul leans against the arm of the couch. "As I mentioned, the family who usually stays here for the summer had to cancel their booking at the last minute. In fact, it was while I was at the airport waiting to board the flight when I got the news about the cancellation. I was in the middle of reposting this apartment's availability online when you . . . well, you know . . ."

My cheeks heat up, but I giggle. "Hey, you leave the outlet debacle out of this."

Paul chuckles, his eyes shining with mirth. "Anyway, I posted the availability for this apartment online, and you booked your reservation less than a day later."

"Okay," I draw out the word. I still have no idea where Paul is going with this. "Go on."

"Within another few days, I expect this apartment to book up for the rest of the summer." Paul's tone is back to all-business. "If that happens before you've sorted out things with this Stuart guy, though—if your week's reservation ends and for any reason you're not ready to fly home yet—you'll probably have a tough time finding another decent place to stay in Rome . . . or anywhere in Italy, for that matter, since it's in the middle of tourist season."

My insides twinge with anxiety. Paul brings up a valid point. I don't yet know if I'll be ready to return home at the end of this week. Will I be ready to leave Italy and end my first taste of seizing the moment? Will I be ready to return to reminders of Stuart? I have no idea.

Paul goes on. "Alternatively, I could remove this apartment's listing from the travel website until you've figured out what you're going to do. You would be able to stay here for as long as you need."

"Are you serious?" I gasp with relief. "That would be wonderful! I . . . but wait, won't that make things harder for you?" I don't hide my concern. "Don't you want to lock in guaranteed renters for the rest of the summer, and do so as soon as possible?"

Paul tips his head in acknowledgement. "Admittedly, securing renters for the rest of the summer would be preferable, but I'll figure something out."

I exhale again. "Then I don't know what else to say except *thank you*. I can't tell you how much I appreciate this. Of course I'll pay . . ." I trail off when I notice that the mischievous gleam has returned to Paul's eyes. I frown. "There's a catch to this, isn't there?"

The corners of Paul's lips curve upward. "A little one."

"What is it?"

"In return for having indefinite access to this apartment, you'll come with me tomorrow to visit my grandparents."

"Huh?" I'm now peering at Paul in total bewilderment. "Why on earth would you want me to do that?"

"I need you to pretend to be my fiancée."

My expression goes deadpan. "You need me to pretend to be your fiancée."

"That's correct."

"You're joking."

"I'm not joking."

I glance around for the nearest exit. "It sounds to me like I've just discovered I'm in the apartment of a crazy man."

Paul chuckles again. "No, I'm not crazy. I just want my grandparents to stop trying to marry me off."

I do a double take. "Huh?"

"I don't want my grandparents worrying about trying to marry me off." Paul's smile fades. "They have enough to worry about as it is."

I open and close my mouth a couple of times as I study Paul in return. Admittedly, *crazy* isn't the first adjective that comes to mind when I look at him. I would still use something more along the lines of *hot* or *sexy* or *intelligent* or . . . the point is, I'm fairly certain Paul isn't insane, which means there must be a semi-decent reason behind what sounds like a completely ridiculous scheme. With a resigned sigh, I wave my hand in his general direction.

"All right. Tell me more."

Paul's grin returns. He takes the chair at the table opposite me and goes on. "Tomorrow morning, I'm heading to Pago Veiano to visit my grandparents. It's typical for me to go back-and-forth between here and there while I'm in the country. I spend my time in Rome getting my grandparents' legal affairs in order and managing their rentals, and I spend time in Pago Veiano updating my grandparents, helping them with things they need, and enjoying my grandmother's cooking."

I smile a little at that. "And tomorrow's the first time you'll be visiting them on this trip."

"Yep."

I sit back in my chair. "I'm still not hearing the part that explains why a supposedly sane individual such as yourself would feel the need to bring a fake fiancée on your visit."

In response, Paul focuses on his phone and taps the screen a few times. He then turns his phone around so I can see what he has on the screen.

"Explanation Number One," Paul says dryly.

He's showing me part of a text message chain that's between Paul and one other person. The other person is labeled as *Gramps*, so I'm guessing it's Donato Conti. The texts by both Paul and Donato are written in Italian, so I have no idea what they say, but attached to one text from Donato is a photo of an elderly woman. She's standing outside a small stone house. She has a cigarette hanging from her mouth and numerous open wine bottles on a table behind her. She's dressed in a loose-fitting tank top, which shows more skin than it probably should, and extremely short shorts.

"Is that, um, your grandma?" I inquire as tactfully as I can.

Paul coughs a laugh. "Definitely not. No, this is the first potential bride my grandparents found for me. She lives in a different village, so my grandparents have never met her, but word is that she's seventy-eight, smokes like a chimney, drinks more than a fraternity on a weekend, and has, at last count, over twenty cats."

My eyebrows shoot up. "Oh my."

Paul turns the phone back toward him and scrolls through the text message chain. He soon shows me another photo. "Explanation Number Two."

I lean forward to study the picture. "But she looks like she's . . ."

"At least fifteen years younger than me? I know." Paul shudders. "She's the great granddaughter of Explanation Number One."

My eyes flick between the picture and the disgruntled expression on Paul's face, and I can't help snickering. "Let me guess: your grandparents haven't met her, either?"

"Nope, they most definitely have not." Paul heaves a sigh. "They haven't seen any of these pictures."

I start massaging my temples. "This whole story is getting weirder by the moment."

"I'll back up." Paul sets the phone on the table. "Recently, I turned thirty-two. Without notifying me, my grandparents decided it was time for me to get married—to an Italian girl, of course—and being the industrious, resourceful individuals that they are, they decided to take matchmaking matters into their own hands."

I snicker. "Sounds dangerous."

"It is," Paul answers immediately. "Extremely dangerous. I love my grandparents, but they're the most persistent people I know. Once they set their minds on something, they're impossible to deter." He sighs again. "Apparently, my grandparents' elderly neighbor told them about the concept of online dating, and my grandparents created a profile about me on an Italian dating app."

"Are you serious?" I break into loud laughter. "And they didn't tell you?"

Paul shakes his head.

I wipe tears of laughter from my eyes. "So how did you find out what they were doing?"

"Once women began responding to the dating profile, Gramps and Grandma didn't know what to do from there. Their neighbor helped them change a setting in the app so communications from interested women started coming directly to me via text and email. Meanwhile, my grandparents continued meddling with the profile on their end, setting me up on dates with women whose profiles they never reviewed."

I put a hand over my mouth in a half-successful attempt not to laugh again.

Paul shakes his head as he goes on. "Anyway, when I started getting alerts from an Italian dating app, let's just say that it didn't take long for me to figure out the gist of what was going on. I called my grandparents, and they fessed up." He glances at his phone, which is still on the table, and grimaces. "Despite me asking them to take down my profile, however, they haven't. They're determined to find me a bride. In fact, I think they've set me up on four dates just for tomorrow night." He rubs his forehead. "Needless to say, this is something else I intend to clear up while I'm in town."

Another laugh escapes my lips. "Sorry." I quickly put a hand over my mouth again.

"It's all right." Paul's stern expression relents, and he breaks into an amused smile of his own. "Trust me: I've had more than a few good laughs about this myself. I—"

Paul's phone pings. He pauses, picks up his phone, and reads a new message. He blinks several times while he stares at the screen.

"Is everything all right?" I ask.

Paul turns his phone so I can see it. "Behold: the latest contender for wedded bliss."

I shift my gaze back to his phone. "Oh. Wow. She's . . . a nun."

"Yes. A nun. On an Italian dating app." Paul places the phone back on the table and quickly withdraws his hands, as if he's afraid it'll burn him. "I'm not sure what to make of that one."

Laughter erupts out of me again, causing my sides to ache. More tears fill my eyes. "At least your grandparents' intentions are good," I utter between laughing fits. "They're trying to do what they think is best for you."

"True." Paul laughs easily, too, the sound making my heart dance again. "However, the fact remains that they won't stop worrying about me and meddling in my love life until I'm married—or, at least, engaged."

I instantly fall silent. "And this is where I would come in."

"Precisely." Paul is also once again serious as he props his sculpted forearms on the edge of the table. "I think if I show up tomorrow with a fiancée, it will be enough to assure my grandparents that they can stop worrying about me. I'll tell them we're newly engaged, so they won't hammer us with questions about wedding details." He looks away, and his forehead creases. "All that matters is getting them to stop worrying about me; they have far more serious issues on their plate."

I study the unmistakable concern that's etched into Paul's expression. "I'm sorry your grandparents are going through a hard time."

"Thanks." Paul swallows and puts his eyes back on mine. "I know how strange this sounds, but alleviating my grandparents' worries about my love life will be a big help for them."

I take a second or two to ponder this, and then I say, "Speaking of your love life, before I agree to anything, I want to confirm one important detail: You *are* officially single, right?"

Paul's eyes search mine. "I'm officially single."

There's an unexpected flutter inside my chest, which I do my best to ignore.

"And you don't have any shady past relationships?" I'm trying to stay focused and not get lost in Paul's dark-eyed gaze. "No ex-girlfriends who will stalk me at Trevi Fountain or something?"

"Nope." Paul continues watching me closely. "I broke up with my girlfriend a year ago. Actually, she broke up with me. She wanted to focus on her career and not, as she put it, 'Stay bogged down with a boyfriend.'"

I flinch. "Ouch. That's harsh. I'm sorry."

"It's okay. I'm glad she was honest about her priorities." Paul sits back in his chair. "I wouldn't want to stay in a relationship where the other person didn't value it as much as I did."

There's another tug in my chest, this time a disconcerting one. I opt to change the subject:

"So back to this completely weird idea of yours: what about the fact that I'm not Italian? It sounds like your grandparents won't be satisfied unless you find yourself an Italian girl."

"Hmm. Good point." Paul starts drumming his fingers on the tabletop. "I'll claim you have Italian ancestry. Your hair is so dark and gorgeous that you could definitely pass off as . . ." he trails off and looks away. "Anyway, we should be able to pass you off as having Italian heritage, especially since we only need to keep up the charade for a day. Italian ancestry will be good enough for my grandparents."

My mind resumes working the problem. Much like when I'm in Lakewood's emergency department, I'm trying to anticipate where problems might arise and figure out ways to prevent the problems before they happen.

"What if your grandpa and grandma contact your parents while we're visiting, and they bring up your new fiancée? Don't you think your mom and dad might freak out or blow our cover?"

"I'll warn them ahead of time," Paul replies without missing a beat. "They'll definitely understand. Dad is my grandparents' oldest child, and he's not only worried about them, too, he knows better than anyone how persistent his parents can be. Mom will simply think it's hilarious."

I look out the windows. The summertime sun is fully up now, and it's evident it is going to be another bright, beautiful, blazingly hot day here in Rome. After a long while, I look across the table at Paul once more.

"Despite how preposterous this plan sounds, I actually can't think of any other questions to ask you."

Paul flashes another charming smile. "Does that mean you'll do it?"

I take another moment to deliberate. This whole scheme is beyond absurd. Pretending to be someone's fiancée? It's laughable. It's cheesy. It's cliché. On the other hand, I do need a place to stay while I'm here, and it's not exactly a hardship to be asked to spend one day in a remote Italian village. In fact, it would be a unique sightseeing opportunity. Talk about a way to be spontaneous and seize the moment.

"Okay. I'll do it," I hear myself say. "In exchange for being able to use this apartment for as long as I need."

"It's a deal." Paul keeps smiling as he stands up. "The train leaves from Termini at eight in the morning tomorrow. I'll stop by here around six to pick you up. The train will take us from Termini to a city called Benevento, and we'll travel to my grandparents' village from there."

I also get to my feet, almost feeling like we should shake hands or something. "I'll see you then."

Paul heads toward the entryway, but he halts and looks back. "Oh, I should probably warn you: my relatives can be quite a handful."

"I work in an emergency department," I remind him, unfazed. "I've had plenty of experience dealing with family members who are a handful."

"Good. Because you'll need it." Paul gives me a playful salute. "I'll see you in the morning, Irene."

Paul disappears around the corner. I hear him whistling as he steps out of the apartment and closes the door. Then all is still.

I stay where I am, letting the sunshine that's coming in through the windows warm my skin. Though I'm not moving, however, my thoughts are racing. I'm halfway around the world because I broke up with Stuart, and now

I've agreed to pretend to be another man's fiancée. I'm pretending to be engaged to a man with whom I've shared more honest discussion and laughter in only a few hours than I've shared with Stuart in a long time. It doesn't make sense. Nothing makes sense.

I rub my aching temples. I need to concentrate on something else. Something predictable and within my control.

Work emails. There are always plenty of those.

I head to the bedroom and grab my laptop. Returning to the main room, I put the laptop on the table and boot it up. Pushing aside thoughts of Paul, Stuart, overhauling my life, and fake engagements, I sit down at the table and start to work.

Ten

The five-fifteen alarm on my phone wakes me from a dreamless sleep. I roll onto my back and stare at the ceiling with eyes that are stinging and heavy. Despite getting some sleep last night, and the morning sunlight that's streaming in through the partly open blinds, every instinct is telling me that I should be going to bed now. My body definitely remains confused by the drastic change in time zones.

Resisting the urge to drift back to sleep, I force myself up into a sitting position, mat down my disheveled hair, and reach over to my laptop, which is on the nightstand. Waking the laptop from its own slumber, I find that I've received a few Lakewood-related emails, but they're all messages that can wait. There are no voicemails or texts waiting for me. In other words, I'm caught up on everything from home . . . everything but my relationship status, that is.

Yesterday, after Paul and I struck our bizarre agreement, I had a productive day. Rather than sightseeing, I chose to spend the day getting settled in for my week-long stay in Rome. I figured dedicating a day to tying up loose ends would help me jettison my angst and look ahead with excitement for whatever the rest of the week might bring.

Over the course of the day, I caught up on my backlog of emails. I then logged into the Lakewood system remotely to check in on how my v-tach patient was doing. To my delight and relief, he has been progressing even better than expected, and he's scheduled to be discharged soon from the hospital. Reading the patient's story again also stirringly reminded me of why I came to Italy in the first place, rejuvenating my soul and re-inspiring me to live to the fullest while I have the chance.

Later in the day, I went to the local grocery store, which proved to be an easy two-block stroll from the apartment. The store wasn't as huge as a grocery store in the US, but it had everything I needed. Including chocolate. There was lots of chocolate. In the spirit of embracing the moment, I made an executive decision that while traveling in Italy and overhauling my life, food indiscretions were completely acceptable. I therefore stocked up on chocolate of numerous forms and varieties, and then I finished loading my nifty shopping-basket-on-wheels with all sorts of other delicious foods and ingredients. The only hiccup came during checkout, when it took me a while to understand that I was being asked to pay for the grocery bags, but once I got that figured out, I successfully returned to the apartment with my grocery-store haul. Dinner consisted of chocolate, a chunk of Gouda cheese, more chocolate, and fresh bread. By seven pm last night, the cumulative lack of sleep caught up with me hard, and I crashed into bed.

My laptop slips back into sleep mode, and I long to do the same. Instead, though, I toss aside the bedspread and get to my feet. I shut off the air conditioner, which has kept the room comfortable through the night. I make my way into the bathroom and crank on the shower, making sure to tuck the evil white string out of reach. After I'm done showering, I towel dry my hair, opting to leave it down. Since Paul suggested my hair would be key in convincing his grandparents that I have Italian heritage, I want to make it as visible as possible.

Paul also said my hair was gorgeous, but that doesn't matter.

I return to the bedroom to get dressed. I have no idea what a woman should wear when pretending to meet future Italian grandparents-in-law. Eventually, I decide on my green blouse and the nicest pair of dark jeans I brought. I head back to the bathroom and apply some mascara—I grabbed makeup while I was in the store yesterday, too, figuring it would give me a more polished look for the grandparent meet-and-greet.

Once I'm ready, I check the time. Paul should be here any moment. The thought causes several feelings to surge inside me: nerves, renewed awareness that the day's plan is crazy, and something that feels a lot like excitement at the prospect of seeing Paul again. Doing my best to tuck away all emotions, I slip my phone into the back pocket of my jeans and grab my wallet.

There's a knock on the front door. My heart skips at the sound, in spite of myself. I head to the entryway and open the door. Paul is standing right outside. When he sees me, Paul does a double take, his eyebrows rise for a fleeting moment, and his lips part slightly. I stare back at him in confusion. Have I done something wrong? Is there something bad about the way I look? Am I overdressed? Underdressed?

I do a rapid analysis of what Paul is wearing: a blue, button-up shirt and jeans. As best as I can tell, I struck the right note with my clothes, so I'm not sure why Paul is staring at me.

I also note that Paul looks particularly attractive this morning, but that's beside the point.

Paul clears his throat and smiles. "Good morning, Pretend Fiancée."

I roll my eyes. "Let's not get carried away."

"Sorry." Paul chuckles and steps back from the door. "I admit, though, I wasn't sure you were actually going to go through with this."

I exit the apartment. "Well, I did have second thoughts. Guilt, primarily. Are you sure it's right for us to mislead your grandparents like this?"

Paul's grin fades. "I'm sure. It's the only way to get them to stop worrying about me. They have enough things to worry about as it is." He exhales. "I'll tell them the truth once more pressing issues settle down."

I shut the apartment door and lock it. "You really can't just tell them how you feel and assure them that they don't need to worry about you?"

Paul smiles again. "I really can't. Once you meet my grandparents, you'll understand. Like I said before, when those two get their minds set on anything, they never take *no* for an answer."

I face Paul squarely. "And is their grandson the same way?"

Paul peers right into my eyes for a long moment. "You'll have to figure that out and let me know."

My body tingles under his gaze. Quickly redirecting the conversation, I motion past him in the direction of the stairwell.

"Well, I suppose we should get going."

"Agreed." Paul nods. "There isn't another direct train to Benevento for hours, so we don't want to miss ours."

Paul and I take the stairs to the ground floor. As we cross the foyer, Paul steps ahead to reach the main door first, and he holds it open for me. We share a glance as I slide past him and step outside.

I stop in the courtyard and take in the scene. The neighborhood is quiet. The early morning air is already warm. I hear birds chirping and the occasional sound of a car somewhere in the distance. Everything feels hopeful, calm, and peaceful, which thankfully helps sooth my unsettled emotions.

Paul steps outside, shuts the door, and comes to my side. Together, we pass through the green gate to leave the courtyard and start retracing the path that I took from the metro station the day I arrived in Rome. On both sides of the street, little shops with charming awnings are opening up for the day. The aroma of coffee is strong in the air. Through open windows, I can hear lively conversations, confirming that Italian is the most beautiful language I've ever listened to.

Paul and I turn onto the next street, and I slow my pace. Paul shoots me a questioning look. In response, I gesture toward the street market that's on the other side of the road; it's the open-air market that I passed when I first made my way to the apartment.

"Do we have time for me to get a purse?" I hold up my wallet and keys, which I'm holding in my hands. "I would love to get one, so I don't have to carry my things all day."

Paul checks his watch. "Sure. We've got time."

Saying no more, I dart across the road to reach the long row of tables that span the entire length of the sidewalk. The tables are arranged into smaller groupings, which are collected under large, reception-style canopy tents that indicate the boundaries between the different "stores" that make up the market. Despite the early hour of the day, several people are already browsing the seemingly endless piles of purses, jewelry, suitcases, hats, scarves, and trinkets. Meanwhile, the sellers in each "store" are strolling back and forth within their designated sections, keeping a close eye out for their next potential customer.

I hurry to a table where purses are on display. It's readily apparent that the purses are knock-offs, as I assumed they would be, but I don't mind. A knock-off purse is better than no purse at all. Immediately, a cute purple purse catches my eye. Before I can pick it up, however, the seller whose territory I entered—a short man who has a dazzling number of gold chains around his neck—dashes to my side.

"Good morning!" the seller greets me in accented English. "Yes, good morning!"

I frown. Apparently, my effort to appear Italian hasn't fooled him in the slightest.

"We have a good deal today!" The seller rummages through the mountain of purses on the table. He lifts up a yellow clutch that doesn't stay closed and a large black shoulder bag with a strap that's falling off. "One purse for fifty euros. Two purses for eighty."

I hesitate. This seller's prices are a lot higher than I want to pay for a knock-off bag. I glance down the sidewalk, deciding to go search for a better deal under one of the other tents. I cast a final, fond glance at the cute purple purse, and then I show the gold-chain-wearing seller a polite smile and say while walking away:

"Thanks. I'll take a look around."

"Ah! I see you like this one!" The seller darts into my path, cutting me off. He has the purple purse in his hand, and he holds it up with a victorious smile. "Fifty euros! A good deal!"

"I'll think about it," I tell him, speaking more firmly this time. "Thank you again."

I take another step to leave. The seller blocks my path again and shoves the purse into my hands.

"This is one-of-a-kind! You will not find it anywhere else in all of Italy! It is genuine! Try it! Try it!"

I eye the purse in my hands. Though it's most certainly not *genuine*, it's exactly what I'm looking for. Plus, it is adorable.

"Fifty euros!" the seller bellows in my ear. "The best price you will find—"

"Hey, honey, there you are," I hear someone say.

I look up in surprise and spot Paul strolling my way. His demeanor is casual, yet there's a focused gleam in his eyes. Keeping his gaze on mine, he subtly tips his head toward the street.

"Do you see anything you like?" Paul asks.

Understanding Paul's silent cue, I place the purple purse back on the table. "No. There's nothing that's quite my style."

Paul puts a hand lightly on the point of my elbow and starts leading me out of the seller's area.

"Wait!" The seller shuffles after us. "One purse for forty euros! Forty!"

I peek at Paul out of the corner of my eye. He's still looking straight ahead, and he isn't slowing his strides.

"Thirty!" the seller shouts.

Only after we've reached the road does Paul come to a stop, bringing me to a stop beside him. Paul glances my way and flashes a lightning-fast grin. He then turns around to face the seller.

"Fifteen euros," Paul says calmly.

"Fifteen?" The seller scowls. "That is not enough. These are genuine."

Paul only shrugs, puts a hand back on my elbow, and gently urges me to continue walking away.

"Ten euros," an elderly seller at the next area over unexpectedly calls out.

Paul halts again. I do the same.

"Did you like that purse?" Paul asks me in a low voice.

"The purple one?" I reply. "Actually, yes."

Paul nods before he strides over to table where the elderly seller is stationed. Meanwhile, the seller with the gold necklaces mutters something under his breath and storms away. I return my attention to Paul, and I realize the elderly seller is showing him a purple purse that's exactly like the one the first seller was trying to get me to buy. Running my eyes farther down the sidewalk, I see another purple purse at the next tent over . . . and another at the seller's table beyond that. I chuckle at my rookie-traveler mistake. Clearly, all these sellers get their goods from the same vendor, and the purple purse isn't as one-of-a-kind as I was tricked into believing.

Chatting politely in Italian with the elderly seller, Paul checks to make sure the purse's zipper works and then hands over some cash.

"*Grazie*," Paul tells the elderly seller. He comes back to my side and gives me the purse. "Here you go."

"Thanks—I mean, *grazie*." I smile. "I appreciate you saving this travel novice from drastically overpaying." I sling the strap of the cross-body purse over my shoulder, and I drop my phone, wallet, and keys inside. "I have some cash on me. I'll pay you back as soon as we get on the train."

"Don't worry about it. It's on me." Paul's eyes flick to the purse on my hip. "That being said, I'm not sure I want to be known as a guy who gifts knock-off purses to beautiful, intelligent women."

I stop arranging the things in my purse and snap my eyes back to Paul's face. Paul meets my gaze. A rush of breath-stealing warmth expands inside me, filling me from my head to my toes.

"Oh, well, um, thank you again," I utter; it's the only thing I can think of to say.

Paul's dark eyes are searching mine. "My pleasure."

I spin on my heels and resume making my way down the sidewalk. Paul falls into step beside me. We stroll in silence until, out of the corner of my eye, I see Paul pull something out of his shirt pocket. He holds it out to me and stops walking while he says:

"I almost forgot about this. I guess you could say it's another cheap gift. I bought it at the market, thinking it would be a good idea to have it today. I hope it fits."

I look Paul's way and stumble to a halt. Paul is holding out a ring . . . a ring with what is undoubtedly a fake emerald-cut diamond set in a band of fake gold. Fake or not, though, the ring is beautiful. In fact, it's exactly the style of ring I would hope to receive if I ever got engaged. As I take in the sight of it, I'm shocked to feel an unexpected lump of emotion swiftly form in my throat. I blink hard as I work down a swallow.

Paul's brow furrows while he watches me, and he shoves the ring into the front pocket of his jeans. "Hey, I'm really sorry, Irene. I forgot about that Stuart guy and . . ." He exhales hard. "I was only thinking it would help keep up appearances with my grandparents, who will undoubtedly toss me out on the street if they think I proposed without a ring. I didn't mean to bring up a painful subject. Again, I'm sorry."

"Don't apologize. I understand," I tell him. "I agree the ring . . . is a good idea."

I put on a smile and extend my hand. Paul appears to hesitate before he removes the ring from his pocket and gives it over to me. For a second or two, I hold the ring between my fingers, studying how it glistens in the sunlight. I can't help wondering why—how—such a tiny object can trigger such huge emotions. Finally, I slip the ring onto the fourth finger of my left hand.

"The ring fits, and I think it will successfully avoid you getting chucked to the curb by your grandparents," I remark, trying to lighten the mood.

Paul only nods before focusing his attention straight ahead. We resume walking, and we don't say anything more. When we reach *San Giovanni*, we leave the sunshine behind and head down into the crowded underground station. Paul buys me a metro ticket and explains he already has a metro pass for himself. He then leads the way through the turnstiles, navigating the station like a pro. Soon, we're on the platform for the next train to Termini. Thankfully, it's so noisy in here that it's not worth trying to talk, so we're able to maintain our silence without things becoming even more awkward than they already are.

The train emerges from the tunnel and comes to a squealing stop. The doors slide open. Paul gestures for me to go first. I board the packed car; Paul follows close behind me. The doors slide shut, and the train resumes rolling. As I'm rocked by the motion of the train, I look down at the ring on my hand. I'm so distracted by it that I don't notice when we reach our stop. Paul gently taps me on the shoulder, bringing me to awareness. We exit together, and I stay near Paul as we follow the foot traffic out of the metro station, through the underground mall, and up the escalator to the main part of Termini.

"I purchased our long-distance train tickets online last night," Paul tells me above the din. He motions toward a nearby café. "We've got a couple of minutes. Do you want anything to eat before we go?"

"No, I'm good." I fake another smile. "I had breakfast at the apartment this morning. Thanks, though."

This is not entirely true. Actually, it's not true at all. The truth is, I've lost my appetite. My churning thoughts are making my stomach churn, too, and I don't want to eat a thing.

Paul is studying me with a searching gaze. "Would you like some coffee, at least? I'm buying."

Churning stomach or not, I could definitely use coffee. A massive coffee.

"Actually, yes. Thanks." I peer up at the menu on the wall, which I can't read. "I'll take the closest thing they've got to a *venti* vanilla double-shot latte, please."

Paul suddenly seems be trying hard not to smile. Clearing his throat, he turns from me to face the woman behind the counter. He speaks with her in Italian, and the only word I can distinguish during the exchange is "*caffe*." Paul hands the woman a couple of euro coins, and she gets to work preparing our drinks. Soon, rather than giving us two humungous drinks in recycled take-away cups that have brown cozies wrapped around them, however, the woman slides two tiny white porcelain cups on saucers across the counter toward Paul and me. The miniscule cups are filled with a shot of dark, strong-smelling espresso.

Paul lifts one of the miniscule cups to his lips. "Forget your double-shot whatevers; this is how coffee is done in Italy. So tell your taste buds to beware that this isn't the watered-down stuff you're used to sipping at a leisurely pace back at home. In Italy, things are quick, strong, and pack a punch."

I raise my eyebrows. Paul grins before he throws back his drink. Eyebrows rising higher, I glance around at other patrons who are standing at the counter. Everyone is downing itsy-bitsy shots of caffeine. So this is not a joke. This really is how it's down around here.

I focus again on the little cup in front of me. When I lift it off the saucer, the thick, intense aroma of coffee hits me hard. I cast a last look at Paul, who's now shamelessly watching me with unmasked amusement. Frankly, I don't know what Paul thinks is so hilarious about this. Coffee is coffee, regardless of what country you're in. I tip back my head and down the drink in one go.

Oh.

Oh my.

I think I've been struck by lightning.

"Holy smokes, what is this?" I cough.

Paul puts a hand on my arm. "Are you all right?"

"Yes, I'm fine." I laugh, fanning air past my face. "Apparently, though, I wasn't as ready for that as I thought. I sure hope it wears off before we get to your grandparents' house." I retreat from the counter, my heart thumping from the stimulant that's charging through my bloodstream. This is the most wide awake I've been since flying to Italy. "The way I feel at the moment, I could probably run to Benevento. Or to the moon."

Paul laughs again before saying, "Now that we've got you energized for a day with my grandparents, how about we head to the train?"

I give him a thumbs-up. "Sounds good."

Paul and I leave the café and take a look at one of the huge digital reader boards that's displaying the constantly updating train information. Our train to Benevento is listed as departing from Platform Three, so we start walking that direction.

"Our assigned seats are in Car Seven," Paul tells me.

We reach Platform Three, where a sleek, silver-and-red train is waiting. We make our way down the platform until we reach the car that has a large number seven painted on its side. Paul presses a button on the doors, triggering them to slide open. We climb the stairs, and as soon as the doors shut behind us, the commotion outside is replaced by soothing quiet. Our train car is only about half-full, and most of the passengers are reading books, snoozing, or texting on their phones. No one is talking above a near-whisper.

Paul shows me our assigned seats, and then he steps aside to allow me to have the chair by the window. I slide into the row and sit down. To my pleasant surprise, the chair is comfortable—far more comfortable than sitting in row thirty-four by the lavatory on an airplane.

"This is great," I tell Paul, keeping my voice down like everyone else is doing.

Paul sits on the aisle seat beside me. "Yeah, the regional trains are pretty good here."

I know I'm still jittery from the caffeine bolus, but Paul's nearness is making my heart beat even faster. My face flushes. I quickly turn and stare out the giant window, distracting myself with watching the never-ending parade of people passing by on the platform.

There's a shrill blast from a whistle somewhere outside. The train begins pulling away from the platform, making almost no sound as it starts rolling along the tracks.

"The ride takes about two hours," I hear Paul tell me. "Once we reach Benevento, we'll take a taxi to my grandparents' place in Pago Veiano."

I face Paul once more. "You *did* notify your grandparents I was coming, didn't you?"

"Uh, no. Not exactly." Paul's expression becomes sheepish. "I only told them I would be bringing a guest."

My eyes widen. "Why didn't you tell them you were bringing your fiancée? It's kind of a big deal!"

Paul sets his phone on the armrest of his chair, and he now appears pensive. "Well, I thought about what I would do if I was really engaged, and I think I would surprise my grandparents with the news." He motions between us. "Just like this."

My heart does another little patter. "Oh. I see," I reply softly before hurriedly looking outside again.

It's a while before I dare to steal a glance Paul's way. He has put in earbuds, and it looks like he's listening to a podcast on his phone. He seems lost in thought as his eyes survey the train car, and his forehead is creased in a ridiculously attractive expression of concentration. I pull my gaze away from Paul once more, before he catches me staring at him, and I resume watching outside, swiftly becoming immersed in my own thoughts.

Gradually, the scenery that's flying by the windows starts to change. No longer am I seeing the grit and dramatic beauty of Rome. Instead, rolling green hills, stone farmhouses, tobacco fields, and groves of olive trees are dotting the landscape, and low-lying mountains are rising up in the distance. The pleasant ride passes fast, and as the train rolls into the station at Benevento, the other passengers get up from their seats and collect their belongings.

I look down at my fake engagement ring and then over at Paul. His expression is serious as he removes his earbuds and meets my gaze.

"Are you ready?" he asks.

I draw in a breath. This is only for a day. "I'm ready," I reply.

Eleven

I step off the train, and I'm clobbered by the heat. Paul, however, seems unbothered by the scorching temperature as he and I walk into the train station. In stark contrast to Termini, this clean little station is nearly empty. Paul and I pass the manned ticket booths and exit the building via its glass front doors. We're met by a lovely view of a circular fountain and cars passing by on the road just beyond. Old buildings line both sides of the narrow streets, some of them made of gray stone and others painted happy shades of yellow and pink. Most buildings have quaint shops or eateries on their ground floors, and apartments with little balconies and flower-filled window boxes are on the upper two or three stories.

"Let's head toward the café across the street. I can usually hail a taxi from there," Paul tells me.

"Usually?" I echo while Paul and I make our way up a tree-lined sidewalk.

Paul nods. "There's not always a taxi in Benevento, but I'm usually able to grab one."

"What do you do when you can't find a taxi?"

"I walk."

"Oh. Right."

I glance up at the sun-filled, cloudless sky and fan some air past my flushed face. I certainly hope Paul and I won't have to make the trek on foot in this scorching heat. If I arrive to his grandparents' house as a flushed, sweaty mess, they'll probably insist on Paul marrying that nun, instead.

We reach the outside of the café, and we hover in the shade that's provided by the building. I'm now smelling potent espresso and mouth-watering pastries, and I hear the sounds of clinking glasses and friendly conversations. Somewhere not far away, a bell tower has begun ringing. Occasionally, a car zips by on the street in front of the shop, otherwise things are quiet and peaceful.

An older woman appears from around a corner on the opposite side of the road. She's wearing a floral-patterned dress and sandals, and she's taking a buff-colored cocker spaniel on a walk. When she notices Paul, she breaks into a broad smile.

"Paulo!" the woman exclaims, waving.

"*Ciao*, Claudia." Paul waves back with a friendly, familiar air.

The woman shifts her attention to me. She then looks back at Paul, wags her eyebrows, and says something to him in rapidly spoken Italian. Paul laughs politely and responds. Claudia lets out a delighted gasp, and she rattles off something else. While Paul and Claudia continue chatting—undoubtedly about me—all I can do is keep a smile plastered on my face. Eventually, Paul waves again to Claudia and says to her:

"*Buonasera.*"

"*Ciao, Paulo!*" Claudia calls out. She then gives me a smile. "*Ciao!*"

I clear my throat. "Oh, um, *ciao!*"

Claudia resumes walking her adorable dog up the road. After she rounds the corner and disappears from view, I shift Paul's way, eyeing him curiously.

"Paulo?"

Paul nods. "Everyone around here calls me that. Paulo was my great-grandfather's name. I was named in his honor."

"That's really neat." I slide farther into the shade. "Should I call you that, too, while I'm here?"

"No. Paul is fine." He leans against the building and crosses his arms over his chest. "You're from the US, so it makes sense for you to keep calling me Paul."

"Fair enough." I keep observing Paul-slash-Paulo. "Okay, now you need to fess up: what were you and Claudia talking about?"

Paul smiles. "You, of course."

"I figured as much." I groan. "What, exactly, was Claudia saying?"

Paul tips his head to one side. "She wished us well on our upcoming marriage."

I suddenly remember that I have a fake engagement ring on my finger. My spirits sink. "I suppose we're going to have to lie to a lot of people while I'm here, aren't we?"

Paul nods again, and this time his expression is tough to decipher. He doesn't appear upset, but he certainly doesn't appear amused. "Yeah. I'll be making a mental list of all the people I need to fess up to later with the truth."

I hear a car coming up the road behind me at what sounds like an alarmingly excessive rate of speed. Paul, however, remains calm as he looks past me and raises his arm. I turn around and exhale with relief: the small white vehicle that's flying toward us is a taxi. Phew. Walk in the stifling heat avoided.

The taxi skids to an idling stop at the curb, leaving a smell of burning rubber in the air. Paul opens the back door for me, and I climb inside. Paul slides in next to me, situating himself behind the driver. The driver looks in the rearview mirror, and his face lights up. Whipping around, the driver gives Paul an emphatic greeting and handshake. He and Paul banter, and then Paul motions my way and keeps talking. I put on another smile; I'm still not sure if I'm supposed to act like I understand what's being said or not (I need to clarify this with Paul). Thankfully, the driver doesn't try to converse with me. Instead, he simply gives me a cheery smile before he faces forward, puts the car in gear, and pulls away from the curb with car tires screeching.

It takes about one split-second for me to realize that every horror story I've ever heard about Italian drivers is true.

Gripping the steering wheel with both hands, the taxi driver swings the little car around a corner like he's maneuvering a racetrack. The vehicle rattles as it continues gaining speed. The driver starts weaving from side-to-side to avoid hitting the cars that are parked along the narrow, bumpy road, causing me to get thrown around in the backseat in the process. Skidding around yet another turn, the driver accelerates even more, takes a roundabout with so much momentum that I'm smashed against the door, and merges onto a highway.

Righting myself, I glance with wide eyes at the dashboard. The speedometer is ticking upward into a range of kilometers I can't convert to miles. I resume staring out the windshield in horror while I start fumbling to find my seatbelt.

There's no seatbelt.

I'm in the middle of an emergency medicine doctor's nightmare.

The driver continues speeding along the countryside highway like he's attempting to outrace an erupting volcano. I reach down and clutch the front of my seat with both hands, flinching each time the driver pulls a heart-stopping move to pass a vehicle that's in our path.

The taxi begins making a gradual ascent up a green mountain. I'm sure there are spectacular views of Benevento and the valley behind us now, but I'm not interested in scenic views at the moment. I'm too busy making a mental list of all the injuries Paul and I will sustain when our driver loses control of the car. I wonder if they have CT scanners in Pago Veiano. Or trauma surgeons who manage splenic lacerations.

I think I hold my breath for the entire twenty-minute ride into Pago Veiano. As we pass the sign that indicates we've reached the city's outer limits, the driver mercifully slows the car. I dare to release my grip on the seat and breathe. Once my pulse finally comes down to normal, I'm able to relax enough to start peering around at the sights.

Without question, Pago Veiano is the most charming place I've ever seen. Situated atop a lush, green mountain, the village has nearly a three-hundred-sixty-degree view of farmlands, homesteads, and olive tree groves that stretch out across the surrounding landscape. The village's main streets are paved, and the side roads are cobblestoned. Buildings that are centuries old line the little streets; some of the buildings are painted bright yellow and orange, and others are gray stone with big wood doors and shutters. Occasionally, we pass someone who's out for a walk, but for the most part, the village is quiet. As we wind farther into town, we pass a pub, and our taxi driver taps the car horn while waving to those who are drinking and smoking outside the building. The pub's patrons call out boisterous greetings as they wave back.

Rounding a curve, we approach what appears to be the village center. There's a building at our left that's clearly newer construction, and based on the signage in its windows, I'm guessing the building houses the village's government offices. Paul doesn't direct my attention to that building, however, Instead, he leans close to me and points out the window to my right.

"That church is dedicated to *San Donato*. It's one of the landmarks of the village."

I look out at the church, and I'm enchanted by what I see. The church is a tall, two-story structure with a bright yellow exterior accented by ornate white detailing. A small crucifix sits atop the roof. The church sits directly across the road from the government building and its adjoining plaza, which has a fountain and provides a breathtaking vista of the valley beyond.

"It's absolutely beautiful," I tell Paul, looking his way.

Paul sets his eyes on mine. "I'm glad you like it."

I suddenly realize how close Paul is to me, and his nearness sends my pulse flying. A tremulous, thrilling feeling explodes inside my chest. I—

Jarring bumps begin shaking the car, causing both Paul and me to lean away from each other and check out the windshield. Our taxi driver has diverted onto an unpaved side street, taking us away from the center of the village. The roads out here are all gravel and dirt. We begin passing old stone homes that are situated on expansive pieces of property filled with rows of olive trees. There are clothes lines in people's front yards; the colorful garments hanging from them are waving in the gentle breeze. We pass a huge stone well that must have been dug hundreds of years ago. Farther in the distance, perched on an outcropping that overlooks the valley, there's an abandoned tower house covered in green ivy. I can't stop smiling as I take it all in. Truly, the setting here is nothing short of idyllic.

The driver makes an abrupt left turn, hurling me off balance as the car flies down another gravel road and through an open iron gate. The next thing I know, our taxi is coming to a stop.

"This is it," Paul tells me.

My stomach knots up. For a few minutes, I had forgotten why I was here. Now the reality of the situation is crashing down upon me once again.

Paul pays the taxi driver, opens the door, and gets out. I slide out after him. After Paul shuts the door, the driver gives us an enthusiastic wave, honks his horn, and speeds away, his car tires churning up rocks and dirt as the vehicle disappears in a cloud of dust.

Everything becomes quiet but for the chirping of the birds and the wind that's softly rustling the trees. I take in a few breaths, still working to calm my unrest, grateful there's something innately soothing about this place.

Putting up a hand to shade my eyes, I turn to view the house. It's a lovely white, two-story home, which is larger than most of the other houses we passed on our way here. I'm guessing it underwent updates and renovations not too long ago, but the work has been carefully done to preserve the home's original character. There's a stone walkway leading up to the front door. A little table and chairs are situated on the porch. Flowers are in bloom everywhere, some in pots and others growing wildly. The lawn is green and well-maintained, without being rigidly manicured. Olive trees dot the rest of the property, which has another postcard-worthy view of the valley behind it.

"What a gorgeous place." I face Paul. "How long have your grandparents lived here?"

"They moved into the original home that was on this property when they got married sixty years ago." Paul's expression is one of quiet pride as his eyes survey the land. "Over the years, they renovated and expanded the home, making it what it is today." He smiles reminiscently. "I spent a lot of summers here as a kid. This place has always been the true heart and soul of the family."

Before I can reply, I hear the front door of the home being opened. I jump and spin back toward the house.

"*Ciao!*" Paul calls out from beside me.

I swallow hard when I see my pretend grandparents-in-law appear.

Twelve

An instant later, I'm swept up by a whirlwind of noise and activity when two people—a short man and an even shorter woman—rush out of the house and scurry toward Paul and me, waving their hands enthusiastically and speaking in rapid-fire Italian. The woman reaches me first, clamps me in a tight embrace, and pauses talking only long enough to stand on tiptoe and give me a peck-kiss on each cheek. The man then gives me a gentle hug while greeting me with words I can't understand. The next thing I know, I'm being pulled toward the house.

A blink later, I'm immersed in the welcome, cool shade of the indoors. Energetic talking continues all around me as I'm tugged through a kitchen, which is filled with the delicious aroma of something baking in the oven, and into a large main room. As the blizzard of hand gestures and animated talking continues, I realize I'm being invited to sit down. I promptly take a seat on a chair at a long dining table, still trying to process what's happening. Paul's grandparents continue chattering over one another as they rush around to the other side of the table and sit across from me. The grandmother asks me another question, and then she clamps shut her mouth, sets her folded hands on the table, and peers at me expectantly. The grandfather, too, goes quiet and observes me. The room falls totally silent as they wait for my reply.

I take a split-second to view Paul's grandparents properly. They both appear to be in their mid-eighties, making the agility with which they were just moving especially impressive. Donato Conti is exactly how I expected him to be, based on his photo on the travel website. He has wispy white hair, a round face, and dark eyes that twinkle much like his grandson's. His smile is warm. He has a kind, wise aura. He's dressed in a pale green button up shirt and tan slacks. Immediately, my heart warms with affection for this sweet man, who I realize probably got dressed up in his nicest clothes to meet his company.

Seated to Donato's left, Paul's grandmother is also radiating a warm, inviting spirit. There's also something playful about her demeanor, which reminds me of Paul. Despite her age, she has naturally dark brown hair, which she has swept into an up-do. Her gaze is curious as she observes me through her round glasses. She's wearing an apron over her black shirt and pants. A string of pearls is around her neck.

"Grandpa, Grandma, Irene doesn't speak Italian," Paul interjects in English, breaking the silence as he sits beside me.

The grandmother's eyes widen, and she starts looking between Paul and me while her lips form into the shape of a circle. Donato doesn't appear quite as taken aback, at least; he continues smiling while his curious gaze also starts shifting from Paul to me and back.

Paul turns my way. "Irene, these are my grandparents, Donato and Rita." He motions across the table. "Grandpa, Grandma, this is Irene Thatcher. She—"

"A ring!" Rita blurts out in accented English. She leaps to her feet. She's staring at my left hand as she clasps her own hands to her chest. "Oh, Paulo, you are getting married!"

Paul and I exchange a fast glance. Before either of us can reply, Rita rushes around the table, scoops me up to my feet, and traps me in another huge hug.

"Oh, my Paulo has found himself an Italian girl, at last!" Still gripping my arms, Rita leans back and peers up at me. She makes a clicking sound with her tongue while nodding with apparent approval. "You are very beautiful. Your ancestors are from Italy, yes? Where in Italy did they come from? *Napoli*? *Roma*?"

I clear my throat. "Oh, um, my . . . great-grandparents came from . . . the north." I flinch. Paul and I really should have ironed out the details of this façade before we got here.

"The north?" Rita reaches up and pats my cheek affectionately. "Well, do not worry, Irene.

It is all right. We are still happy to have you as part of our family." With tears brimming in her eyes, she pulls me into yet another mighty hug. "And you are a Catholic girl, yes? Of course you are. My Paulo would only marry a Catholic girl."

I bite my lip. I'm not Catholic.

"Now, now, Rita. Not so many questions at once." Donato laughs quietly as he gets up and shuffles around the table to join us. Rescuing me from his wife's hold, he takes my hands in his and gazes up at me. His eyes also start to glisten with tears. "We are very pleased to welcome you to the family, Irene."

Guilt crashes down upon me; it feels completely wrong to be lying to these dear people. I have to remind myself that Paul didn't concoct this scheme for his amusement. He's not trying to be cruel. Paul genuinely believes that lying to his grandparents is for the best.

"Thank you," I tell Donato softly.

Rita is beaming as she nudges her spouse. "Oh, now we can stop using the app! We do not need any more women from the app!"

Rita spins around, grabs a cell phone from off a nearby cabinet shelf, and slides to my side. When she shows me what's on her phone, I have to hold back a giggle. The Italian dating app is open on the screen.

"Here, you see?" Rita swipes fast through women's photos without actually taking time to view them. "All of these women are trying to marry Paulo!"

While Rita continues swiping from one picture to the next, I hear Paul's phone start pinging just as rapidly. I glance his way. Paul shoots me a playfully exasperated look before he stands up and pulls his phone from the back pocket of his jeans. He heaves a sigh.

"Grandma, you've just scheduled me for twelve more dates," Paul tells her.

Rita stops what she's doing and fixes a wide-eyed stare on her grandson. "What? You have more dates?"

"Unfortunately, yes." Paul puts away his phone. "So you should probably stop whatever it is that you're doing over there. My social calendar is definitely booked."

Rita nods. "Of course I will stop! You do not need the app anymore! You have Irene!" She begins humming to herself as she returns her phone to the shelf. She comes back to my side and pats my hand. "I am so glad to be done with the app. It is a very strange thing."

I bite the insides of my cheeks to stop from laughing, and I nod to Rita in reply.

Rita looks Paul's way again and shakes a chastising finger at him. "You did not tell us you were getting married! Shame on you!"

Paul's smile doesn't reach his eyes. "I wanted to surprise you and tell you in person."

"Oh, you are a mischievous boy!" Rita pinches Paul's cheek hard, and I nearly snicker again. "We will tell everyone the good news when they come for lunch!"

"Everyone?" I echo, my smile vanishing. I shoot Paul a panicked look. "Who's *everyone*?"

Paul turns my way. "Family members who—"

"*Ciao*, Paulo!" someone bellows from the front door.

I whip around, my eyes getting huge when I see a herd of people charging into the room. I dart out of the way, narrowly avoiding getting trampled as the room becomes filled with renewed commotion while everyone shares loud, lively greetings, exchanges kisses on the cheek, and uses their hands to gesture as they talk. Hovering in the corner, I count that five new people have arrived: two men and a woman, who all appear to be somewhere in their fifties, and a young man and a young women who are probably in their late teens.

Observing the scene, my shock starts fading, and I break into a smile. There's no question that this is a loving, tightly knit, vivacious group. They share a family dynamic unlike anything I've ever witnessed. While I'm close to my parents and twin younger sisters, we're not particularly close with any extended family members. In fact, I've never been to a family reunion or spent a holiday with aunts, uncles, or cousins. So as I watch everyone greeting Paul with embraces of joy and familiarity, I feel a pang of envy. Paul is lucky to have so many supportive family members in his life.

"This is Irene!" Rita's declaration, spoken in English, yanks me from my thoughts. "She is

Italian, and she is Catholic, and Paulo is getting married to her!"

Instantly, everyone freezes. The house becomes pin-drop silent. Then, almost in unison, Paul's family members turn toward me. I only have time to gulp and brace myself before the herd stampedes my direction. A breath later, I'm surrounded. I begin getting jostled around as everyone hugs me and kisses my cheeks while talking at me in a mixture of English and Italian.

I feel a hand wrap around mine, and I look up. Paul has made his way to my side. Keeping my hand in his steady grip, Paul gently draws me closer to him. The room quiets down, and the family members back up, giving Paul and me a little breathing room.

"Irene, I would like to introduce you to some of the members of my family," Paul says evenly. He motions first to the two men. "These are my uncles—my father's younger brothers—Mateo and Lorenzo."

Both men have dark hair sprinkled with gray. They're a couple inches taller than I am. Mateo has a round face, like his father, while Lorenzo looks more like Rita. Nonetheless, there's an obvious family resemblance between the two brothers, and there's also a resemblance with Paul. Both men show me friendly smiles.

"Our wives are sorry they could not be here," Mateo tells me with a thick accent. "They are working at the store."

My eyebrows rise with curiosity. "The store?"

"Our family runs a store in the nearby town of Pietrelcina," Paul interjects. "Everyone in the family takes different shifts throughout the week."

"That's wonderful you're all able to work together." I smile at the whole group and then focus on the brothers once more. "I look forward to meeting your wives soon."

Paul smiles again and next motions to the woman. "This is my aunt, Francesca."

Francesca and I make eye contact. She has short hair and cute glasses, and she's dressed in a striped shirt and jeans. She strikes me as someone who's quiet and good-hearted; a natural peacemaker. Smiling at me, she gives me a hug and a peck-kiss on the cheek.

"I am so excited that you and Paulo will be married," Francesca tells me.

I have to shove aside more guilt as I return her embrace. "Thank you. We're . . . excited, too."

Paul quickly gestures to the two youngest members of the group. His smile becomes more playful. "And these are Lorenzo's kids, my cousins, Violetta and Rafaele." He glances at me. "They're about to graduate from high school, and they're going to be trouble."

Rafaele chuckles and gives Paul a high-five.

Violetta, who has been staring at me this entire time, steps closer. She pushes her curly, dark hair from her face. "When are you getting married? Will it be in a big church or a small one? What will your dress look like? Are you going to have bridesmaids?"

Everyone else leans in, waiting for my response.

"Oh, well . . ." I shoot Paul a look.

"We haven't worked out the details yet. I proposed only the other day." Paul puts an arm around my shoulders. "Once we return home, we'll start wedding preparations and keep you posted."

Immediately, every single person in the group starts shouting opinions about when the wedding should take place, which church we should get married in, whether or not we should invite the neighbor who's always intoxicated, and what family recipes should be used for the food at the reception.

I look up at Paul, who still has his arm around me. He meets my gaze. I can see the strain behind his eyes, yet there's conviction in his look, too. Somehow, it's enough to assure me that we're doing the right thing for Donato and Rita.

I also realize how natural and comfortable it feels to be at Paul's side.

A beat later, I come to my senses. This isn't natural. Nothing about this is natural. Paul and I aren't together. This is only a façade, and I can't let myself get swept up in it.

I slide out of Paul's embrace and address the whole group. "I'm impressed by how well everyone speaks English. I don't speak any Italian, but hopefully I'll be able to learn."

Everyone promptly gathers more tightly around me, and they all start loudly reciting Italian phrases in over-enunciated syllables while waving their hands for emphasis. Apparently, my first Italian lesson has begun. I grin and attempt to parrot back a few phrases, causing the others to laugh good-naturedly at my fumbling speech. I giggle along with them, amazed to find that I already feel as though I'm part of this extraordinary family.

Paul's eyes are now sparkling with amusement as he leans down and speaks in my ear so I can hear him over the din. "Years ago, my father decided to move to the US to attend college, and when he married an American woman and chose to stay in the States, the rest of my family took it upon themselves to learn English."

"Wow, really?" My affection and admiration for these people are growing by the moment. I look around the group. "You're an incredible family."

"And now you are part of the family, too!" Lorenzo declares. He turns and playfully punches Paul on the shoulder. "Kiss her, Paulo! Kiss her! This is a celebration!"

My heart skids to a stop.

Everyone begins cheering for Paul to kiss me. Out of the corner of my eye, I see Paul slowly shift my way. A shockwave runs down my spine. Hardly breathing, I face Paul in return. Paul is peering directly into my eyes as he leans down, bringing his face close to mine. My lips burn with anticipation. My skin tingles at his closeness. Paul draws even nearer and pauses again. He then plants a soft kiss on my forehead. Everyone cheers. Paul slowly pulls his eyes from mine to look at his relatives. He puts on a grin.

"That's all you get to see," Paul tells them with a chuckle.

Paul's uncles, aunt, and cousins continue laughing and clapping. Rita appears delighted as she uses a handkerchief to dab tears from her eyes. Donato looks curiously between Paul and me, and for a moment or two, I swear I see a gleam in his eyes.

I still haven't moved, very aware that the place on my forehead where Paul kissed me remains hot from the memory of his touch. Somehow, that one simple kiss from Paul has generated more of a thrill and a sense of passion within me than any kiss I've shared with Stuart in long, long time.

"Time to eat!" Rita declares, yanking me back to attention.

The group moves over to the long dining room table while everyone continues their spirited conversations. Donato takes a place at the head of the table, and he motions for Paul and me to sit on the chairs on each side of him. Paul goes around the table to sit at Donato's left. I take the chair at Donato's right. Glancing around, I sense myself relaxing and smiling once more. I now understand why Donato and Rita have such a big table; nearly all the seats are occupied, and not everyone in the family is even here.

After everyone is settled, Rita promptly gets back to her feet. Francesca and Violetta do the same, and all three of them scurry into the kitchen. I begin hearing the sounds of clanking dishes, sink water running, and the oven being opened.

"I'll go help them," I tell Paul, pushing back from the table and standing up. I figure it's the least I can do.

Paul opens his mouth to reply, but he's cut off by a collective gasp from the others who remain at the table. I freeze. Everyone is staring at me. I have no idea what I've done, but I've apparently made some sort of profound dining-table mistake.

Rita and Francesca poke their heads out of the kitchen, and when they see me, they both begin motioning for me to sit back down.

"What is happening?" I ask Paul under my breath.

Paul chuckles as he observes his grandmother and aunt. "Around here, it's considered an honor to host a guest. Unlike what we're used to in the US, guests here don't typically help with cleaning, making or serving meals, or paying for things. It's almost insulting to the host to do so." He playfully tips his head toward Donato. "And you don't want to offend Gramps!"

"Of course I don't!" I quickly sit back down, my cheeks getting warm as I laugh. "I'm sorry!"

The others laugh along with me. Rita and Francesca smile before disappearing back into the kitchen.

Donato reaches out and pats my hand. "You are a good girl, Irene."

I meet Donato's gaze and feel another rush of affection in my heart. "Thank you, and thank you for having me for lunch."

I note the slight tremor of Donato's hand as he keeps it rested on mine. He watches me closely as he smiles and quietly replies:

"You are most welcome. I hope this will be the first of many meals we share together as family."

I have to blink away tears, and in the periphery of my vision, I'm almost certain Paul blinks a time or two himself.

Those who have been in the kitchen reappear carrying plates that are piled high with food. Rita serves me first, placing in front of me the largest and most delicious-looking piece of homemade lasagna I've ever seen. It's beautifully presented on a blue-and-white porcelain plate. Donato is served next, followed by Paul, and then the others. Once everyone has their food, the eating commences amidst more laughter and conversations spoken in both Italian and English. Lost in the bliss of the most incredible meal I've ever enjoyed, I stay quiet for the most part, simply taking it all in. It's like being part of that idyllic Norman Rockwell painting of the family at Thanksgiving . . . Italian style.

After everyone has finished their lasagna, Rafaele and Violetta clear the plates and head into the kitchen. I sigh contentedly and sink a little lower in my chair. My stomach is so full, I can hardly move. And I wouldn't change a thing.

I look down the table at Rita. "That was the most wonderful meal I've ever eaten. Thank you so much for lunch and . . ."

I trail off when Rafaele and Violetta reappear from the kitchen carrying more plates of food. My eyes get even bigger when Violetta sets down a plate in front of me that has been loaded with a giant slice of roast drizzled in gravy, and lots of fresh, steamed vegetables. I cast an astonished look around the table only to discover that the others are already back to eating. Astoundingly, that gargantuan lasagna was only the first course.

I pick up my fork, hoping I'll somehow be able to consume at least a couple of bites so I don't come across as rude. My concern soon proves to be completely unnecessary, however, because once I taste the rich, delicious roast, I manage to polish it off with ease. Same with the vegetables.

Two more courses follow. I eat it all: salad, freshly baked bread, exotic fruits I've never heard of before, rich cheese, and gelato. My stomach goes from stuffed to ready-to-explode, yet I joyously keep shoveling it in. Part of the reason, of course, is that the food is extraordinary. Yet there's something more than that. There's a joy and a spirit of camaraderie here, and I love being a part of it.

By the time we're finishing the gelato, over two hours have passed since lunch began. The time definitely wasn't wasted, though. Quite the opposite. Without question, this was the most fantastic dining experience I've ever had in my life. I'll never forget it.

The teens start cleaning up the table, and Rafaele jokingly snatches away his father's gelato dish before Lorenzo can eat the last bite. Lorenzo chastises his son in Italian, causing Violetta and Rafaele to snicker as they dart into the kitchen. Lorenzo chuckles and shakes his head, but then a serious expression comes over his face. He shifts in his chair and poses a question to Donato. The only word I pick out is, "*appartamento.*"

A hush falls over the table, and everyone looks Donato's way with apprehension etched in their expressions. I follow the others' gazes to Donato, and I discover that the happy gleam in his eyes has dimmed, and his brow is deeply furrowed. He glances at me before he stands up from the table and says something to his three children. They all get up and head into the kitchen, talking together in low voices.

Strained silence follows. I shift my eyes to Paul. He's staring down at the table, the muscles of his jaw working. With growing unease, I look at Rita.

"Is everything all right?" I dare to ask.

Rita puts on a smile. "Yes. Just a little trouble from the business."

I look Paul's way once more. "The store in the nearby town?"

Paul shakes his head. "No. Trouble with their rental properties."

I keep my attention on Paul, willing him with my eyes to tell me more. Paul seems to understand, for he glances at Rita, who gives him a permitting nod. Paul focuses on me again, and he starts to explain:

"My grandparents have owned the store in Pietrelcina since they got married. Gramps inherited the store from his father, who inherited it from his father before him. The store has been successful enough to allow my grandparents to renovate this home over the years, turning it into the family gathering place we enjoy now." He pauses to give Rita a smile. "With the ongoing success of their store, my grandparents also decided to pursue their dream of investing in other real estate. They purchased two apartments in Rome to use as rentals: the apartment where you're staying, and the place I'm currently using. Through it all, my grandparents had a great estate agent who handled most of the details, which allowed them to oversee things from here."

"And they were fortunate to have your help, too," I surmise.

Paul shrugs. "I helped a little. Italian estate laws aren't exactly the same as in the US, but I chipped in however I could."

"Paulo is being too humble," Rita interjects. "We would not have been able to do any of this without him."

There's a distinct flicker in my chest when I hear that. I turn back to Paul, and when my eyes meet his, the flickering grows stronger.

"Rita?" Donato's voice interrupts the conversation.

Donato has reappeared in the open doorway between the kitchen and the main room. Rita looks at her husband, and I see the two of them exchange a worried glance. A cold sense of unease comes over me. Yes, something serious is definitely wrong for Donato and Rita.

Rita focuses on me again, puts on a gracious smile, and stands up. "Please excuse me."

Paul also gets to his feet, but Rita holds up a hand in a halting gesture.

"No, Paulo, we are all right. You stay here with Irene."

Rita slips out of the room with Donato and shuts the door behind her, leaving Paul and me alone. Paul exhales hard as he takes his chair once more.

I watch him, not hiding my worry. "Are your grandparents in trouble?"

Paul puts a turbulent gaze on me. "Not legal trouble, but they're at risk of losing two new rental properties they recently invested in. It's going to be a devastating blow if the transactions fall through."

"That's awful," I reply in almost a whisper. "May I ask what happened?"

Paul's eyes go to the window. "Like I mentioned, Gramps and Grandma's dream has always been to own and manage rental properties. They've loved having the rentals in Rome, and for years they've longed to acquire additional rentals in Florence and in Venice." He glances toward the kitchen and grins a little. "I don't know where they get their energy from, but like I've said before, once they get an idea in their heads, they're impossible to discourage."

I can't help laughing at that. "So I've gathered."

Paul laughs, too, but his levity soon fades. "However, their health isn't what it once was, especially not with Gramps, but they still refuse to slow down." He runs a hand through his hair. "I don't know where Gramps would be, though, were it not for the fact that Mateo, Lorenzo, and Francesca, as well as their spouses, took over running the store in Pietrelcina."

"And I assume some of them even gave up careers of their own to do it?"

Paul nods. "For example, Mateo gave up running his own store to work at his parents' shop instead."

"And what about your dad?" I venture. "Is he involved?"

"Definitely." Paul sits up. "Dad manages their finances, and though he has lived his adult life in the US, he visits here several times a year. My grandparents are lucky they don't have to worry that their money is being handled by someone they can't trust." His eyes drift toward the kitchen once more. "Anyway, thanks to the help from their kids, and the support of a great estate agent, my grandparents were able to purchase the two apartments in Rome some years ago and start living their dream of owning rental properties."

"And as I said before, I'm guessing they had some invaluable help from their grandson, too," I chime in with a smile.

"Nah." Paul shrugs. "Grandma exaggerates. I'm happy to help as much as I can, of course, but I can't take any credit for their success."

Paul's humility is as sincere as it is endearing. I'm convinced he has done far more for his grandparents than he's letting on, but I'm not going to argue the point at the moment.

Paul continues, "In addition to their two rentals in Rome, my grandparents wanted to acquire a rental property in both Florence and Venice. True to their character, they saved for years to do it. A few months ago, they finally got to the point where it was financially feasible." He breaks off from what he's saying and frowns. "To be honest, none of us wanted them to do it. Gramps' health has continued to wane, and we worried the strain of managing two more properties would be too much. They were both so insistent and excited, however, that we finally had to throw our support behind them."

I nod, staying quiet.

"Thankfully, through it all, they had their great estate agent," Paul resumes. "He was always willing to do the leg work, including property visits and negotiating on my grandparents' behalf."

I nod again, this time uneasily. I'm starting to get a terrible feeling that this is where the story takes a turn for the worse.

Paul exhales hard. "Not long ago, a great property became available in Florence. Shortly afterward, one became available in Venice. My grandparents were thrilled, and things were put into motion for them to acquire both properties. Unfortunately, their estate agent had a health crisis of his own and had to step down."

I cringe. Yep, this is definitely where things get worse.

"My grandparents rushed to find a new estate agent so they wouldn't lose the properties they had dreamed of acquiring for so long. They hired someone without telling us, and my grandparents paid him a huge advance without notifying my dad." Paul's expression darkens. His jaw clenches. "Turns out, this so-called estate agent was a con-artist. After receiving my grandparents' money, he disappeared. Obviously, my grandparents were devastated, both because of the loss of their hard-earned money and because they would likely lose the new properties they longed to buy."

I need a few seconds to absorb what I've heard, and then I want to cry for Donato and Rita. And I seriously want to punch whoever stole their money.

Paul lets out another sigh. "Everyone has seen the effects that the stress of all this is having on Gramps, but he refuses to give up. He still wants to acquire those two new properties.

That's why I flew out here this week. I'll be visiting both properties on my grandparents' behalf to keep the negotiations going. Meanwhile, Dad is trying to track down the stolen funds. Until those funds are recovered, though—and there's no guarantee they ever will be—the pressure is on to get the new rentals purchased and up-and-running. If my grandparents don't quickly earn money to make up for the advance that was stolen from them, they'll have to sell all their rentals, including the ones in Rome."

"That can't happen," I declare, my eyes widening with dismay. "What can I do to help? I want to help somehow."

Paul shows a strained smile. "You've helped immensely already. As trivial as it seems, I know that relieving my grandparents of their worry about me has taken one weight off their shoulders."

"It's not enough, though," I insist. "I want to do more."

Paul starts observing me more closely. "What do you propose?"

I clasp my hands together in front of me on the tabletop. "Well, if I'm understanding correctly, it sounds like your grandparents need to get the rental properties in Florence and Venice purchased soon, and then they need to get all their rental properties booked up for the foreseeable future, right? This is the only way they'll be able to achieve their dream of owning those properties while earning enough money to compensate for what was stolen from them, correct?"

"Correct," Paul responds.

I unclasp my hands and start tapping a finger on the edge of the table. "Then for starters, your grandparents need to expand their advertising—particularly about the new apartments they plan to acquire in Venice and Florence—in order to get the word out and make their rentals stand out from the crowd." I stop tapping. "Who manages their website and advertising, anyway?"

"No one, really," Paul replies with frankness. "My grandparents don't have their own website or any advertising campaigns. They just pay to use that third-party travel website where you found the apartment's listing a couple days ago. I manage what's posted on there."

"Hmm." I press my lips together. "I'm no expert in marketing, but I think your grandparents would benefit from having their own website; it could still link to the third-party travel website where the rentals would also be posted. Additionally, your grandparents need a dedicated advertising campaign." I show Paul a grin. "Plus—and no offense—the photos and descriptions about the Rome rentals that are currently on the third-party website could use a significant facelift."

Paul snorts a laugh. "Are you inferring my photography and creative-writing skills aren't good enough?"

I laugh along with him. "While you undoubtedly have a great legal mind, let's just say there could be some improvement in the artistic department."

Paul laughs again. Eventually, though, his expression becomes pensive. "These are great ideas, Irene, but it will take time—and money— to hire a web designer, advertising guru, and professional photographer. Unfortunately, it's both time and money my grandparents don't have." He leans back in his chair, his brow furrowing. "Financially, my dad and I have both offered to help, but my grandparents adamantly refuse. As for the time . . . well, no one can give them more of that, I'm afraid. The clock is already ticking."

"Then I suppose that means we're going to have to do it," I state.

Paul quirks an eyebrow. "We're going to have to do what, exactly?"

"You and I are going to give your grandparents the help they need. You'll do the site visits and handle the legal side of things. I'll accompany you on your visits and take photos that we can post online; my phone's camera is as good as any professional's . . . at least, that's what the guy at the store told me when he convinced me to buy the upgraded—and markedly more expensive—device."

Paul's other eyebrow rises. "What about that new website and its content? And the advertising campaign?"

I open my mouth but close it again, drawing a blank. Clearly, neither Paul nor I have web-development skills, and I have no idea where on such short notice we could possibly find someone who . . .

Actually, I take that back. Finding someone who's tech savvy might be the easiest part of all.

I lean back in my chair and call toward the kitchen, "Rafaele? Violetta?"

The two teens come bounding into the room. Paul shoots me a perplexed look. I just smile at the duo and ask:

"Do you two know how to design a website?"

Violetta nods. "Sure. It is easy. We learned in school."

"Yeah. Really easy," Rafaele adds nonchalantly.

"Perfect." I shift my attention back to Paul. "So here's what I suggest: I'll go with you to visit the properties in Florence and Venice. While you handle the estate stuff, I'll take photos and write up new descriptions about the rentals. When we get back to Rome, I'll do the same with the two rentals there." I turn again to the teens. "Meanwhile, you guys will create a website for your grandparents' rental properties. The website will include some of the photos I take and the write-ups, as well as contact information and a form to submit a reservation request. The website will also incorporate links to the third-party travel website, to accommodate anyone who prefers to make their reservations through that platform instead. As for advertising, we—"

"I will make social media pages." Violetta motions to her phone. "It is super fast. I will get lots of followers."

"And I will get a domain name and web address, and I will look for other websites we can link to for more advertising," Rafaele chimes in.

"Fantastic." I smile again at them before focusing on Paul once more. "Am I leaving anything out?"

Paul is watching me, his eyes narrowed slightly with a look of concentration. "You're really serious about this?"

"Of course I'm really serious about this," I reply calmly.

Paul slowly breaks into the most genuine, relaxed smile I've seen from him today. "Then I'm going to take you up on your offer, Irene." He turns to his cousins. "So you two need to get to work. By the end of the week, Irene and I will have a lot of content for you to post on the new website."

"That will be no problem," Rafaele tells us, grinning back at Paul.

Without another word, the teens dart out the back door, talking rapidly between themselves as they go. Paul watches his cousins disappear, and then he gets to his feet. He looks at me with a widening smile and says:

"I should probably go tell my grandparents about this scheme you've concocted."

I push back from the table and stand up. "I'll come with you."

Paul unexpectedly reaches across the table and gently takes one of my hands in his. "Irene, thank you."

I draw in a silent breath, the feel of Paul's hand around mine awakening my senses in a way I've never experienced before. Paul and I gaze at one another, neither of us moving or speaking, until the quiet is shattered by the sounds of the other adults making their way back to the room.

I slip my hand from Paul's and say, "You're welcome, Paulo."

Thirteen

The warm nighttime breeze is stirring the trees that line the sidewalk as Paul and I make our way from the *San Giovanni* station back to my apartment. We've just returned to Rome from Pago Veiano, and though it's late in the evening and shops are closed, the restaurants are still bustling. So in addition to the whispering of the wind, the air is carrying the sounds from the restaurants, including music, clanking glasses, cheering from those who are watching soccer—I mean, *calcio*—on television, and lively conversations. Meanwhile, the lampposts have come on, their soft glow mixing cozily with the flickering candles that are on the restaurants' outdoor tables.

Neither Paul nor I have said much during our journey back to Rome. I'm trying to tell myself that the reason for our silence is simply because we're both worn out. After all, we got up early this morning, traveled to Pago Veiano, concocted a plan to save Donato and Rita's real estate dreams, convinced the family to go along with our plan, went on a jam-packed, whirlwind sightseeing excursion of Pago Veiano and

Pietrelcina in the scorching heat, and maintained our façade of being engaged the whole time. So of course we're tired.

Yet something is telling me that fatigue isn't the reason for our silence.

If I'm being honest, during the train ride back to Rome, I felt anything *but* tired. As soon as Paul and I were seated next to each other on the train, the intense feeling of attraction between us that had been swelling all day became more palpable than ever. I kept my head down and passed the time using my phone to answer emails and surf the Internet, yet I remained completely aware of Paul's presence beside me. He remained quiet, too, reading articles on his phone and listening to music through his earbuds, but the glances he periodically sent my way were more than enough to convey that he was totally aware of me, too. So although we said little, we communicated plenty. It was like Paul and I were sharing some sort of thrilling, confusing, frustrating, powerful dance that neither of us dared to acknowledge. We couldn't acknowledge it. Because what's going on between Paul and me isn't real. It's an act. It's temporary.

And I'm planning to talk with Stuart.

Paul and I turn a corner and start walking past the closed-for-the-night street market where we got my knock-off purse and fake engagement ring. At the sight, I brush my left thumb against the ring; I've lost track of the number of times I've done that today. This little ring has come to symbolize the blur of events that have transpired over these past few days and led to this moment: deciding to live more fully, breaking up with my boyfriend, traveling alone to Italy, and agreeing to pretend to be someone else's fiancée. The ring is also a reminder of how attached I've become to Paul's loving, vivacious, generous, tight-knit family, and how I'm determined to help save his grandparents' dreams.

Most notably, the ring is a reminder of Paul, a man who has proven himself to be witty, handsome, respectful, kind, caring, and intelligent. A man with whom I've already shared more candid, heartfelt discussions than I've shared with Stuart in a long time. Paul makes me laugh; I can't recall the last time I laughed with Stuart. With Paul, I feel listened to and understood, and that's something I haven't sensed with Stuart lately. Paul and I have a natural chemistry, which has been brewing since the moment we met. I'm not sure what kind of chemistry I share with Stuart anymore.

Stuart.

Only a few days ago, I was dreaming that he would travel to Rome with me. Now I find myself doubting if we ever had the relationship I thought we did. Have I been wrong? If so, when did things go awry between us? I can't say. After these past few days, I don't know what I think or believe anymore.

A loud squeak of hinges yanks me back to the moment. Paul is pushing open the green gate that leads to the courtyard in front of my apartment building. Paul holds the gate ajar for me, and as our eyes meet, he and I share an electrifying look before I slide past him to enter the courtyard. Paul follows, moves in front of me, and uses his keys to unlock the building's main door. Paul again turns my way as he pushes open the door. Our gazes lock once more, and now my legs are shaking as I step by him to go inside. Paul enters after me, and the sound made by the closing door echoes up the stairwell and fades away. Then all is still.

Without a word, we climb the stairs while the quiet seems to thicken around us. My heart is drumming, and an impossible-to-ignore sense of anticipation is coursing through me. I work to steady my breathing, and I keep my gaze directed straight ahead, though my concentration is completely focused on the man beside me.

"You're sure you're okay with going to Venice tomorrow?" Paul asks, breaking the silence once we stop in front of my apartment door. "It's going to be a long daytrip."

"I'm sure." I dare to face him. "I want to help your grandparents. They're wonderful people. Your whole family is wonderful, Paul. I had an amazing time with everyone today."

Paul takes a step closer to me and lowers his voice. "I can't tell you how much I appreciate what you're doing."

I flush at his intoxicating nearness. "You don't need to say anything," I reply in practically a whisper. "I know how you feel."

For a heartbeat, we're both completely still, gazing at each other in the near-darkness of the hallway, and then the fiery, magnetic pull that has been building between us all day finally erupts. My heart starts pounding so hard that I can barely breathe. I see Paul's respirations quicken. Gazing right into my eyes, he reaches out and places a hand on my cheek, his touch igniting a blaze within me. My lips part. Paul leans down, bringing his face toward mine.

"Wait," I hear myself utter.

Paul freezes. My legs are threatening to give out as I stagger back from him, my face brushing his fingertips as I step out of his reach. I look away, working to catch my breath. My mind is reeling as I attempt to process what just happened. What almost happened.

As fast as it came on, the energy between Paul and me vanishes. The silence becomes heavy and strained. Forcing down a swallow, I dare to look at Paul once more. He's still standing in the same place. His chest is rising and falling with his respirations. He lowers his arm back to his side, and he shuts and reopens his eyes.

"Stuart," he says.

"Stuart," I repeat in almost a whisper, a terrible ache pressing upon my chest.

Paul retreats a step, putting more space between us. "I'm sorry, Irene."

"Don't be sorry." I resist the urge to move closer to him again. "You have nothing to be sorry for. I mean that."

Now Paul is the one who looks away. I can see a muscle twitching in his cheek. "Perhaps it would be better if I went alone to Venice tomorrow."

"No, don't go without me," I object. "I said I would help your grandparents, and I intend to do so. I want to do so."

"I know." Paul still has his gaze averted. "But maybe it's not a good idea to—"

"If you leave without me, I'll hop the next train to Venice and search for you there."

Paul's eyes immediately leap back to mine. "Don't do that. It wouldn't be safe."

"Then take me with you."

Paul rubs the back of his neck. "Are you sure?"

"I'm sure," I say, barely managing to keep my voice steady.

Dropping his arm, Paul focuses on me with an expression that's now devoid of emotion. "Then I'll see you at four in the morning like we planned."

"I'll see you in the morning." I fumble around in my purple purse to find my set of apartment keys. "Goodnight, Paul."

Without waiting for him to reply, I jam the keys into the lock, heave open the door, dart into the dark apartment, and shut the door behind me. I turn the lock while keeping one ear near the door. After a second or two, I hear Paul start making his way down the stairs.

Turning around, I slide down to the floor and hang my head. What has happened to my life? In only a few days, everything I thought I wanted or understood has been called into question. What do I really want to do with my life? Who do I want to be with? What do I believe about love?

I don't know, but I have to figure it out.

I get to my feet, find the light switch, and flip on the entryway light. I stagger into the main room and drop onto the couch. I'm not even thinking anymore as I tug my phone from my purse and rapidly, impulsively compose a text to Stuart:

Guess what? I'm in Rome!
I'm staying at a rental apartment owned by a wonderful man named Donato Conti.
Any chance you're able to talk sooner than Saturday night?

I don't bother to reread the message before I push the *send* button. I don't care what my text said. Stuart and I just need to talk. I need to know where we stand. I need to know if there's any chance of a future between us.

I don't know how much time passes while I wait for Stuart to reply. Finally, my emotions ebb, and exhaustion gets the better of me. I slip off my shoes and lie down on the couch. I set my phone on the floor, still listening for the sound of a text alert. My eyes close.

Fourteen

A pounding sound wakes me from sleep. My eyes flutter open. Why am I on the couch? What's making that noise? When—

My mind clears, and memories of last night come back to me in a rush: the moment when Paul and I nearly kissed, the moment my resolve to be patient broke down and I impulsively sent Stuart a text, and the agonizing moment when I realized I have no idea what to believe anymore.

With a groan, I turn onto my side. I didn't close the drapes before I fell asleep, so I have a view out the windows of the balcony and skyline beyond. I can see the faintest hints of sunlight beginning to touch the dark sky. Sunrise isn't far off. It's got to be—

I sit up with a gasp.

Venice. Paul and I are going to Venice.

I hear the same pounding again, and this time I register that it's someone knocking on the front door. I snatch up my phone from the floor. The first thing I notice is that Stuart didn't reply to my text. The second thing I notice is that it's four in the morning.

Paul is here. It's time for us to go.

There's another knock, and my body jolts. I leap to my feet, rush to the entryway, and yank open the door.

"I'm so sorry! I forgot to set an alarm!"

Paul is standing a couple feet back from the doorway with his hands in his pockets. He's dressed in a black shirt and jeans. He hasn't shaved this morning, and there's darkness under his eyes; I'm guessing Paul got less sleep last night than I did. Not that Paul looks bad, though. Not in the slightest. To the contrary, in fact, Paul's rugged appearance is profoundly attractive.

"No worries." Paul adjusts the laptop bag that's hanging from his shoulder. His demeanor is friendly but formal. Restrained. Cautious. "I still feel badly about dragging you out of bed to go all the way to Venice just for a day. Why don't I make the trip alone, and I'll fill you in when I get back?" He clears his throat. "You can stay here to catch up on things and finally get in some *Roma* sightseeing."

I shove my disheveled hair from my face. "No, I want to go. I only need a couple minutes to get ready. I'll be right back."

I retreat from the door. Paul appears to hesitate before he comes inside. I shut the door behind him, spin away, and charge into my bedroom. Flinging my door closed, I proceed to yank out from the closet the first articles of clothing I get my hands on: a gray, short-sleeved top and jeans. After I change, I dash into the bathroom. I wipe off the makeup that's smeared under my eyes, brush my teeth, and pull my hair half-back with an elastic. Returning to the bedroom, I stuff what I need into my purple purse. Once I'm ready, I return to the entryway. I find Paul staring into the main room, looking out the windows and watching the sun come up. He jumps slightly when I approach, as if hadn't heard me coming.

"I probably set a record for the fastest get-ready time in history, but I think I'm good-to-go." I sling my purse across my body.

"Fair enough." Paul starts heading for the door. "Let's head out."

The fact that we're rushing to catch our train provides a good excuse for us not to attempt conversation. Even without words, though, it's acutely evident there's a barrier of uncertainty between us that neither of us dares to venture over. Rather than warm, invigorating, and exciting, the sense of restraint we share is now uncomfortable and strained. I hate it.

Part of me is starting to wish things would go back to the way they were before. Back to when I thought I was content to spend all my time working in the Lakewood ED. Back to before I realized how desperately I needed to do more with my life. Back to when Stuart and I were happily in love . . .

My thoughts screech to a halt.

Stuart and I *were* in love . . . weren't we?

I draw in a shaky breath and try to distract myself with the sights and sounds of the now-familiar route that Paul and I are taking to the metro station. The cafés are starting to open. The smell of coffee is wafting through the air. The street lights are flickering off as the sun continues rising. The sellers at the street market are setting up, and when I see them, I'm reminded that I'm still wearing the fake engagement ring. I consider taking it off and stashing it in my purse. But I don't.

Paul and I arrive at *San Giovanni* and head underground. We navigate the metro station, get on the train, and arrive a few stops later at bustling Termini. Still without a word, we maneuver through the underground mall, reemerge above ground, and weave through the crowds to reach the platform where the long-distance train to Venice is scheduled to depart. Once again, Paul has already bought our tickets, and he leads the way to our designated train car. Our reserved seats are part of a grouping of four, where two seats face forward and the other two face backward. Paul takes the backward-facing seat on the aisle. My seat is the forward-facing chair by the window. There's no one else in our grouping, leaving space between Paul and me. I can't help wondering if Paul bought four seats to set it up this way on purpose.

As soon as the train rolls out of the station, Paul promptly puts in his earbuds, pulls his laptop from his bag, and begins working on something, his brow furrowed with a look of concentration. I clear my throat and focus my attention outside. Rocked by the steady motion of the train and warmed by the sunlight, I lean my head against the window. I sense my eyelids drooping, and then they shut.

***

A shrill whistle causes me to open my eyes. My face is mashed against the window, and based on how kinked my neck muscles feel, I'm guessing I've been sleeping like this for quite a while. How glamorous.

People are moving about inside the train car, causing me to sit up and look around. To my surprise, the other passengers are gathering their belongings. Even Paul is putting away his laptop. I check out the window again. The train is rolling into a large station, and there's a blue-and-white sign hanging from an awning that reads, *Venezia S.Lucia*.

"We're already in Venice?" My eyes are wide as I look at Paul. "I slept the entire ride?"

Paul stands and slings his computer bag over his shoulder. The first hint of a grin I've seen from him today appears on his lips. "You were out like a light the whole time."

"I can't believe it." I get to my feet and adjust my purse on my hip. I start rubbing the side of my face where it's undoubtedly indented from the window frame. "I guess I was more sleep-deprived than I realized."

The train doors open. Paul and I make our way out of the train car and step down onto the platform, becoming swallowed up in heat and crowds. Paul stays at my side as we follow the flow of pedestrians into the station. We cross the station's central hub and exit out the other side. Immediately, I stumble to halt, staring straight ahead in stunned disbelief. I then put a hand to my chest and gasp with complete and utter delight.

Paul and I are only steps away from the Grand Canal of Venice.

In person, the gorgeousness of this place almost defies description. Down some stairs and across a small plaza that's filled with people, the wide, building-lined Grand Canal is sparkling a lovely hue of green under the summer sunshine. I'm first riveted by the staggering amount of boat traffic that's moving along the water. The canal is clearly Venice's version of a highway. Countless small boats of all shapes, sizes, and colors are cruising the canal in both directions, including open-air boats packed with selfie-taking tourists, commuter boats for the locals that make frequent stops at the docks that stick out into the water, and fancy boats with tinted windows. The air itself is humming with the sounds of boat engines, chatting tourists, and singing gondoliers.

Gondolas.

I pull in another breath of giddy excitement. I'm looking at real gondolas. Several of the famous long, ornate black boats that lie low to the water are also floating along the canal, carrying romance-minded tourists. The gondolas are being steered by gondoliers who are dressed in striped shirts and round-brimmed hats. Happy tears fill my eyes as I watch the scene. Gondolas might be touristy and cliché, but they're iconic. I've always dreamed of seeing them.

In the periphery of my vision, I realize Paul is studying me. He probably thinks I'm ridiculous for getting emotional, but I don't mind. This moment is too magical to pretend to feel otherwise. So I continue soaking it all in, trying to imprint this scene upon my memory forever.

Finally shifting my attention from the boats, I gaze about, watching the people who are going in and out of the train station and tourists who are taking selfies near the canal. At last, I put my focus on the most stunning sight of all: the buildings themselves, which sit on the edge of the canal.

Rising up prominently almost directly across the canal from where we're standing is a massive, strikingly gorgeous white church with tall pillars and a huge green dome on its roof. Meanwhile, countless other stunning, centuries-old buildings line both sides of the canal for as far as the eye can see. The buildings are flat-fronted, square or rectangular in shape, and four or five stories tall. Some have pedestrian alleyways between them, and others are immediately adjacent to their neighbors. Most buildings have wooden docks extending from their front doors into the canal, where little boats are tied up and waiting to be used. Some of the buildings show their age more than others, but this only adds to their beauty. What I love most is that each building has its own unique color scheme, window shape, and ornate detailing, and yet, amidst the variety, they all maintain the Venetian motif, making a cohesive and incredible visual array.

"What do you think?" Paul nudges me gently.

I put my hands to my flushed cheeks. "This is the most amazing thing I've ever seen." I drop my hands and look Paul's way. "Thank you for letting me join you today. This is a dream come true."

Paul's eyes reignite with their usual soulful warmth. "I'm glad you like it." He tips his head toward the canal. "What do you say we take a little journey on the water?"

"Yes," I reply. "One hundred percent yes."

Paul smiles, and I practically skip alongside him as he leads me to a small, free-standing, rectangular-shaped building that's nearby. The building has white siding, a bright yellow stripe near its roof, and signs hanging on its exterior walls. The structure isn't ornate or particularly pretty—it looks almost like a big shipping container, and it's clearly centuries newer than the buildings on the canal itself. Only once we get close to it do I realize it's a ticket booth.

Paul steps up to the ticket booth's window and speaks to the woman behind the glass. He pays, and she issues him two tickets. Giving me another smile, Paul guides me through an open doorway and into the little building, which brings us to a covered waiting area that's right beside a dock. With a squeal of glee, I dash forward and hang over the dock's railing as far as I can to get another view of the canal. To the left, there's a footbridge arching high over the water; it's crammed with pedestrians, most of whom are taking selfies. Watching the scene, I can't help sighing with total contentment.

"This is our *vaporetto*," I hear Paul say.

I lean back and shoot Paul a perplexed look. "Our what?"

Paul chuckles and points past me. "Our water taxi."

Returning my attention to the canal, I spot a large, white, open-air boat chugging toward our dock with enough speed to make me nervous. Somehow, though, the driver manages to drop the speed at the last moment and skillfully navigate the boat so it glides up parallel to the dock, touching it with no more than a light bump. While the boat idles in place, a woman who's dressed in a baby blue polo shirt and black shorts jumps from the boat onto the dock. She uses a thick rope to tether the vessel, and then she makes a loud announcement to those waiting in line with Paul and me.

"Time to board." Paul gestures for me to go first.

I'm grinning from ear-to-ear as I step on the boat. Paul stays right behind me. I glance around, noting that while there are a few chairs at the stern and bow, it's clear most people are expected to stand . . . and I don't mind at all. I venture over to the starboard side of the boat, making room for people who are boarding behind us, and lean out to resume taking in the magical vista of buildings, boats, sunshine, and people. The boat is soon crammed with passengers (far more than a boat of similar size would be allowed to hold in the US, I suspect), and then the woman in the polo shirt gets on and unties the boat from the dock. A second later, our journey is underway.

Can this be real? Surely, this is too perfect to be true! The sun is shining. The wind is tousling my hair. I'm riding a *vaporetto* down the Grand Canal of Venice! I break into another thrilled smile. After years of dreaming of coming here, I'm really in Italy. I'm in Venice!

Out of nowhere, my mind recalls the time when Stuart insisted that a hotel stay in Las Vegas would be enough to satisfy my desire to see Venice. Gazing about me now, all I can do is shake my head. Oh, how wrong Stuart was.

The *vaporetto* is steered up a side canal, which is narrower than the main waterway though still nearly as busy. More stunning, iconic buildings line the route. There are people everywhere, strolling the sidewalks, going in and out of shops, and waiting at various docks for boats to arrive, much like they're waiting at a bus stop. A water ambulance flies past us with its siren blaring. I spin around and keep watching it until it disappears from view, and I can't help wondering what it would be like to work in an emergency department here, speaking fluent Italian and expertly handling all sorts of *vaporetto*-related injuries.

I realize that I've been so busy admiring the breathtaking scenery that I haven't taken a single picture today. I reach into my purse, find my phone, and begin capturing pictures, though I know photos will never do this place justice. Soon, I hear the boat engine roar, and I look up. Our *vaporetto* is stopping at a dock to allow passengers to board and disembark.

I look over at Paul. "Is this our stop?"

"Not quite yet." Paul motions to the phone in my hand. "Would you like me to take your picture with some of the buildings in the background?"

"I would love that," I answer without hesitation. "Thank you."

I give Paul my phone and turn around so my back is against the railing and the buildings that line the canal are in full view behind me. I'm already smiling. Paul takes a picture.

"I'm sorry you're stuck traveling with such a giddy tourist." I sheepishly push off from the railing and take the phone back from Paul. "Please forgive me. I've always dreamed of coming here, and I'm overjoyed."

Paul's dark eyes are sparkling in the sunlight. "I'm glad you came. This place is special to me, too."

Under Paul's spell-binding gaze, my heart rate rises. My head gets light, and I suddenly can't think straight. All at once, every ounce of me is drawn to Paul more powerfully than ever before. My breathing hitches. I have to do something. I have to say something.

"Do you want to take a picture with me?" I blurt out.

Paul keeps peering right into my eyes in a way that is sending tingles shooting down my spine. "I would love to."

As our boat gets underway, Paul comes to my side and turns the same direction as I am. I feel the heat of his nearness and inhale the scent of his cologne, and I swear I get a little weak in the knees. I have to concentrate on holding my arm steady as I lift my phone and frame the picture. My mind flashes back to the few instances when Stuart begrudgingly agreed to be in a selfie with me; those pictures were always awkward and forced. In stark contrast, as I stand next to Paul, everything feels carefree, natural, and . . . perfect.

I take the picture.

I lower the phone to my side, taking a moment to make sure my emotions are in check before I look up at him again. He gazes at me for another second or two, and then he simply says:

"Our stop is next."

The *vaporetto* emerges from the canal to enter the vast lagoon on the north side of Venice. Veering right, we start sailing through open water, with the lagoon on the boat's port side and the buildings of Venice to the starboard. After a while, our boat approaches a dock on our right that's marked by a sign that reads, *F.te Nove.*

The boat gently bumps the dock, and the gal in the polo shirt hops out and secures the vessel once more. As passengers start to disembark, Paul puts his hand lightly on my back, cuing me to follow the others. Stepping onto the dock, Paul and I weave through crowds, cross a wide stone walkway, and reach the shade provided by a lovely white building that's rising up toward the perfectly blue sky.

"This is the lagoon side of Venice." Paul's eyes are surveying the scenery. "This is my favorite area of the city. It's a little removed from the main tourist hubs on the Grand Canal, yet it's still easy to get to the Grant Canal from here, either by *vaporetto* or on foot."

I survey the lagoon, the locals strolling past us, the shops and restaurants that line the walkway, and the beautiful bridges that reach over little canals that run between some of the buildings.

"I can definitely understand why you like it." I shift Paul's way. "It's beautiful, and as you say, it's also quiet and peaceful."

Paul smiles before he motions to a café. "We arrived a couple minutes early. Do you want to get anything before we go check out the apartment?"

I laugh and shake my head. "Thanks for asking, but I should probably avoid consuming anything unknown before we meet a potential seller. You never know what it might do to me."

Paul laughs along with me. "Good point. We'll wait until afterward."

Paul is still chuckling as we start walking together with the open water of the lagoon at our left and the buildings at our right. Paul soon points to a small island that's not far off shore; it has a stone wall all the way around it.

"That's the cemetery for Venice, *San Michele*," Paul explains.

The fabulous impromptu tour of this area of Venice continues as Paul and I stroll while he describes the sights. Frankly, between the magnificence of Venice and Paul's intoxicating presence at my side, I'm not sure how I manage to keep my wits about me as we go. Paul and I cross two lovely bridges, venture up a walkway to our right, and finally approach a building on the left that has a big front door painted a bright shade of blue.

"This is it," Paul says.

Paul pushes the doorbell. I note there are five last names listed on the panel beside it, indicating there are five apartments within the building. As the sound of the doorbell fades away, I hear what sounds like someone coming down a staircase, and then the door is pulled open from the inside. A middle-aged woman with glasses and gray, chin-length hair pokes out her head and greets us. Paul says something to her in reply, and then he motions to me and continues speaking. While Paul and the lady converse, I mirror their facial expressions. Since I am supposed to be Paul's fiancée-with-Italian-heritage, I figure I should try to keep up the act.

The woman motions for Paul and me to come inside. Stepping through the doorway, we enter a foyer that has a wood floor and a high ceiling. Sunlight is streaming in through a window that's above the door. The woman keeps talking as she leads Paul and me up a steep staircase. When we reach the first-floor landing, the woman inserts a key into the lock of a wood door. She pushes open the door and steps aside, allowing Paul and me to enter first.

It takes me only a blink to fall in love with the place, but I maintain a poker face. I have no clue how property transactions go in Italy, and so I don't want to make the mistake of seeming too eager, in case there are still negotiations to be had.

To the right of the entryway is a spacious kitchen with an adjoining main room. A nicely renovated bathroom is close by. The long hallway that stretches out from the entryway has gorgeous parquet flooring. Halfway down the hallway, on the right, is the first bedroom, which is large and full of natural light, thanks to two windows that give a wide view of the bustling walkway down below. At the far end of the hall is an even bigger bedroom, and this one provides a spectacular, unobstructed view of the lagoon itself. This room has an accent wall painted blue, which ties in perfectly with the nautical ambiance. I smile as I finish taking it all in. I'm somehow sure Donato and Rita will love this place, and it will undoubtedly be a huge draw for tourists who are seeking a great rental in Venice.

That is, assuming we can secure this rental soon enough for Donato and Rita to make back the money that was stolen from them.

My smile fades, and spurred on by determination, I get to work. Leaving Paul and the woman in conversation, I go from one room to the next while taking pictures—some to use for reference when I write about the apartment, and other more artistic shots for Rafaele and Violetta to post online. I'm so preoccupied with what I'm doing that I'm not sure how much time has elapsed when I hear footsteps coming my way. I take a last picture of the view of the lagoon through the window of the main bedroom and then turn toward the sound. Paul is walking toward me.

"The owner and I have wrapped up things on our end." Paul gestures to my phone. "How are things going for you?"

"Great." I slip my phone into my purse. "I think I got some useful pictures."

The owner calls down the hallway to us, and Paul and I look her way. She's opening the front door. Apparently, our tour is over. Paul and I return to the entryway and exit the apartment. The woman follows us down the steep staircase and sees us outside. After saying something to Paul, she gives us both a wave, goes back inside, and shuts the door.

Fifteen

"So what did you think?" I look up at Paul, immensely curious to hear his opinion. "Will the apartment work for your grandparents?"

"Definitely. They'll love it." Paul glances back at the building, appearing satisfied. He pats his hand against his computer bag as we start walking away. "I still need to write a few emails and get some documents signed, but I think the deal will go through. The best part is that we negotiated a price below what my grandparents were hoping to pay."

"That's wonderful!" I exclaim. "Your grandparents will be thrilled!"

"I admit I'm looking forward to when we let them know. They definitely could use some good news." Paul fixes his attention straight ahead for a few steps before shooting me a side-glance. "The appointment went quicker than expected, which means we have several hours before the last train departs back to Rome. If you're up for some sightseeing, I have an idea of something we could do with the afternoon."

"Are you serious? I would love to do some sightseeing!" I clap my hands excitedly. "What are we going to do?"

Paul adopts his trademark mischievous grin. "It's a surprise."

My anticipation is soaring by the time Paul and I make the short walk back to the dock and board a *vaporetto*, which soon commences with another glorious trip on the water. Retracing our earlier route, we sail along the lagoon, cruise up a side waterway, and merge into the vibrantly busy Grand Canal. Our boat comes to a stop at the dock by the train station. With impressive familiarity of the scene, Paul leads me off the vessel, through the crowds, over to a different dock, and onto a different *vaporetto* that's pointing in the direction opposite from where we just came.

"I thought you might enjoy seeing the rest of the Grand Canal," Paul explains once we're on board. "And there's no better way to do so than by taking another ride on the water."

I beam at him. "I can't think of anything else I would rather do."

The smile Paul gives me in response sends a quivering sensation all the way through my core and down to my toes. He slides closer to me as more passengers continue to board. Before long, the *vaporetto* pushes away from the dock, and we're underway, the renewed breeze a perfect antidote to the rising temperature of the day.

Our excursion on the water proves to be the most awe-inspiring, dream-come-true thing

I've ever experienced: a perfectly leisurely, forty-five minute trip covering almost the entire length of the Grand Canal. Surrounded by the gorgeous buildings, boats, people, and Venetian ambience, I take a few more photos but mostly just try to appreciate the beauty around me. Emotion is flowing through me freely. This is one of those wondrous, life-changing moments that I've been missing out on for far too long, and I'll do all that I can not to miss out on such meaningful opportunities ever again.

I realize I'm smiling giddily, as I'm sure I've been doing since our *vaporetto* left the dock. How could I not be smiling, though? I've got sunshine and blue sky overhead, the breeze brushing past my face, the most picturesque scenery I've ever beheld all around me, a wonderful guy at my side . . .

Hang on. *What* did I just think?

I grip the railing of the boat as my own startling thought replays in my mind. Like a shot in the arm, it hits me again: being here with Paul is one of the reasons I'm so profoundly happy right now.

I lower my eyes to the water. What is happening to my mind? To my heart? Once upon a time, I dreamed that Stuart and I would visit Venice together. Now, though, the thought of having Stuart here instead of Paul is nearly enough to sap the joy out of this beautiful experience. How can my feelings change so powerfully and so quickly?

My own question is answered with another sobering thought: perhaps this change in my heart didn't happen quickly at all. Perhaps my feelings for Stuart slowly started fading long ago, but I was too busy with my mundane, work-filled life to realize it.

The boat's engine revs, shaking me from my contemplation. Most of the passengers begin shifting toward the port side of the boat in anticipation of getting off. I stand on tiptoe to see over everyone's heads, and I spot a sign on the dock that indicates we've arrived at *San Marco*.

"St. Mark's Square?" I spin toward Paul. "Is this where we're getting off?"

"Yep." Paul has a gleam in his eyes. "After all, if you've only got one afternoon in Venice, I figure this is where you should spend it."

The boat comes to an idling stop at the dock, and Paul and I disembark with the throngs of excitedly chatting, picture-taking tourists. Turning right, we walk in the shade of a tree-lined path that's lined by vendors in little booths who are selling magnets, umbrellas, watercolors, ornaments, t-shirts, baseball hats, and about every other type of memento one could think of. At our right, the canal opens up, stretching out forever toward open water; I can see a small island in the distance with a church dominating its skyline.

Farther up the walkway, immediately at our right, several empty gondolas are tied to docks and bobbing in the water. I can't resist jogging closer to them and taking some pictures.

I then put my camera away and rejoin Paul, who's watching me with a grin on his lips. Resuming our route, we veer left around a corner, and we're suddenly met by the staggering sight of St. Mark's Square.

"Oh my goodness, this is incredible," I utter, almost at a loss for words.

Nothing could have prepared me for the feeling of being at St. Mark's in person. Up ahead on our right, the ornately decorated, light pink Doge's Palace sits grandly under the sunshine. Past the palace is the enormous St. Mark's Basilica itself, with its eastern-influenced architecture, recessed portals, stunning mosaics, and domes topping its roof. To our left, across from the basilica is the famous *Campanile* bell tower. Straight ahead, farther in the distance, is the clock tower that sits above an archway, marking the path into the shop-lined, cobblestoned streets beyond.

Paul faces me. "Before we go into the buildings, may I buy you some lunch? It's the least I can do to repay you for your help."

I turn Paul's way. "You don't have to repay me for—"

"Irene." Paul peers right into my eyes. "I want to."

Paul's tone and the way he's looking at me cause a tingle to rush down my back. "Then I . . . I would love that," I say softly.

Paul breaks into another smile. "Good. Because I've got the perfect place in mind."

I give him a curious look. Paul only smiles again before he resumes guiding me forward into the sea of picture-taking sightseers. Paul rests a hand on my low back as we weave through the fray. His touch nearly takes my breath away.

After passing between the palace on our right and the bell tower to our left, we reach the heart of St. Mark's Square itself, and I come to another stop to drink in the view. This place is massive. It's incredible. Somehow, though, despite its size and the crowds that fill it, this area also retains an atmosphere that's intimate. With our backs to the basilica, ornate sixteenth- and seventeenth-century buildings enclose the square on its other three sides. There's a covered promenade around the perimeter of the square that's lined with glass-fronted stores. As a finishing touch, live piano-and-string music is being performed somewhere close by.

Paul and I begin walking the checkered stone floor of the covered promenade. The piano music gets louder, pulling my attention toward it. In yet another delightful sight, up ahead on the right, I see a small stage just outside the promenade. A man dressed in a tuxedo is playing a grand piano, artfully moving through a medley of elaborate arrangements of famous songs, and he's being accompanied by other fantastic musicians who are playing the violin, viola, and cello.

"Here we are," I hear Paul say.

I pull my eyes from the musicians and look Paul's way. He has brought us to a place called *Caffe Florian*. I'm instantly mesmerized.

The café's outdoor seating consists of marble tables with fancy place settings, and the plush, black chairs at the tables are positioned to provide patrons with an unobstructed view of the musicians. The café itself has lovely glass doors and tall windows trimmed in black and gold. I peer shamelessly through the windows at the gorgeous interior, which consists of small adjoining dining rooms. Each room has fancy chandeliers, gold detailing on the ceilings, elegant furniture, and old portrait paintings on the walls.

"This place has been open since the early seventeen-hundreds," Paul informs me. "It's considered by many to be the oldest café in the world."

"It's magnificent." I keep gazing through the windows, watching as waiters in crisp white jackets bustle to-and-fro.

Paul moves nearer to me, making room for people who are walking the promenade to pass. "I know you think I have no talent for creative writing, but this place has served the likes of Goethe, Lord Byron, Proust, and Dickens."

I stop, processing what Paul said, and then turn toward him. "Are you serious?"

"I'm serious."

"Wow!" I throw my arms around Paul, giving him an enthusiastic hug. "That's amazing! I . . ."

I fall silent when I register the fact that I've got my arms wrapped around Paul's neck and my cheek pressed against his. For one moment, I don't speak, move, or even breathe. Paul is also completely still. With my pulse flying, I let go of Paul, step back from him, and avert my gaze.

Long pause.

I shift my eyes back to Paul. He has his arms raised slightly, as if he froze just before hugging me in return. Peering at me, Paul slowly lowers his arms to his sides. There's another beat of silence. Paul then clears his throat and inquires in a steady voice:

"Would you prefer to eat outside or inside?"

I do my best to mirror Paul's unflustered demeanor. "Let's sit outside so we can watch the musicians."

Paul steps over to one of the outdoor tables and pulls out a chair. Despite my calm outward appearance, I'm still working to catch my breath as I take the seat. Paul sits beside me, and we settle our attention on the musicians. I'm grateful we have this chance to listen to the music because I need time to collect myself. I can't stop thinking about the amazing way it felt to have my arms around Paul, and yet I also can't stop thinking about how I'm planning to speak with Stuart, potentially even to reconcile with him.

Nothing makes sense.

A waiter approaches our table, bringing me back to the moment. After Paul helps me interpret the menu, he gives the waiter our orders, and as always, the sexy sound of Paul speaking fluent Italian makes me blush a little bit. Paul and I then resume listening to the music, and the silence now feels naturally comfortable. For reasons I still cannot understand, it seems perfectly right to be here at Paul's side.

Our lunch is served, and as I dive into my salad, I take another moment to remind myself this is real. Paul and I are really eating at a historic café, listing to live music, and gazing upon the world-famous sights of St. Mark's Square. I'll never forget this moment, and I'll never forget that the happiness I'm feeling is in large part because Paul is with me.

Would I be this gloriously happy if Stuart were beside me?

I don't know.

"Would you like anything else?" I hear Paul ask.

I again snap out of my thoughts, and I discover that Paul and the waiter are watching me.

"No. I'm great," I reply. "Thank you."

Paul converses with the waiter and pays for our meal. Once the waiter departs, Paul and I gather our things and stroll away from the café. I look over my shoulder, taking one last look so I can remember every detail of this place forever.

The rest of the afternoon passes in a fantastic blur. Paul and I tour the Doge's Palace and St. Mark's Basilica. We watch the clock tower chime, and we proceed underneath the archway to stroll the shops that line the narrow

roads beyond. Paul then leads me into what I
realize is a little eatery, and as soon as we step
through the door, the delicious aromas of sugar
and waffle cones fill my nose.

"Have you ever had gelato?" Paul asks.

I suddenly process the fact that we're
standing in a place that looks very much like the
ice cream parlor back at home. Behind the glass
serving counter, there are large containers filled
with brightly colored gelato, the famous Italian
frozen dessert that I've heard is basically like a
smoother, denser version of ice cream. My
mouth waters as I start smelling chocolate,
raspberry, vanilla, mango, and all sorts of other
flavors.

"I've never had gelato," I admit, "but I've
always wanted to try it."

"This is the perfect time." Paul grins.
"How many scoops?"

I pause, an unexpected rush of emotion
hitting me hard. I stare through the glass display
case for a long second or two, and then I focus on
Paul once more.

"Three," I reply. "I'll take three scoops,
please."

Paul nods. "Great minds think alike. I'm
going to order the same thing."

Paul places our orders, and before long
I'm gripping a mammoth cone that's piled high
with three heaping scoops of gelato. When Paul
and I step back outside, the gelato starts melting
in the heat almost faster than I can devour it,
causing Paul to laugh as I speedily attempt to
consume every bite. And I do. I manage to inhale

every bit of the delicious goodness. All three scoops. Without reservation. Because life is too short and too precious not to enjoy moments like this.

With the afternoon growing late, Paul and I retrace our steps back to the dock, hop aboard a crowded *vaporetto*, and begin sailing back in the direction of the train station. About halfway through the journey, the boat stops at a dock near the iconic Rialto Bridge. Paul leans in close to me and says in my ear:

"Let's get off here."

I eagerly nod in agreement. Paul and I disembark the vessel, slide out of the way of the foot traffic, and turn to admire the Rialto Bridge. Spanning over a bend in the canal, the big, ornate white bridge is one of the most famous, romantic landmarks of Venice—of all Italy. Though we sailed underneath it earlier (and I nearly broke my neck attempting to see it from every possible angle), the bridge is even more striking now with the afternoon sunlight playing upon it. My heart swells with joy.

"I was thinking we should travel the rest of the route back to the train station a different way," Paul remarks after a while.

"Oh?" I raise an eyebrow teasingly. "Are we gonna swim?"

Paul is searching my face. "I was thinking something more like a gondola."

My heart skips. "Really?"

Paul keeps gazing into my eyes. "It might be a nice way to end your first trip to Venice. That is, if you're interested."

My voice trembles as I reply. "I would be very interested."

"Great. Then I'll go inquire."

Paul approaches one of the gondoliers who are standing on a nearby dock. Paul and the gondolier chat briefly, and then Paul hands over some cash. While the gondolier climbs into his boat, which is tied to the dock, Paul turns toward me and offers his hand. The sunlight catches Paul's face at an angle, highlighting his breathtakingly handsome features and making his dark eyes shine. I place my hand in Paul's steady grip, sharing a smile with him as he helps me into the boat. Once I'm settled, Paul sits beside me. The gondolier pushes off from the dock. The next thing I know, Paul and I are sailing down the canal. The Grand Canal of Venice. In a gondola.

The water laps against the sides of the boat as we float along. The sun continues drifting lower in the sky, causing everything to glow in its rich, golden light. At times, the gondolier breaks out into operatic song, the melody echoing through the air and mingling with the sounds of life along the canal. Yet again, I find myself thinking this is almost too perfect and magical to be real.

The space between Paul and me is getting smaller as we lean closer and closer to one another. The force drawing us together is impossible to ignore. Every ounce of me wants to finish closing the gap and nestle against Paul's chest, letting him drape his around my shoulders, but I make myself resist.

Before I'm ready, the train station comes into view, and the gondolier glides the boat to a dock and ties it up. Paul stands, steps onto the dock, and reaches down a hand to me. I place my hand in his once more, letting him assist me out of the boat. We gaze into one another's eyes while our hands remained intertwined.

"Thank you for this," I tell him, hoping he understands how much I mean it.

"You're welcome." Paul slowly lets go of my hand.

We cross the plaza to reach the station. In silence, we board the train and get to our seats, which are in the same configuration as before. Soon, the train begins rolling away from the station, and as we cross the water to reach the mainland, I turn to get a last look of the Venetian skyline, which is beautifully backlit by the last remnants of the sunset.

"Is everything okay?" Paul gets up from his aisle seat to take the one beside me.

I look over at him. "Yes. I'm just . . . thinking."

Paul is quiet for a long moment as he studies my face. "Then I'll leave you to your thinking," he says before moving back to his seat and pulling his laptop from his bag.

"Paul?"

He looks up at me.

"Thank you again for a wonderful day."

"It was my pleasure." Paul is again looking right into my eyes. "Thank you for helping my grandparents. It means more than I can say."

Without another word, Paul lowers his head, focuses on his laptop, and gets to work.

Sixteen

I step out of the shower, grab a towel from the rack, and wrap it around me. Pushing my wet hair from my face, I head into the bedroom. For the first time since this trip began, I'm well-rested. Not only am I adjusting to the time change, I had a chance to sleep in today, and I took full advantage of it. It's already twelve-thirty in the afternoon here, which accounts for why I can feel the staggering heat of the summer day hovering in the apartment.

I open the wardrobe and scan the unused articles of clothing I have left, ultimately deciding to spend the day in my burgundy, v-neck t-shirt and jeans. I figure I can keep things casual since I'm going to be spending the day in the apartment.

Paul will be arriving soon so we can work on assembling the information Rafaele and Violetta will post about the Venetian apartment on the website they're creating. After our train ride back from Venice yesterday, Paul called Donato and Rita, put them on speaker phone, and told them the great news about the rental. Though I barely understood any of the conversation, it was evident that Donato and Rita were thrilled. They even began crying, and if I wasn't mistaken, Paul got choked up, too. (Okay, I was as tearful as any of them.)

There was also a moment during the call when I heard Donato say my name. I'm not sure what else was said, and Paul seemed to dodge the issue smoothly, but guilt started gnawing at me again. Though it's for the best, it continues feeling so wrong to be lying to Paul's dear grandparents. It's another reason why I'm anxious to get their estate issues solved; the sooner we do that, the sooner Paul and I will be able to explain to them the truth. I can only hope Donato and Rita will forgive us.

There will be a gut-wrenching downside to disclosing the truth, however: I'll lose my connection to Paul's family. In the brief time I've spent with Paul's relatives, I've come to feel as though they're my family, too. It's crazy, I know, but it's the truth. Unbeknownst to them, Paul's loving, welcoming family members have been a source of joy and light for me when I needed it most, and I'll be forever grateful to them.

With a sigh, I finish getting ready while mentally reviewing my plan for the day. Once Paul arrives, I'll transfer to my laptop the pictures I took of the Venetian apartment, and I'll write informative paragraphs about the rental property. Paul will handle phone calls, paperwork, and the other necessary logistics to get the ownership of the apartment transferred into his grandparents' names. Paul estimated our work will take a few hours, so we should wrap up around suppertime. After we're done, I'm going to go into recluse mode for the rest of the night. I intend to dash over to the grocery store, buy a bunch of pasta, return to the apartment, and immerse myself in tortellini and low-budget Italian television shows.

Yanking up my hair into a bun, I head into the main room and open the drapes. The blue sky is cloudless, and the sun is dazzlingly bright. I crank up the main room's air conditioner. I next shuffle into the kitchen, open the fridge, and pull out the last of my chocolate stash. I make a mental note to stock up on more chocolate, too, when I go to the store.

Chomping on the last of a hazelnut-and-milk-chocolate candy bar, I go back into the bedroom to retrieve my phone. Stuart still hasn't replied to my text. Part of me knows I shouldn't be surprised, since we arranged to talk at the end of the week, and Stuart specifically said he would be busy until then. The other part of me, however, wonders why Stuart wouldn't at least compose a brief response. Doesn't Stuart think what happened between us is important enough? Or did Stuart never care about our relationship as much as I did? The fact that I'm even asking myself these questions is like a punch to the gut. It's getting harder and harder to ignore the fact that Stuart's actions don't strike me as the behavior of a man who's in love . . . or who was ever in love.

Almost under its own power, my thumb swipes my phone screen, bringing up the pictures I took in Venice. I scroll to the selfie that Paul and I took while we were riding the *vaporetto*. Our smiles are so carefree. So natural. So—

A knock on the apartment door causes me to jump. I shove my phone into the pocket of my jeans, lick the remnants of chocolate off my fingertips, grab my laptop, and head to the entryway. I stop to collect my emotions, and then I put on my best attempt at a smile and open the door.

"What's wrong?" Paul asks immediately, his brows snapping together. "Are you all right?"

My smile falters. I was hoping Paul wouldn't be so perceptive, but I should have known I wouldn't be able to fool him.

"I'm just a little sleepy, that's all," I lie. "Believe it or not, I woke up only a few minutes ago."

Reinforcing my smile, I step back so Paul can enter. Paul keeps an eye on me as he crosses the threshold. I study him in return, noting he also went for a casual vibe with his outfit today. He has on a baseball cap that displays the emblem of an Italian sports team, a green t-shirt, and jeans. Once again, he didn't shave, so his facial scruff has grown in even more.

"I talked to Violetta." Paul motions to his phone. "She and Rafaele almost have the website built. It was a genius idea to ask them to do it. I don't know why I didn't think of it."

I shrug. "I guess you're just not a genius."

Paul laughs. "I guess not."

We make our way into the front room, get settled across the table from one another, and power up our laptops. Paul reaches into his bag and pulls out something that's wrapped in brown paper. He slides the little package across the table to me while saying:

"I suspected you might be sleeping in today, and so I figured you might need breakfast."

My mouth is watering even before I've unwrapped the paper, because whatever is inside smells so delicious. When I pull open the packaging, I swear I hear angels start singing. Paul has brought me two croissants. Fresh croissants covered with a chocolate drizzle.

"Are these really for me?" I raise my eyes hopefully. "Both of them?"

Paul chuckles. "Yep. They're all yours."

"What about you?"

"Don't worry: I enjoyed a couple pastries already." Paul jokingly makes a gesture like he's patting his stomach, which only winds up calling my attention to the fact that he clearly has washboard abs under his t-shirt.

My face gets hot. "Right. Um, thank you."

I return my attention to the croissants. My stomach growls. I probably shouldn't eat both of them, but . . .

Without further hesitation, I dive into breakfast paradise. Once I'm done, I head into the kitchen. I wash the crumbs off my hands, fill up water glasses for Paul and me, and return to the main room.

With the sun shining and the air conditioner whirring, Paul and I concentrate on our laptops and start working. I transfer photos, open a few as my inspiration, and begin writing. Before long, I've composed paragraphs of different lengths and styles, which will give Paul and his cousins options to choose from when they decide what to include on the website.

Meanwhile, Paul is answering emails, making calls, and handling something that has to do with document e-signatures. I can't help sneaking peeks at him as he works. I've never seen Paul in business mode before, and it's . . . well, it's immensely attractive. There's something almost irresistible about the way his brow furrows with concentration when he's reading on his computer, or the confident way he talks on the phone, or how he exhales, leans back in his chair, ruffles his hair, and gazes outside when he's collecting his thoughts. Yes, when Paul is in work mode, he's intelligent, thoughtful, confident, and jaw-droppingly handsome all at the same time.

And it's making it a tad hard for me to focus on my own work.

I do my best to concentrate on what I need to do, and nearly two hours pass by the time I'm done with my writing. Paul is still working, so I unplug my phone, push back from the table, and start taking website-worthy pictures of this apartment, which I'll use as I start working on the written info for this place. I even head outside to get a few snaps of the building's exterior, but I don't stay long, since it has got to be a hundred degrees out here. Back inside the shady building, I climb the stairs, re-enter my apartment, plunk back down at the table, transfer the new photos, and begin the writing process again.

"Remind me: how far away is this apartment from the Colosseum?" I stop typing to look across the table at Paul.

Paul meets my gaze. "It's about a fifteen minute walk, and . . . hang on, you haven't gone there yet, have you?"

"Nope." I resume typing.

"We have to fix that."

I peer at Paul again. "Fix it? But you haven't even read what I wrote yet."

Paul laughs. "No, I mean we have to fix the fact that you haven't seen the Colosseum yet." His expression becomes serious. "You've been extremely generous to help my grandparents, but I don't want you missing out on seeing some of Italy's most incredible sights because of it." He leans back in his chair while crossing his sculpted arms over his chest. "How about we finish up here, grab some dinner, and then head to the Colosseum? It'll be early evening by that point, and a lot of the tourists will be gone. The lights will be coming on, too. It's the best time to be there, in my opinion."

Instantly, my plans to spend the night with tortellini and low-budget television vanish from my mind.

"Count me in," I reply.

Paul smiles and resumes working.

I, too, attempt to get back to what I'm doing, but there's a giddy, elated feeling flowing through me now that's extremely distracting. How could I not be distracted, though? I'm going out on a date with Paul, and we're going *to the Colosseum*. I—

My heart punches my chest. A date? Wait a second, are Paul and I going on a date?

I steal another look across the table at Paul, but he doesn't seem to notice. I cough and refocus on my own laptop, frantically attempting to make sense of things. Paul and I aren't going out on a date. Of course we're not. We're just stopping by to see it since we're working together.

I command myself to concentrate on my writing, and another hour or so goes by fast as Paul and I finish what we're doing. I return my laptop to the bedroom, grab my purse, and rejoin Paul, who has collected his things and gone to the front door.

"What would you like to do for dinner?" Paul pulls open the door and waits for me to exit.

I step out of the apartment. "Anything sounds great to me. You choose."

Paul follows me out and locks the door. "In that case, I vote that you let me make you dinner at my place."

The giddy sensation is unleashed inside me again. I gulp. No matter how I try to deny it, this outing with Paul is feeling more and more like a date—and a rather romantic date, at that.

Paul and I make our way down the stairs, head outside, and start walking in a direction I haven't gone before. I'm drowning in the heat of the late afternoon, and while my fair complexion is undoubtedly getting more lobster-like by the moment, I can't help noticing that the sun has been much more favorable to Paul. His skin has bronzed over the past few days, and paired with his dark eyes and dark hair, the effect is intoxicating.

"In addition to the crowds, the heat is one of the reasons why I avoid sightseeing in the middle of the day." Paul seems unaware of the mesmerized way I'm staring at him. "I often get up just before sunrise to enjoy sights while they're still cool, quiet, and fairly empty. Or I visit in the evenings right before they close."

My heart flutters. "That sounds really nice."

Paul returns my look. "It is."

We reach the end of the street, and Paul guides me into an apartment building that's nearly identical to the one where I've been staying. It even has its own itsy-bitsy elevator in the foyer. Paul and I take the stairs to the fifth floor, and we go down a long hallway to a tall door. Pulling keys from his pocket, Paul unlocks the door and invites me to enter first.

I step through the doorway and do a quick scan of the place. The layout is essentially the same as my apartment, but the décor has a playful mid-century vibe rather than the elegant atmosphere of mine. I meander toward the main room, noting a few dishes in the kitchen sink, a couple books and the remote control on the couch, and a jacket hanging over the back of a chair. I smile. Paul keeps things clean without being obsessively particular. I doubt Paul would chastise me for not putting a coaster back under the coffee table where it belongs, for example, the way Stuart often does when I'm at his house.

"What do you think?" Paul sets down his laptop bag in the entryway and flips on the air conditioner.

I pull my phone from my purse. "It's great. I particularly like how it has a different décor than the other apartment. It'll make a great contrast for the website."

"I'm glad you think so." Paul motions in the direction of the kitchen. "While you take photos, I'll get started on dinner. Would you be all right with calzones? I'll be using my grandma's recipe."

I do a double take. "You're going to *make* calzones for dinner? Like, from scratch?"

Paul's eyes sparkle with amusement. "You sound surprised."

"No, I'm not . . ." I break off with a giggle. "Okay, fine, I admit that I'm a little surprised. I didn't have you pegged as a chef."

Paul steps closer to me. "It's just one of my many hidden talents, Irene."

The air leaves my lungs, and my brain goes blank. All I can do is gaze up at Paul in a trance. His eyes linger on mine a second or two more, and then he heads into the kitchen. Only once he's gone do I mange to catch my breath. I start taking photos of the main room, but I'm still tracking the sounds that are coming from the kitchen: clanking pans, water running from sink faucet, the refrigerator door being opened and shut. Each noise is making my pulse tick up higher and my heart beat a little faster.

I need to get out of here. I need to clear my head.

"I'll be back in a few minutes," I blurt out, scurrying toward the entryway.

"What?" I hear Paul call from the kitchen.

I'm at the front door before I stop and spin around. Paul has poked his head out of the kitchen. Steam is swirling in the air behind him. His face is slightly flushed. There's a dab of flour on his cheek.

I gulp as my heart throbs even harder. Yes, I definitely need to vacate the premises.

I pull open the door. "I'll be back shortly. I'm going to go back to my place to get my laptop. I figure I'll start working on the write-ups."

Paul steps out of the kitchen, wiping his hands on a dish towel. "I'll go with you."

"No!" I hold up my hands like I'm stopping traffic.

Paul halts, eyebrows raised.

"I mean, no thank you." I clear my throat and lower my arms. "It won't take me long to go there and back."

"You sure?"

"I'm sure."

I bolt out of the apartment and pull the door closed. Jamming my phone into my purple purse, I scurry down the stairs and charge outside. I think it's even hotter out here now than it was earlier. Or maybe it's just me. It's hard to say.

Keeping my head down, I race along the sidewalk to my building. I run up the stairs to the fourth floor, unlock my apartment door, and charge inside. Only once I shut the door and become immersed in its emptiness do I finally stop to breathe.

I check my phone. My stomach twists hard when I see that I've received some texts. With a trembling hand, I click to read the messages. The first text is from Mom, which reminds me I should probably let my family know that I'm halfway around the world. The next is a message from Adrienne Hayes, who says she wants to take me out for a belated birthday lunch. The last text is from Henry Ingram, another attending at Lakewood; he's inquiring about a possible shift swap next month.

No text from Stuart. Still. So I'm stuck in limbo. Still.

With a groan, I put away my phone and rub my face with my hands. What am I supposed to do? I can't deny my feelings for Paul; I'm attracted to him in a way I've never been attracted to a man before. What about Stuart, though? We were together for six years. Shouldn't we at least talk about trying to fix things?

With another tormented sigh, I trudge into the bedroom, slip my laptop into its bag, hang the bag over my shoulder, and return to the entryway. I take another few seconds just to breathe, and then I leave the apartment. Lost in thought, I return to Paul's building, hike up the staircase, head down the hall, and knock on his door.

"Coming," I hear Paul say.

Before I'm really ready, Paul answers the door. The flour is still on Paul's cheek, and now there's also a smudge of white on his t-shirt. And he still has that dang dish towel over his shoulder.

"Welcome back," Paul greets me as he moves aside so I can enter.

Stepping into the entryway, I'm met by an incredibly rich, mouth-watering collection of aromas that includes tomatoes, herbs, meats, and fresh dough.

"I'm working on the sauce right now." Paul closes the door. "Once I've assembled the calzones, I'll put them in the oven. We should be able to eat in about an hour."

"Everything sounds—and smells— delicious." I trail Paul into the kitchen. "In the meantime, I'll finish taking pictures of your apartment and compose blurbs for the . . ." I trail off as I look around. Flour is scattered across the countertops. The sink is piled high with dishes. Pans with bubbling water are on the stove, juice from freshly sliced tomatoes is puddled on a cutting board, and cheese remnants litter the floor. I snicker. "I suppose I'll wait to take pictures of the kitchen until we do something about this mess you've made."

Paul chuckles. "Hey, don't knock a chef's mojo."

"Oh, is that what you call it?" I use a finger to brush the flour from his cheek. "*Mojo.* Gotcha."

Paul's eyes shift to my hand and back to my face. Suddenly, our gazes lock. Paul makes a move closer. I suck in a breath as my insides ignite. We watch one another while the steam swirls around us. I—

One of the pots on the stove starts boiling over.

Paul blinks fast, spins away from me, and snatches the overflowing pot off the burner. I hastily start retreating while saying:

"I'll, um, go take those pictures."

I whirl around and burst out of the kitchen, which has become more like a pressure cooker. I charge down the hall, dart into the closest room, and slam the door behind me. My face flushes hard when I realize I've just shut myself inside Paul's bedroom.

"This is just work," I tell myself, though I'm breathing fast. "And we're just having a work dinner."

I make myself busy taking pictures of Paul's bedroom, which is as casually tidy as the other rooms in the apartment (minus the kitchen). I then go through the rest of the apartment, photographing what I need. When I'm done, I head to the round table in the main room, set up my laptop, transfer the pictures, and start typing.

Paul emerges from the kitchen with his phone to his ear. My eyes drift his way. Paul is conversing in Italian over the phone while he strides in and out of the main room. As the sexy, staccato sounds of Paul's words mix with the pattering of my fingers on the keyboard, I am fairly certain I'm dangerously close to swooning.

I shake my head hard. I cannot get swept up in feelings for Paul. Our relationship is nothing but a fake business arrangement to help his grandparents. Besides, I promised to speak to Stuart, and I have to keep that promise.

Seventeen

Calzones. Forever.

I use my fork to scrape the last morsel of cheesy goodness from my plate and lick the utensil clean. I would lick the plate, too, were it not for the fact that Paul, who's seated across the table from me, might deem it weird. So instead, I set down the fork and sigh contentedly. Paul is an amazing cook, and Rita's recipe is unparalleled. If meals in this country are always like this, it's yet another reason why I'm seriously going to consider moving to Italy.

"What did you think?" Paul's grin proves he already knows exactly what I think.

I give him a jokingly chastising look. "Don't be cocky. You know it was incredible."

Paul winks before he gets up and takes both of our plates into the kitchen. I remain in my chair for a time, listening to the sounds of Paul moving about in the other room, and then I get up and head into the kitchen to join him.

"How can I help?" I pick up a pan to start washing it in the sink.

"You don't need to do anything." Paul comes across the kitchen and stops right in front of me. He slowly takes the pan from my hands. "You're my guest. Remember?"

As our hands brush, I quietly say, "I remember."

Paul seems to take an extra second before he steps away from me and puts the pan in the sink. "I'll finish cleaning up later. This is about the right time for us to leave for the Colosseum, if you're still interested. What do you say: should we head out?"

My insides cheer with excitement. The Colosseum. I'm about to see the real Colosseum.

"Definitely," I reply.

Paul and I leave his apartment, make our way down the stairs, and head outside. It's evening now, and the blazing heat of the day has evolved into a pleasantly warm temperature, which is made even more pleasant by the breeze. After stopping by my apartment so I can drop off my laptop, Paul and I continue on our way.

Leaving the neighborhood, we venture down a sidewalk paralleling a road that's currently filled with rush-hour traffic. We pass underneath the stunning archway of an ancient Roman wall, go by a small park, and stroll down a street that's lined with bistros. As we go, I remain quiet as I think about, well, everything: Stuart, my hope that Donato and Rita will regain the money they were swindled out of, work, other ways I want to change how I'm living my life, and . . . Paul.

I sigh aloud.

Paul shoots me a glance. "May I ask what's on your mind?"

I hesitate before meeting his probing gaze. "A little bit of everything, I suppose."

"You mean, Stuart." Paul focuses his attention straight ahead.

"Yes. Stuart." I also resume staring down the sidewalk. "Among other things."

Out of the corner of my eye, I see Paul glance my way again. I pretend not to notice.

Falling back into silence, Paul and I pass more restaurants, reach the end of a tree-lined road, and crest a small hill. I stagger to a stop. My jaw drops. My eyes get big.

The Colosseum.

It's only a hundred yards in the distance. It's massive. It's staggering. It's amazing.

Paul tips his head toward a nearby intersection. "Let's head this way. We'll walk around the perimeter of the structure so you can see the entire thing from the outside, and then we'll grab entry tickets. That should work out just about right so we're inside as the sun begins to set."

All I can do is mumble something incoherent, my ability to speak still gone as I remain spell-bound by the world-famous ancient sight towering before us. Gawking at the postcard-come-to-life, I allow Paul to guide me across the busy street to the wide sidewalk adjacent to the Colosseum itself.

The fact that the Colosseum sits smack in the middle of a bustling metropolitan area makes for a striking juxtaposition between the ancient and modern, and the setting somehow further enhances the power and mystique of this awe-inspiring place. There's a powerful energy here, which I suspect has no equal anywhere in the world, as the Colosseum seems to be proudly defying the modernization of Rome around it.

Paul and I commence with making a slow loop around the gigantic structure. Keeping my head cranked back and relying on Paul to make sure I don't crash into anyone, I stare upward at the Colosseum's three stories of massive arches and ornamental columns stacked on top of one another, the crumbling detailing in the stones, and the beautiful façade that so jarringly contrasts to the brutally bloody events that once took place here.

It's nearly an hour before we finish our walk around the outside, mostly because I keep stopping to admire the Colosseum from every possible angle while snapping a few photos along the way. As we complete the circuit, Paul and I weave past hoards of tourist groups returning to chartered buses, locals who appear to be on their way home from work and school, and a construction site for a new metro station.

Paul leads me to a large courtyard, and we approach a ticket booth. I step forward to pay for our tickets, but Paul takes out his wallet, reaches around me, and slides a few Euros over to the person who's issuing the entrance cards. As we walk away from the booth, Paul hands me my ticket.

"I appreciate this, but you don't need to pay for everything," I tell Paul.

Paul rests a hand on my low back, guiding me through yet another wave of tourists who are departing the premises. "I want to."

Once again, the sensation of Paul's hand against my shirt is making it hard for me to keep my voice steady. "As I've said before, though, you don't need to repay me for anything. I'm volunteering my time because I want to help your grandparents."

Paul stops and faces me, causing me to face him in return. "I'm not trying to repay you, Irene," he states. "I'm trying to take you out on a date."

My heart leaps. I know this is the moment when I should emphasize to Paul that I can't be out on a date with him while I'm waiting to sort out things with Stuart. However, once again, I've apparently lost the ability to speak.

Paul breaks into a hint of a grin before he turns from me to give our tickets to a guy who's waiting by a metal detector. Paul and I pass through the detector and walk underneath a mammoth arch to reach a vast corridor that wraps around the entire base of the Colosseum. There are tourists still strolling around, but Paul was right about visiting near the end of the day; already, it's less busy compared to when we first arrived.

Moving to the inside of the corridor, Paul and I walk up a ramp that leads into the arena itself. As we pass from the shade back into the sunlight, I have to stop to take in the view, struck to my core at seeing this ancient place with my own eyes.

One of the first things I notice is how dwarfed I feel by the sheer size of the Colosseum that's rising up around us. Directly in front of where we're standing is a platform for viewing the huge, oval-shaped center of the arena—the place where countless people were once forced to fight to the death. The area is undergoing renovations, so the underground level is also exposed, revealing a haunting labyrinth of stone-walled passageways where gladiators once waited before fights and prisoners were kept in cells until their public executions. Lifting my head, I survey the rows of tiered stone benches that circle the arena—the places where people sat when they came to be entertained by the bloodbaths. Other than the fact that the type of entertainment here was literally sudden death, this arena has a ghostly resemblance to a modern stadium.

Paul and I circle the ground floor, and then we climb ridiculously tall steps to reach the second level and view the arena from a new vantage point. The vista from up here is equally spectacular, if not more so. We make another full lap, and by the time we've reached the place where we started, the Colosseum has grown relatively quiet. Most tourists have departed, and construction down below has finished for the day. The light of the setting sun is pouring into the arena, creating a dramatic scene of contrasting light and dark. I can't resist taking a few more photos, but then I put my camera away to just soak in the view.

"You were right," I tell Paul when he comes up beside me. "This was the perfect time to visit."

Paul's gaze flicks across the scene. "And the best is yet to come."

"There aren't going to be reenactments of gladiator fights or something, are there?"

"Nope." Paul laughs. "It'll be something slightly less gory. Don't worry. I think you'll like it."

We return to the ground level, walk through a dark corridor, and emerge from the Colosseum. It's twilight now, and the sky is taking on gorgeous hues of purple while a few stars are becoming visible in the summertime sky. Guiding me back to the courtyard where the now-closed ticket booth sits, Paul points to a stone wall, which is about waist-high and has a landscaped hill rising up behind it.

"That should be a good spot for us to sit," Paul states.

I'm still not sure exactly what he has in mind, but I nod in agreement. I could definitely use the chance to sit down. I can't believe how sore my feet have become from all the walking. Hiking the Colosseum is almost as fatiguing as racing around Lakewood Medical Center's emergency department.

Paul and I cross the courtyard, headed for the wall. As we go, out of the corner of my eye, I notice a group of guys appear from the shadows. Their hands are full of knick-knacks, which they're clearly hoping to sell to the tourists who are still lingering. One of the guys sets a large boombox on the ground, turns on techno music, and cranks up the volume. The other guys split up to start attempting to convince sightseers to buy their trinkets.

Paul stays close beside me until we're free of the throng. Once we reach the wall, he turns around and boosts himself up so he's sitting on top of the wall and facing the Colosseum. With a playful smile, he uses one hand to pat the empty space beside him. I laughingly pull myself up onto the wall so I'm sitting at Paul's left. Stretching my arms behind me to prop myself up, I lean back on my hands, tip up my head, and gaze at the Colosseum.

"Pretty nice view from here, isn't it?" Paul asks me after a time.

"*Nice* doesn't begin to describe it," I declare softly, enthralled by the sight.

Because it's true. *Nice* doesn't come close to describing the striking beauty of the Colosseum at night. As twilight is deepening, lights in and around the Colosseum are coming on, illuminating the majestic structure and making the evocative power of this place more potent than ever before.

Paul bends at the waist as if bowing to me. "Very well. I shall defer to whatever adjective you decide is appropriate to describe this. After all, as you so clearly implied, you're the better creative writer."

I snort a laugh and punch Paul lightly on the shoulder. "And don't you forget it."

Paul's expression becomes serious. He looks right into my eyes. "I could never forget you, Irene. You know that."

Paul's tone makes my body get hot. My heart starts dancing. I draw in a breath, finding it's impossible for me to look away from him. Almost before I realize what's happening, the space between Paul and me narrows as we slowly lean in closer to each other. I—

Paul's phone rings.

Paul and I jump and pull away from one another. My heart is pounding. With shaky hands, I yank my own phone from my purse and make myself busy taking more pictures of the Colosseum. Paul clears his throat, retrieves his phone from his pocket, and puts the phone to his ear—but not before casting me a look that makes it very clear he's still thinking about our near-kiss, just like I am.

"Violetta?" Paul answers, running a hand through his hair.

I stop and look Paul's way, suddenly worried something bad has happened to Donato or Rita. Thankfully, though, I see Paul's posture relax while he listens to whatever Violetta is saying to him. Everything must be all right.

I glance around the courtyard again. The trinket sellers are still circling, intrusively shoving their wares into people's faces to score a sale. One of them turns up the music another notch, and the obnoxious beat blasts through the air, killing the ambience. Shaking my head, I refocus on Paul, who's still on the phone with his cousin. Paul has his free hand covering his other ear, trying to block out the music so he can hear what Violetta is saying. Paul looks so hot that I suddenly have this crazy impulse to grab him by the shirt and kiss him hard. I nearly gasp aloud at the thought. I promptly scoot myself farther down the wall to get away from him, but it's not enough. I need to put more space between us.

I hop down from the wall and scurry away, pretending like I'm taking more photos of the Colosseum, which is glowing against the night sky. With my attention glued to my phone, I reach a corner of the courtyard and set up to take another picture.

"Hello! Hello, my friend!"

I look up. One of the knick-knack sellers is approaching me. He's wearing a baseball cap turned sideways, a baggy t-shirt, and cargo shorts. He's holding a bunch of bracelets in his hands that remind me of the things I used to weave in elementary school to give to my friends.

"Would you like a beautiful bracelet?" the man demands in a loud voice, stopping right in front of me.

Something about this situation makes the hairs on the back of my neck stand up. "No, thank you," I tell the man firmly.

I turn and begin walking the other direction. The man lunges around me and cuts me off, forcing me to stop. He's now hovering only an inch or two in front of me. With a piercing stare, he shoves a bracelet into my hand.

"Take one as a gift! A gift!"

I shake my head and hold out the bracelet for him to take back. "No, but thank you."

Instead of taking the bracelet, however, the man grabs my hand. I gasp. The man puts a smile on his face, but his stare becomes even more menacing. His grip on my hand gets uncomfortably tight . . . threateningly tight. Alarm swells inside me. I attempt to tug my hand free. The man doesn't let go.

"Take the bracelet." The man is still smiling in a chillingly eerie way.

I cast a frantic glance around the courtyard. Cold panic consumes me when I see that the other trinket sellers are hovering in the shadows. They've made a circle around this man and me, I realize. One of them turns up the music even louder. I pull in a terrified breath and resume fighting to free myself from the man's grip.

"Sir, I said I—"

"She doesn't want it."

Paul seems to appear out of nowhere. Jaw clenched and hands fisted at his sides, Paul has a steely gaze locked on the man who has me in his grip. Paul puts himself between the man and me, lowers his voice, and says something to him in Italian. Though I don't understand Paul's words, there's no mistaking the threatening edge in his tone. The man's smile immediately disappears, and his eyes get wide. He releases my hand and starts retreating. I'm shaking as I drop the bracelet to the ground.

Paul reaches back, placing one hand on my hip while he continues tracking the man's movements until the trinket seller finishes slinking into the shadows and disappears from view. Paul's nostrils are flared as he scans the courtyard, confirming the other men have also vanished into the darkness. The music fades away. All is still.

Paul turns around to face me. His brow is deeply furrowed. He puts his hands on my shoulders. "Irene, are you okay?"

I don't reply. I can't reply. All I do is stare at nothing while repeatedly opening and closing my hand, as if doing so will rid it of the sickening memory of that man's touch.

"Irene?" Paul puts a finger under my chin and tips up my head, so I'm looking into his eyes. He repeats, "Are you okay?"

I blink and manage a nod.

Paul's jaw clenches again. "Let's get out of here."

Paul keeps one arm around my shoulders and starts guiding me from the courtyard. We cross to the other side of the intersection and begin retracing our route back to the apartment. I stay close to Paul as we go, letting him lead the way. My mind is foggy, and I feel sick to my stomach. All I can think about is that man's unrelenting grip and the threatening look in his eyes. A shiver rolls down my spine.

"Street hawkers have become a problem at major sights, especially at night." Paul's strides are fast and certain. His eyes are leaping across the shadows. "Many of them are selling illegally, which can result in an unwitting buyer being issued a substantial fine by the police for participating in the transaction. Even worse, many hawkers aren't really trying to sell anything at all. They simply use it as a cover to harass unsuspecting tourists . . . or to do worse." He glares and works down a swallow. "They scatter like rats when the *polizia* appear."

I shudder, and another wave of nausea rises up inside me. What would have happened if Paul hadn't been there? As the horrible possibilities play through my mind, I bury myself against Paul's chest. Paul holds me tightly and kisses the top of my head. He doesn't let me go until we've reached the apartment. I reach into my purse for my keys, but I'm trembling so much that I drop the keys to the ground. They land with a jarring clatter.

"Sorry. I . . ." I trail off weakly.

Paul scoops up the keys and uses them to open the door. He puts his arm around my waist and escorts me into the apartment. Locking the door behind us, Paul places my keys on the entryway table and flips on a light. Without slowing his pace, he takes me into my bedroom and sits me down on the edge of the bed.

"I'm no doctor, but I think you're in some degree of shock." Paul turns on the lamp and the air conditioner. He drops to one knee beside the bed and begins taking off my shoes. "Why don't you lie down?"

I comply, resting my head back on the pillow while Paul swings my legs up onto the bed. Paul studies me, concern remaining etched in his features.

"How are you doing now?"

I attempt a reassuring smile. "I might be a little stunned, but I'm okay."

Paul exhales. "I'm not," he mutters. He gets to his feet and motions in the direction of the kitchen. "Can I get you something to eat or drink?"

"Actually, yes. Hydration would probably be a good idea. Thank you."

Paul leaves the room, and I hear a kitchen cupboard being opened followed by the sound of water running from the faucet. I then hear Paul rummaging around in refrigerator.

"You're probably not going to find much in there," I call to him, my mouth dry. "I'm overdue for a grocery run. Even my chocolate stash has run out."

"No chocolate? Yikes. We'll definitely have to do something about that." Paul finally shows a hint of a smile as he returns to the room. He has a glass of water in one hand and the last of the Gouda cheese in the other. "Drink up, Doc."

I prop myself up on one elbow, take the glass from Paul, and swallow a few sips of the water. Deciding my stomach isn't quite settled enough to try cheese, I set the glass on the nightstand and lie back down.

"Please don't feel as though you have to stay on my account." I smile again. "I'm already doing much better."

Paul sets the cheese next to the water glass. "If it's okay with you, I'll stick around for a bit. I'll be worrying about you, otherwise." He cracks another grin. "Besides, I want to make sure you're not going to deliriously pull the shower alarm or something."

I snicker. "I'll try not to."

Paul laughs, goes to opposite side of the room, and sits in the chair by the window. Saying no more, he pulls out his phone and begins reading something. I roll onto my right side so I can see him. There's something immensely reassuring about his presence, and as time passes, my body gradually relaxes, and the fog lifts from my mind. Eventually, a yawn escapes my lips as the remnants of jet lag set in.

"Violetta sent me screenshots of the website. It's looking great," Paul remarks, raising his head to look at me.

"That's awesome," I tell him, my words coming out in a sleepy slur. "I . . . can't wait . . . to see what she sent."

My eyes drift shut.

Eighteen

I open my eyes, and the first things I see are a piece of Gouda cheese and a half-empty water glass on the nightstand. All at once, the events of last night return to my mind. Thankfully, the shock of what occurred has worn off, and though the awful memory of the trinket seller will stick with me, I'll remember Paul's chivalry far more.

I'm lying on my left side on the still-made bed. One of the cozy, soft blankets that are kept in the main room is draped over me. I hear the gentle hum of the air conditioner, which is keeping the room pleasantly cool. The ambient natural light in the room is letting me know the sun has come up.

I roll onto my back and push myself up into a sitting position. I barely manage to stifle a startled gasp when I see Paul. He's sound asleep, still seated in the chair by the window. His baseball cap is on the floor at his feet. His chin is resting on his chest, his arms are crossed, and his respirations are slow and measured. The daylight leaking in around the edges of the closed drapes is falling upon his face, illuminating the way his long-lashed eyelids flutter while he sleeps.

I realize I would otherwise be swooning over how alluring Paul looks while he sleeps, but right now, my chest warms with a different emotion: gratitude. I'm sure passing the night on that chair couldn't have been comfortable for him, but his presence allowed me to rest comfortably. With a soft, thoughtful sigh, I draw my knees in toward my chest and wrap my arms around them. Yes, Paul makes me feel safe. And it's much more than just making me feel safe from men who are pretending to sell knick-knacks. When I'm with Paul, I feel safe to be myself. I feel safe to show my emotions. To try new things. To be honest with myself and my feelings. Paul is a major reason why, in only the course of a few days, I've started living with more purpose and meaning.

So what does that say about how I felt when I was with Stuart?

As quietly as I can, I locate my phone on the bed. It's about eight-thirty. I don't have any new texts, but I find this doesn't bother me. I don't even have the desire to check my emails. Instead, I toss the phone aside.

Paul stirs. I look his way once more. He drops his arms and lifts his head. His eyes open. He blinks a few times as he observes me.

"Good morning, Sunshine." I grin.

Paul yawns a laugh and slowly rolls his head from side-to-side, stretching his neck. "Good morning to you, too."

"You stayed all night."

"I did." Paul gets to his feet. "I wanted to make sure you were okay."

"Thank you."

"You're welcome." Paul bends at the waist and picks up his baseball cap from off the floor. Standing up straight again, he goes on. "I'll head out." He strides to the doorway, but then he stops and looks back. Now there's a gleam in his eye. "What do you have on tap for today?"

I take a second to think. "Not much, actually."

"Good." Paul breaks into a smile. "Because seeing the Vatican and St. Peter's Basilica will probably take us the entire day."

"What?" I do a double take. "We're going to—"

"I'll pick you up in ninety minutes."

Still grinning, Paul leaves the room.

***

Paul and I have been making our way through the magnificent halls of the Vatican Museums for several hours, and I remain as mesmerized as I was when we started. Despite the heat and the mobs of headphone-wearing tourists who are dutifully following the signs that point the way from one room to the next, Paul and I have remained in our own little world. Sometimes chatting quietly, other times in thoughtful silence, we've taken our time venturing through the incredible galleries these museums contain. I've seen more beautiful, historical paintings and sculptures in one morning than I've seen over the course of the rest of my life combined. Even the building itself is an amazing work of art, with its ornate architecture, high ceilings, tall windows, and decorative floors.

Paul and I go through a doorway into yet another room, which is smaller than some of the others and has a particularly tall ceiling. Paul puts a hand on my arm and pulls me to a stop.

"Turn around," Paul says. "There's something you should definitely see."

I do as instructed and set my eyes on the massive wall to the right of the doorway we just came through. Instantly, I'm riveted by what meets my eyes: a huge work of art painted directly on the wall. The fresco shows the inside of a vast building, which has towering archways, statues in recessed portals, and a soaring ceiling dome. Hints of clouds in a blue sky can be seen outside the building. At the center of the painting, two men dressed in colorful, ancient-style garments are walking side-by-side, and they're engaged in conversation. The man on the left is pointing a finger upward. The man on the right has a hand outstretched. Around the two men are several groupings of other people who are reading, writing, and talking amongst themselves.

"*The School of Athens* by Raphael," Paul tells me. "It's my favorite piece in the entire museum."

I continue gazing upon the gigantic fresco, deciding this might very well be my favorite work of art, too. There's something majestic, fascinating, and a little mysterious about it. The more I study it, the more detail I notice in the poses, actions, expressions, and activities of the many people who are portrayed. I can't help but sense there's a powerful message in this work—a hidden meaning behind each person. It compels the viewer to try to understand the artist's message from hundreds of years ago.

"Raphael was commissioned to paint this work for the Vatican in the early fifteen hundreds," Paul explains. "Many believe Raphael depicted every famous Greek philosopher, including Plato and Aristotle, who are in the middle, and others such as Socrates, Archimedes, and Pythagoras. It's possible even Michelangelo is represented."

I exhale a breath. "I think I could look at it all day."

"I agree." Paul is also peering up at the wall, his head tipped slightly to one side. "No matter how many times I see it, I can't help but stop and observe it for a while."

I don't know how long Paul and I remain rooted in place while hoards of people pass by us as they continue moving through the museums. Finally, Paul and I also resume our tour. The rooms get smaller, and the halls become increasingly narrow. Eventually, we reach a bottleneck where tourists must file through a small doorway. Once we're through, Paul and I go up a wide staircase and make a couple of turns.

Suddenly, we've entered the Sistine Chapel.

The rectangular-shaped room is large, though it's not as huge as I expected. Natural light is coming in through numerous tall, arched windows that are high up on the walls. The room is packed with standing-only tourists, who are maintaining respectful quiet while cranking back their necks to view the ceiling.

I stick close to Paul, who does a masterful job weaving through the throng to reach a vacant corner near the back. Turning around, we now have a full view of the room without being crammed in the middle with everyone else. I don't look up at the ceiling just yet, though. First, I spend time admiring the gorgeous paintings on the walls. Then, at last, I raise my gaze upward.

In person, the ceiling of the Sistine Chapel is more glorious than the pictures. Michelangelo's Renaissance-era depictions of Biblical scenes, which are done in rich, vibrant colors and exquisite detail, span the entire length and width of the ceiling. Situated near the center of the ceiling is the most famous work of art in the entire Vatican—one of the most famous pieces of art in the history of the world: the thought-provoking, *The Creation of Adam*.

I point up at it. "Did you know many people speculate that the shapes and figures behind God were intended to portray a profile view of the human brain and brainstem?"

Paul, who has also been looking upward, glances at me and then returns his focus to the ceiling. He becomes still. At last, he fixes his eyes on mine once more. "I've never heard that before. You're right. It *does* look like the human brain."

"While it may be coincidence, it's hard to deny that it's pretty anatomically correct." I peer upward again. "I like to think it was a way of showing a harmonious blend of religion and science, and that all those years ago, perhaps Michelangelo was trying to say those two things aren't mutually exclusive."

When Paul doesn't reply, I look at him again. He's watching me closely with his dark eyes.

"That's really beautiful, Irene," he says.

I suddenly become extremely aware of how closely Paul and I are standing to each other, and how his hand is almost touching mine. I—

One of the Vatican workers makes a loud announcement that echoes throughout the chapel. I hear the worker say, "*foto*," and I notice several people scrambling to hide their phones. I grin, guessing the worker is chastising tourists who are trying to sneak pictures of the ceiling, which is against the rules.

Paul checks his watch. "What do you say we head over to St. Peter's? There's a great café along the way where we can grab lunch."

I nod my agreement, and Paul and I begin what proves to be an immensely lengthy journey to get out of the museums. Following the signs and crowds of tourists, we leave the Sistine Chapel and proceed to pass through several hallways and galleries, and a couple of gift shops. Once we finally reach the main hall, we pass an info desk and another gift shop, and then we wind down a gigantic circular ramp before getting to the ground floor and the exit.

Stepping outside into the sweltering heat, I slide on the sunglasses that I purchased from a street vendor this morning. Paul and I take a right turn and start meandering along the sidewalk that follows the massive wall that surrounds the grounds of Vatican City. We take another right to reach a wide promenade that leads toward St. Peter's Square, which is rising up in the distance.

"Paulo! Irene!"

The unexpected sound of someone shouting our names causes me to halt. Eyebrows rising, I peer through the sea of tourists and street vendors, trying to figure out who could have possibly called to us.

Paul, however, doesn't seem surprised in the slightest. He looks across the road and casually waves while shouting, "*Ciao*, Violetta! Rafaele!"

Following his line of sight, I'm astonished to see Paul's cousins waving back at us from the street corner.

"Surprise," Paul says to me with a mischievous gleam in his eye.

"You knew they were coming?" I break into a broad smile, delighted to see members of his family again.

"Yep," Paul replies, grinning. "This is what Violetta called about yesterday while we were at the Colosseum. She and Rafaele have the day off, and they wanted to meet up with us. Violetta, in particular, was excited to see you again. I think you've made a great impression on her."

"Really?" My smile widens even more. "I'm honored and thrilled your cousins are here."

Paul and I share another smile before we cross the road. As we draw closer to his cousins, however, my excitement is displaced by sorrow and guilt. It doesn't matter how much I adore Paul's family. My relationship with them has been built on a lie. In only a few days, the façade will be over. I'll be telling Paul's family members the truth and leaving them all behind.

My chest grows heavy. Is that what I really want? Is saying goodbye to Paul and his family part of the life I want to live?

"Irene!" Violetta gives me a hug, jarring me from my thoughts. "I am happy to see you!"

"I'm happy to see you, too. What a wonderful surprise." I hug Violetta in return and then turn to Rafaele, who's giving Paul a high-five. "Great to see you also."

Rafaele shows a grin that's markedly similar to his cousin's. "We thought it would be good to sightsee with you, and then we can talk about the website."

"I also want to talk about the wedding!" Violetta's eyes are sparkling with excitement. She motions to her phone, which she's gripping in her hand. "Perhaps we can look at dresses on the Internet!"

My eyes flick to Paul and then back to Violetta. "That would be . . . great."

Paul causally interjects into the conversation. "How about we head to the café to get something to eat?"

The siblings voice their agreement, spin around, and race down a nondescript side street. Paul and I exchange another glance before following after them.

The café proves to be an adorable little eatery that's quiet, cool, and filled with the delicious aromas of fresh foods. The four of us place our orders at the counter and then take a seat at a table by a large window. Before long, we're enjoying a late lunch of chilled sandwiches, salads, and, of course, gelato. Once again, the meal is a home run. It's yet another culinary argument for why I need to stay in Italy forever.

Even more wonderful than the food, though, is the company. Over the course of our meal, not only do the four of us talk about the new website for Donato and Rita's rentals, we get to know one another better. We swap email addresses and social media invites. We show each other pictures on our phones. We talk about what life is like in the Lakewood area compared to Pago Veiano. As silly as it sounds, I'm beginning to feel like a big sister to Rafaele and Violetta, and I love it.

Amidst my joy, however, remorse gnaws at my heart. After this trip, I won't see Rafaele or Violetta ever again. I won't see Paul again, either. With a silent sigh, my eyes drift Paul's way. Seeming to sense my gaze, he looks back at me. From the subtle furrow in his brow, I can't help wondering if he's thinking the same thing as I am.

"I got tickets so we do not have to wait in line." Rafaele proudly pulls a couple pieces of paper from the back pocket of his jeans, which I see are ticket vouchers that have been printed off the Internet.

"Awesome." Paul gives his cousin an appreciative nod. "If everyone is ready, we can head over there. With the sun getting a little lower in the sky now, the lighting inside should be just about perfect."

We exit the eatery and rejoin the crowds on the main promenade. Soon, we reach the giant columns that ring the front of St. Peter's Square, and we pass between the columns to enter the square itself. As I've found myself doing over and over on this trip, I have to stop to take in the majestic, striking, iconic view.

St. Peter's Basilica is an amazing sight to behold. The massive church, with its ornately capped columns and statues, and enormous dome on the roof, is gleaming proudly in the sunlight. No matter what one's religious background, there's no denying the historical importance and staggering beauty of this place.

Somehow, too, despite its overwhelming size, there's also a peaceful ambience here.

"Thoughts?" Paul comes up beside me.

"I don't know if there are words that can describe it," I reply, still in sensory overload. "And that's coming from someone who claims to have a knack for writing."

Paul chuckles. "If you think this is good, wait until you see the inside."

"Irene! Paulo!" Violetta calls to us from behind. "I want to take your picture!"

Paul and I share a fast look, and then we turn around.

With her phone in one hand, Violetta is using her other hand to enthusiastically gesture for Paul and me to stand closer together. "I will get a picture with the *basilica* in the background!"

Paul and I both fall still for a long second. Paul then clears his throat and adjusts his stance so he's standing right next to me. His eyes flick my way as he drapes an arm over my shoulders. Before I even realize what I'm doing, I slip my right arm around the back of Paul's waist. Paul's breathing hitches almost imperceptibly as I do so, and by the time I process what I've done, it's too late to let go. Instead, I keep my arm where it is, my heart racing at the sensation of Paul's firm body underneath his shirt.

Violetta holds up her cell phone. "Smile!"

I do. I smile with both happiness and sadness. With certainty and confusion. With the awareness that this is one of the most wonderful and most agonizing moments of my life.

"Now a closer picture!" Violetta jogs nearer to Paul and me. "Show the ring, Irene!"

I'm not exactly sure how one is supposed to pose to show off a ring, so I turn in even more toward Paul and rest my left hand on his chest. My heart rate rises even more when I feel his sculpted pec muscles under my hand.

Violetta giggles with delight and takes more pictures. "I cannot wait for your wedding!"

Thankfully, Rafaele wanders over and joins us, interrupting the wedding talk, and Violetta finishes taking pictures. My eyes meet Paul's as we slowly let go of each other and step apart. Pulling our gazes away from one another, Paul and I join the teens as they race over to the person who's taking the entry tickets. Once through the armed checkpoint, we climb the steps to reach the towering, dark wood doors that lead into one of the most famous places of worship in the world.

Stepping inside St. Peter's Basilica is an experience that is unlike any other. The building looked huge from the outside, but nothing could have prepared me for the true size of this place. It's absolutely enormous. Its walls seem to stretch up forever before finally meeting the arched ceilings that are high overhead, and the building feels like it stretches out for miles around me. This gorgeous-beyond-description building is so gigantic, in fact, that even though there are hordes of tourists inside, there's still plenty of room to move around. The sheer size alone of the basilica is simply incredible.

As if its astounding size wasn't enough to take my breath away, this is also the most ornately, intricately decorated building I've ever beheld. The gray-white walls, arched ceilings, and central dome are covered with gold, recessed sculptures, and religious paintings. More stunning artwork makes up the marble floor itself. Basically, there's a masterpiece every few feet in here, and one of the most stunning of them all is to the right of the main doors and behind bulletproof glass: Michelangelo's poignant *Pieta*. Meanwhile, at the far end of the nave, directly underneath the soaring dome, is the giant canopied altar, which at this moment is gorgeously lit by the sunlight that's streaming in through the dome's high windows.

"Violetta and I are going to go climb the dome," Rafaele tells Paul and me. "Do you want to come with us?"

Paul looks my way.

I cast another look around at the overwhelming splendor. I then give Rafaele an appreciative smile while shaking my head. "Thanks, but I think I need some more time to try to take it all in from down here."

Rafaele gives me a thumbs-up before he slips away, soon becoming lost in the crowds as he goes to wait in line for a turn to climb up to the viewing area in the dome. Violetta scurries after her brother, her head down as she busily starts doing something on her phone.

Paul faces me. "I don't blame you for wanting a little more time to soak in everything. Would you like to take another slow lap?"

"Yes," I tell him gratefully. "I would love some time to process it all."

"Me, too," Paul says, observing me. "Me, too."

Nineteen

Florence might be the world's most perfect city. Granted, that might be a rather sweeping declaration to make considering Paul and I only arrived here by train an hour ago. However, after taking a taxi from the train station to the heart of old downtown, there's no question that I'm falling hard and fast under Florence's spell.

Paul and I are standing on a lamppost-lined walkway, looking out over the wide Arno River, which is sparkling in the sun while it flows through the city. From our vantage point, Paul and I have a sweeping view of the buildings on the river's opposite shore and of the *Piazzale Michelangelo* farther in the distance. Not far down the river to our right is one of the most iconic landmarks of Florence: the *Ponte Vecchio*, the bridge that has stretched over the water since medieval times. Almost directly behind where we're standing is the courtyard of the famous Uffizi Gallery, which is lined with statues of several world-famous Italians, including Leonardo da Vinci, Galileo, and Donatello. Only a few blocks up the street sits the world-renowned *Duomo di Firenze*, and mere blocks beyond that is the Accademia Gallery, which holds Michelangelo's *David*.

In other words, this city is a powerhouse of Renaissance history, food, architecture, and art. Nonetheless, somehow, Florence still feels intimate and peaceful. The end result is that the energy here is a perfect blend. Florence is carefree yet refined. Relaxed but sophisticated. Adventurous but quiet. Historical yet modern. Touristy but authentic. Fun yet elegant. And I am utterly enchanted.

There are countless things to do and see here, but Paul and I actually didn't come for the sightseeing. Instead, we're about to do a walk-through of the apartment Donato and Rita hope to buy. As always, I've got my fully charged phone in my purse so I'm ready to take pictures, and Paul has his laptop bag on his shoulder.

"Looks like the apartment is on this side of the river and only a couple blocks east from here," Paul tells me while referencing a map on his phone. "Are you ready to check it out?"

"Definitely." I nod. "Let's do it."

We start strolling along the river while following the map on Paul's phone. Despite this breathtaking location and the reason for our visit, however, my thoughts soon start wandering. In truth, my mind has been a loose cannon all morning. Tomorrow will mark one week since I arrived in Italy, and it will be time for me to talk to Stuart. I don't yet know where the conversation will lead, but Stuart and I may try to make things right.

So why does it feel completely wrong?

My mind tells me I should be willing to consider giving my six-year relationship with Stuart another chance. My heart, though, insists that Stuart and I fell out of love a long time ago, and we were simply too busy with our work-controlled lives to notice . . . that is, if we were ever truly in love at all.

My heart also knows that Paul has ignited amazing, liberating, thrilling feelings inside me that I've never experienced before. I've shared more heartfelt moments, genuine laughter, and candid discussions with Paul in a week than I've shared with Stuart in a long time. I can be myself around Paul. I feel safe and secure with him. There's a natural chemistry that is undeniable. Truly, amidst my vow to live more fully and not let opportunities pass me by, the most incredible opportunity I have may be Paul himself. Or is this is all still a façade? I'm not sure.

Paul and I begin venturing down a quaint side street while my heart and mind continue to battle. I glance Paul's way, trying to get a sense of what might be going through his mind. His sunglasses are hiding his soulful, dark eyes, however, so I can't read what he's feeling or thinking. I sigh silently and focus straight ahead once more.

We soon reach our destination: a narrow, five-story apartment building that sits in the middle of a long row of attached dwellings. I smile when I see it; this place is beautiful, and it's a perfect representation of this gorgeous city. The building is made of light gray stone. Fancy millwork frames the tall, dark double doors, which are flanked by ornate sconces. Each story has two tall windows facing the street, and all the windows are adorably trimmed with shutters. Yes, barring any catastrophic surprise on the inside, this place will be another perfect rental for Donato and Rita to own. It's stunning, and the location couldn't be more ideal.

Paul lifts his sunglasses onto his head, steps to the front door, and presses one of the buttons on the panel beside it. A few seconds later, the door is unlocked from the inside. A short man who's wearing round spectacles opens the door. Speaking in Italian, Paul sounds as though he's introducing us. I put on a smile. The man looks at us both, grunts with approval, and motions for us to follow him inside.

After stepping into the shady foyer, I become even more excited for Donato and Rita to own an apartment in this lovely building. While Paul and the man continue talking, I commence taking pictures of the stone floor and a brick archway that leads to the staircase. I keep documenting with my camera as I trail Paul and the man up three flights of stairs, around two left turns through a decorated landing, and to a closed door. The man uses a fancy key to unlock the door, and then he steps aside. Paul motions for me to go ahead of him. I cross the threshold.

I'm absolutely in love.

The gorgeous apartment is big and laid out in an open floor plan. The towering windows at the front of the building have an unobstructed view of the street where Paul and I were standing, and also of the river beyond. The light-colored parquet floor, soft gray tone on the walls, and impressively high ceilings make this apartment feel elegant and airy, while simultaneously giving it a warm and comfortable ambience.

Straight in front of me is a large sitting room. As I go farther inside and look to my left, I get a view of the main sleeping area, which is on the opposite side of the apartment. There's a queen-sized bed with tall cabinets on each side of it, and a chandelier hanging from the vaulted ceiling. Turning toward the back of the apartment, I'm met by the sight of a modern kitchen. I peek through doorways that lead into a second bedroom and a spacious bathroom. I make a mental note to tell Paul to put up a sign that warns tourists about the alarm cord in the shower.

Paul comes up behind me, and I shoot him a glance that lets him know how much I adore this apartment. His glance in return tells me he's as impressed as I am. The silent exchange between Paul and me lasts no more than a moment, and it goes unnoticed by the man who's with us, yet it's enough. Paul and I understand one another without saying a word.

Paul and the man resume conversing. I break away to get more pictures. When I'm done, I migrate over to one of the comfortable couches in the sitting area. I pull out my phone so I can start jotting down notes about things I want to remember to highlight in my write-ups, but I pause in surprise when I see that I have a ton of new voicemails. Scrolling through the list of callers, I see the names of various family members and friends. I then note that I have several new texts, too. For a second, I fear something bad has happened back at home. Thankfully, though, my fear is short-lived when I realize that all the texts and voicemails came through within a short period of time. Evidently, it's just a data dump. Messages and voicemails haven't been getting through to my phone reliably while I've been overseas, and they all finally came through at once. Conspicuously, there's still no communication from Stuart.

I decide to ignore my messages for the time being. I need to make my notes about this apartment while things are fresh in my mind. On Sunday morning, Paul and I will be meeting to finish working on the info about this rental, and then we'll pass along everything to Rafaele and Violetta, who will be standing by to add the data to the website. If things go according to plan, the estate deals will be closed, the third-party travel website will be updated, Donato and Rita's own website will go live, and all the social media promotion and advertising will hit the Internet by the end of Sunday.

Also on Sunday—specifically early Sunday morning, which will be Saturday night back at home—is when I'll be talking to Stuart.

I turn to look out the window. The sunshine that's coming in through the sheer drapes warms my face as I watch pedestrians strolling along the river. The peaceful scene makes a striking contrast to the confusion that's swirling within me.

"Irene, if you've gotten everything you need, I think we're ready to go."

I whip up my head. Paul is standing beside the couch, and he's observing me with a pensive gaze.

I get to my feet. "Yes, I think I'm set."

Paul's eyes seem to linger on mine before he turns to the man, puts on a smile, and says something to him. The man shakes Paul's hand and then leads us out the door. We all go back down to the ground floor. The man opens the main door, and Paul and I step outside. With a final wave, the man shuts the door behind us.

Paul makes a slight tip of his head in the same direction from where we originally came. We start walking along the street, and once we're a distance from the apartment building, Paul asks me:

"So what are your thoughts?"

"I think it's fabulous," I gush. "The location is close to the major sites in the city, and the apartment itself is beautiful. I wouldn't hesitate to stay there myself, if I were traveling in Florence."

Paul slides his sunglasses back down in front of his eyes. "No, I mean what are your *thoughts*?"

I do a double take. "You mean . . . about Stuart?"

"About Stuart." Paul's tone reveals nothing. "Tomorrow is the one-week mark for you being here in Italy, isn't it?"

"Yes." The word catches in my throat. "It is."

Paul continues staring straight ahead. "So have you decided what you're going to do?"

Just then, we emerge out from the shady side street and into the sunshine. Paul and I wander to the walkway that parallels the river. I stop, lean against the waist-high wall, and peer out over the water. Paul stands close beside me, also keeping his attention on the river. A nearby street performer starts playing an accordion, and the melancholy melody makes the ache in my chest expand. I pull my own sunglasses from my purse to hide my eyes.

"Stuart and I arranged to talk, and I need to follow through with that," I eventually say. I look Paul's way. "I owe at least that much to both Stuart and me."

Paul is still staring out at the water. "I see."

"I won't let that affect our plans for your grandparents, though, I promise," I add. "We're still going to get our work done, and as soon as I've spoken with Stuart, I'll . . . I'll let you know how much longer I need to use the apartment."

Paul's cheek muscle twitches. "This isn't about the apartment, Irene," he says in a low voice. "You know that."

Before I can reply, Paul turns his back to the river so he's facing the Uffizi Gallery, and when he speaks again, his tone is aloof and businesslike:

"There are several trains that go to Rome over the course of the day, so we don't necessarily have to rush back to the train station right now." He looks at me. "Would you like to tour some of the highlights first? It sounds like this might be your last opportunity to see Florence before your trip is over."

I gaze at the Uffizi Gallery, aware of all the incredible works of art that are contained inside. I think, too, about the other amazing sights this city holds, and I ponder how many off-the-beaten-path treasures Paul and I would also discover today. I would normally drop everything for a chance to spend a day absorbing the beauty and culture of Florence—especially with Paul. Today, though, I can't bring myself to do it.

"Thank you for asking, but I . . . would prefer to go back to my apartment," I say, speaking softly. "I have some work emails to catch up on."

"There are some things I should probably get taken care of, too." Paul takes off his sunglasses, and he gazes intently into my eyes. "I do hope you'll come back here one day, though, Irene. I know you would love it."

My breathing hitches. "I hope so, too."

Twenty

My apartment feels particularly quiet in this early morning hour. I'm standing in the entryway, staring at the front door while running my hand along the strap of my purple purse, which has my phone inside. At times, I feel numb; other times, I feel achingly resigned as I contemplate what I'm about to do.

The earliest hints of morning sunshine are streaming in through the apartment's main windows and filling the entryway with light. I'm glad the time difference is such that I'll be talking with Stuart before the bustle of the day gets underway here in Rome. I'm hoping the serenity of the early hour will help me keep my head clear and my emotions under control. This is, after all, potentially the most important conversation of my life.

I decided to leave my apartment to make the call because I can't be here, talking to Stuart, where everything reminds me of Paul. It's painfully ironic that only a week ago I was fleeing my condo because I didn't want to be surrounded by reminders of Stuart, and now I'm seeking out a place where I can try to connect with him again.

I open the apartment door, step out into the hallway, and lock the door behind me. Nearly on tiptoe, I venture down the empty stairwell to the ground floor, tug open the main door, and step outside. The temperature is comfortably warm. A soft breeze is stirring the trees. The songs of the birds are carrying through the air. The streets are empty but for a few locals who are already going about their day. Were it not for what I'm about to do, this morning would be idyllic.

I navigate the familiar route past the closed shops and the street market to reach the *San Giovanni* metro station. I head underground, buy a ticket, and push through the turnstiles. I'm comfortable navigating the metro station now. I've come to feel at home with everything around here, which makes my heart hurt even more to ponder that my trip might be coming to an end.

The station is relatively quiet; not surprisingly, there aren't many crowds around on an early Sunday morning. I reach my platform, and soon the train emerges from the dark tunnel at my left. After the train comes to a stop, I step into an almost-empty car. I take a seat.

I stare out the window at the walls of the tunnel as the train resumes rumbling along the A line. The third stop is Termini, but I don't get off. Instead, I ride the train another two stops and get off at the Barberini station. When I exit the station, I find myself on an unfamiliar street. I pull my phone from my purse and follow the map that I downloaded last night, taking a route that consists of several turns down surprisingly tucked-away, narrow, tree-and-building-lined roads. About fifteen minutes later, the street opens up, and I'm suddenly staring at the place I set out to find: Trevi Fountain, one of the most famous fountains in the world.

The stunning Baroque fountain was created in the seventeen hundreds. Its size is jaw-dropping, but what's even more impressive is that it's carved into the side of a palace. This giant white fountain, with its pillars, statues, and gushing, crystal-clear water, is flanked on both sides by the symmetrically spaced windows of the building it's structurally a part of.

I glance around. The little square around the fountain is nearly empty—a true rarity, as this place is notoriously jam-packed with tourists, day and night. Putting away my phone, I walk down the steps to reach the front of the fountain. For a while, I let my eyes wander across the sculptures and watch the water flow. A cool mist touches my face, and the soothing sound of the fountain fills my ears. Once I'm ready, I take a step toward one of the benches to sit down, but I stop once more. There's something else I want to do before I make the call.

Digging around in my purse, I find my wallet and pull out a penny. Turning so my back is to the fountain, I toss the penny over my shoulder. Quickly spinning around again, I watch the coin splash softly into the water and drift down to the bottom of the fountain, joining the countless other coins that are resting there. They say tossing a coin into Trevi Fountain guarantees you'll return to Rome one day. I can only hope the legend is true.

Retreating from the fountain, I take a seat on one of the stone benches. I pull my phone back out of my purse. I have more new voicemails, but none of them are from Stuart. I close my eyes and take another moment to breathe. I then pull up Stuart's contact info and press the button to make the call. My heart is racing so fast that it hurts as I put my phone to my ear.

The call goes directly to voicemail.

I end the call without leaving a message. For a long time, I stare at the fountain, trying to sort out what to do. This was supposed to be my opportunity to finally talk to Stuart. This was when I was going to decide if Stuart and I have any chance of reconciling and moving forward together. This should have been the end of the angst, confusion, and worry, for this was when everything was going to be resolved once and for all.

Why isn't Stuart answering? He knows we scheduled this time to talk, and he never forgets anything on his calendar. I shake my head in frustration. I can't stay in limbo. I cannot continue wondering. I can't keep getting pulled back-and-forth between my sense of loyalty for Stuart and my feelings for Paul.

I quickly call Stuart again and put the phone back to my ear. My foot is tapping the ground as I wait. Again, the phone goes directly to voicemail.

"Hi, Stuart," my words shake as I start leaving a message. "I'm calling because we planned to talk now, remember? Please call me back ASAP."

I end the call, drop my phone to my lap, and exhale hard. Now what do I do? Just wait here for Stuart to call? No, I refuse to keep waiting. The uncertainty is unbearable. I need answers. How, though, can I get answers without Stuart?

I sit up taller as the answer hits me: I'll fly home. Today. I need to talk to Stuart, and if showing up by appointment at his office on Monday morning is the only way I'm going to get some time with him, then that's how I'm going to do it.

My pulse rate picks up as my plan continues forming in my mind. I'll return to the apartment, pack, and head to the airport. I'll grab a seat on the first-available flight back home. Once I'm home, which should be some time on Sunday over there, I'll unpack and catch up on sleep. First thing Monday morning, I'll call Stuart's secretary and schedule an appointment to meet with him. His office is the one place where I know I'll be able to find him.

Springing to my feet, I take a few hurried steps before stopping abruptly in my tracks. There's one major flaw in my plan: I'm supposed to work with Paul today. We're going to work on finishing the information for Donato and Rita's rental unit in Florence, and no matter how desperate I am to get answers from Stuart, I will not abandon Paul and his grandparents.

My mind churns as I continue thinking over the situation. Paul is planning to come over fairly early this morning, so we should be finished with our work by early afternoon at the latest. Once we're done, I could head immediately to the airport. I should still arrive back home by Sunday night, which means I'll be able to stick to my plan of seeing Stuart on Monday.

Though my plan will still work, however, that doesn't stop the profound grief and heartache from setting in. I'm going to tell Paul goodbye today. I won't be with Paul when he explains to Donato and Rita why we misled them about being engaged. I'll never see his family again. Nothing about this is how I wanted things to end, but I have to go home. I have to talk to Stuart.

I look over at the iconic fountain one last time, and then I start retracing my route back to the metro station. More people are strolling the streets now, and cafés are opening up. I inhale the aromas of pastries and coffee, but I walk past the shops without even slowing my pace. I'm not hungry.

Reaching the station, I head back to the platform for the A-line trains. It isn't long before I'm on board. Though there are more passengers on the train than earlier, there are still plenty of places to sit down. I take a chair and rest my forehead against the window as the train courses along the underground tracks back to *San Giovanni*. By the time I'm off the train and walking back to my apartment, I'm almost dizzy at the thought of everything the next twenty-four hours will entail: working with Paul to finish assembling the information for his grandparents' website, blindsiding Paul by telling him goodbye, taking a last-minute oversees flight, and meeting with Stuart. It will be a brutally exhausting, agonizingly emotional time, but at least the horrible unrest and uncertainty will be over.

I reach my street and continue heading toward the green gate that leads into the courtyard in front of my building. I note the gate is slightly ajar. When I reach it, I push open the gate farther and step through, shutting the gate firmly behind me. I then shift my eyes to the building's front doors. And I freeze.

Stuart is standing there.

Twenty One

"Stuart! What are you . . . how did you . . ." I trail off while feeling the color drain from my face.

Stuart is here. In Italy. He's standing less than ten feet away from me.

I force myself to blink, as if doing so will somehow prove this is only a hallucination, but there's no question about it: Stuart is standing in front of the building's main doors. He's wearing a maroon, button-up shirt and black slacks. He has his suit jacket draped over the handle of his roller suitcase, which is situated beside him. His hair is atypically a bit ruffled. I can also see the faintest hints of facial scruff on his upper lip; I can't remember the last time I saw Stuart with anything other than a perfectly clean shave.

"Surprise," he tells me, sounding tired, without a smile.

I have no idea how long I gawk at him in my stunned stupor before I manage to collect myself enough to voice a reply. "How did you find me?"

"From the text message you sent a few days ago." Stuart motions to his phone, which he's holding in his hand. "You mentioned you were staying in an apartment in Rome that was managed by someone named Donato Conti. It wasn't hard to narrow down things from there, since only two apartments in a website database matched those search criteria. I found the addresses for both apartments, and I took a taxi from the airport here first. If this turned out not to be where you were staying, I was going to try the other apartment next."

Once again, I find I can't speak. I can't even move or breathe. My thoughts are flying faster than I can keep up with. My emotions are all over the place. Stuart came to Italy. To find me. It doesn't seem possible. It doesn't feel real.

"I can't b-believe you're here," I finally stutter. "I'm extremely surprised."

"You're surprised?" Stuart asks while blinking at me.

"Yes, I'm surprised." I stand up straighter, forcing my thoughts into focus. "How could I not be surprised? You haven't exactly been acting like someone who would be willing to fly halfway around the globe just to find me. Only a week ago, you had no desire to travel to Italy at all. You also didn't seem to care when I called you to talk, and you never responded to my texts, which you clearly received." I finish with a pointed glance at his phone.

Stuart massages his forehead with his free hand and lets out an exaggerated sigh. "I needed time, Irene. We had just gone through a significant life restructuring, which necessitated stepping back and reassessing the situation in order to determine the best course of action."

My stern expression relents a little. "So you *have* been thinking about me . . . about us?"

Stuart drops his arm to his side and frowns. "How could I not think about you when I discovered you were engaged? We may have broken up, Irene, but I wasn't going to sit back and let you foolishly rush into a marriage with some guy you were recklessly flirting with on the rebound." He shakes his head. "Look, I know you have dreams of being more spontaneous, but there's a point when doing so is stupid and foolish—even dangerous."

My mouth is slowly dropping open as I process Stuart's words. "What are you talking about? I haven't been . . . what in the world makes you think I'm *engaged*?"

Stuart motions matter-of-factly to my left hand. It takes another second for the confusion to clear from my mind, and then I swallow hard. The ring. The fake engagement ring that's on my finger. I've gotten so used to wearing it that I didn't remember I had it on.

I open my mouth to explain, but Stuart beats me to it. Maintaining an air of diplomacy, he goes on:

"A day or so ago, I started receiving a flurry of calls from several of our mutual acquaintances regarding a photo you were tagged in on social media. Imagine my shock when a screenshot of the photo was sent my way, and I learned you were engaged. I saw you posing with some guy in front of St. Peter's

Basilica, clearly making a point of showing off your engagement ring. As if that wasn't absurd enough, the person who posted the picture even wrote you were the guy's fiancée."

My stomach crashes to the ground. Violetta. Violetta must have posted one of the pictures she took of Paul and me. With a groan, I close my eyes as a sickening wave of panic washes over me. Everyone I interact with on social media now thinks I'm engaged to Paul Conti. No wonder I've been getting so many voicemails and texts these past few days! What must my family and friends be thinking? How can I possibly explain to everyone what really happened? Will I ever be able to clean up this mess? I groan again, feeling queasy. This is a disaster. What am I going to do?

I push my hair from my face. All I can do is tackle one catastrophe at a time. And first up is Stuart's unexpected arrival here in Rome.

Opening my eyes, I concentrate on Stuart once more. I rack my brain for a straightforward way to explain everything that has happened, but all I hear myself say is:

"It's not what you think."

Stuart's eyes narrow. "Are you saying you were *familiar* with this guy before you came out here?"

My posture stiffens in reaction to his thinly veiled accusation. "Absolutely not! I didn't meet Paul until the day I flew out here."

"Paul," Stuart repeats flatly. "His name is Paul."

"Yes, his name is Paul." I draw in a breath. "But no, I'm not engaged to him. He's the grandson of the owner of the apartment I'm staying in, and we've been pretending to be engaged to help his grandparents. I know it sounds crazy, but I swear it's the truth." I wearily motion to the doors. "Let's go inside, and I'll tell you the whole story."

Stuart keeps staring at me. "Irene, I obviously have no idea what's going on here, but it's evident you're going through a really difficult adjustment." He takes a step closer to me. "To be honest, I've been going through a difficult time, too. That's why I came to find you. Seeing a picture of you with another man caused me to do some serious introspection. I realized I didn't like how we left things, and I wanted to talk with you in person."

I nearly drop the keys as I pull them from my purple purse. "I agree we need to talk. Let's head up to the apartment, okay?"

Stuart nods, appearing satisfied. He takes a firm hold of his suitcase handle. "Great. Before we talk, though, I could use some rest. First-class seats aren't nearly as conducive to sleeping on an airplane as one would think."

I refrain from commenting about trying to sleep in the back of a plane near the lavatory, and I instead unlock the door. I take my time doing so, however. Still reeling from Stuart's arrival, I'm trying to give myself a chance to sort out what I think and how I feel. The only emotion I can discern out of the mess, though, is how uncomfortably strange it seems to have Stuart here. It doesn't feel right.

I push open the door and step into the foyer. I keep the door held open for Stuart, who strides in behind me with his suitcase rolling loudly on the floor, the sound echoing obnoxiously up the stairwell. I wince at the noise, hoping no one gets woken up by it.

"We can take the stairs, or you can use that elevator if you prefer." I point toward the accordion doors while closing the building's main door.

"That's an elevator?" Stuart turns my way with a smirk. "I know you've always had rather romantic dreams of what Italy would be like, but I'm guessing you've probably come to realize that the sooner you get home, the better."

I feel the sting of his words but keep my expression impassive. I'm going to give him a wide berth, at least for now. Stuart is jet-lagged, and he came a long way to see me. Not to mention, a chance to have his undivided attention is what I've been longing for, so I'm not going to throw away that opportunity now. If Stuart and I are going to sort through things, both of us need to be especially forgiving.

"I assume that means you'd prefer to use the stairs," is my unaffected reply.

Stuart grunts with effort as he lifts his suitcase. "Do I have any other choice?"

I turn without responding and start making my way up the stairs. Behind me, I hear Stuart breathing hard as he carries his luggage. I reach back an arm to help him with the small suitcase as we climb the rest of the way to the fourth floor. Once we reach the landing, I release my hold on the suitcase, unlock the apartment door, and enter. Stuart drops the suitcase back onto the floor and pulls it behind him as he follows me inside.

"This is it." I set the keys on the foyer table. "Isn't it wonderful?"

Stuart continues pulling his luggage as he ventures into the main room. His nose wrinkles as he looks around. "It's . . . quaint, I suppose."

I hold in an exasperated sigh. "Would you like something to eat or drink before we talk?"

"No, I'm all right." Stuart faces me. "As I said, I've been anxious to talk, and now I'm immensely curious to hear what possessed you to start wearing a fake engagement ring. However, also like I already alluded to, I do want to be fully present, both mentally and physically, for our meeting. So I would prefer to take a nap first."

I blink a couple times. "Right. Of course. There's, um, a second bedroom you can use. Let me show you the way."

Stuart resumes pulling his suitcase as we leave the main room and go into the other bedroom. After Stuart gets his suitcase tucked away to his liking, I give him a brief tour of the rest of the apartment. While we're in the kitchen, I fill up a glass of water for him (without ice . . . Stuart doesn't like ice). Finally, we return to his bedroom. I set down the water on the nightstand and show him how to use the air conditioner. I then retreat for the doorway.

"Let me know if you need anything," I tell him, still attempting to process the fact that Stuart is actually standing inside this apartment.

Stuart grabs earplugs and a sleeping mask from the front pocket of his luggage. "I will. Thanks."

"You're welcome."

I stagger backward the rest of the way out of the room and shut the door. Spinning around, I charge into my bedroom. I flop down, face-first, onto the bed and squeeze shut my eyes. I take in a few breaths, trying to calm myself, but my thoughts are spiraling faster than I can control.

Stuart came all the way here to find me. He made it clear that he's not happy about our breakup. He even implied he's hoping to work things out between us. This should be what I want, and yet—

There's a knock on the apartment's front door. I whip up my head with an alarmed gasp, yank out my phone from my purse, and check the time. My body goes cold. Paul is here for our scheduled work session.

I'm suddenly feeling sick as I shakily push myself to my feet. Paul is here. Stuart is here, too.

What am I going to do?

Twenty Two

"Good morning, Irene." Paul has his eyes on his phone as he steps into the apartment. With his laptop bag slung over his shoulder, he continues reading whatever is on his phone while he heads toward the main room. "Good news: Rafaele sent me screenshots of the new website. The photos you took of the Venetian apartment look awesome, and your write-ups are great." He briefly lifts his eyes to smile at me. "I'll go set up my laptop and load the screenshots onto it, so you can see them in full size. I think you'll be really pleased with how everything turned out."

Paul disappears around the corner, leaving me in the entryway. I slowly shut the door as another wave of intense emotion crashes into me. Paul's arrival has once again unleashed all the thrilling attraction and deep connection I feel toward him. At the same time, I know Stuart is just down the hall, and I can't disregard that; especially not after he traveled all the way here to talk with me. I owe it to Stuart—I owe it to us—to determine if we can fix what has gone wrong between us . . . don't I?

I whimper and bury my head in my hands. With Stuart, there's familiarity and predictability. With Paul, there's passion and chemistry. The situation would make me laugh, if I didn't want to cry. How did I wind up in this position, anyway? It's certainly not what I expected or wanted. Yet somehow, in my effort to start living more fully, I've already found myself grappling to understand what are perhaps life's most profound questions of all: what is love, and who do I want to share that love with?

"Irene?" Paul calls out from the main room. "Is everything all right?"

I slowly lift my head. I have to tell Paul that Stuart is here.

Drawing in a breath, I start moving down the entryway. "Paul, there's something I . . ."

I trail off when I round the corner and wind up nearly running into Paul, who's coming back toward the entryway. Paul and I both halt just before we collide, so now we're standing face-to-face with only a breath of space between us. A hot, tingling sensation zips down my back. My heart starts beating even harder as Paul gazes down at me. Everything becomes very quiet.

Stuart. I need to tell Paul about Stuart.

I force myself to step back. "Before we do anything else, there's something extremely important I need to—"

A sound down the hallway echoes through the apartment like an explosion. Paul and I both spin in the direction from where it came. I suck in a breath when I see the door to Stuart's room getting opened from the inside.

Paul quickly steps forward, putting himself in front of me as he stares down the hallway. "What in the . . ."

Paul falls quiet when Stuart emerges from the bedroom wearing nothing but boxer shorts. Stuart does a double take and freezes, his eyes widening, when he sees Paul. There's a terrible pause.

"Let me guess: you're Paul," Stuart eventually remarks, shattering the stunned silence. He tips up his chin, his expression one of disdain as he observes Paul. "You're Irene's fiancé who's not actually her fiancé."

Paul doesn't respond for what seems like a long time. Standing behind him, I can see his torso rising and falling with his deep, measured respirations. At last, Paul steps aside, moving away from me while keeping his eyes on Stuart.

"You're Stuart," Paul says, his tone and expression giving away nothing.

My legs are shaking so badly that I have to reach out to the wall to steady myself. "Hey, guys, I think this whole thing seems stranger than it actually is." I use one hand to gesture toward the main room. "How about we all go sit down and discuss what's going on?"

Both Paul and Stuart turn my way. I look at Paul, and I see a flicker of hurt in his eyes before his gaze becomes distant and cold, almost as if he's looking through me. I flinch and shift toward Stuart, whose eyes are narrowing as they leap from Paul to me and back.

"Apparently, Paul doesn't think talking things over is important, Irene," Stuart remarks in an unmistakably condescending tone. "I, however, would be happy to participate in a discussion." He again glances pointedly in Paul's direction. "In fact, I think it will be extremely helpful for everyone here to know where they really stand."

"Stop it, Stuart," I snap. "Paul has done absolutely nothing wrong, and this isn't the time for you to—"

"Irene, you don't need to defend me," Paul interrupts, speaking in a low voice. Ignoring Stuart, his vacant eyes remain on mine. "I appreciate you offering to talk things through, but I think it's pretty clear what's going on. There's no need to take up anyone's time to discuss it further. I'll show myself out."

Paul strides into the main room and soon reappears with his computer bag over his shoulder. Keeping his attention focused straight ahead, Paul passes by me, goes to the entryway, opens the door, and steps outside. The sound of him shutting the door behind him causes my heart to feel as though it's going to break.

Twenty Three

"Paul, wait!"

My desperate, anxious plea echoes down the stairwell as I race to catch up with him. Paul doesn't slow his pace until he gets to the ground floor. He then turns around and watches as I finish flying down the stairs. I'm panting by the time I bound off the last step and rush across the foyer to meet him.

"Paul, I didn't know Stuart was planning to come here." I put a hand to my chest while I work to catch my breath. "I left the apartment early this morning, and when I got back, I found Stuart waiting outside the building. I was as shocked to see him as you were."

Paul's eyes flick up the stairwell. "Well, it clearly didn't take him long to make himself comfortable."

I exhale my frustration. "He came directly from the airport. He asked for a chance to catch up on some sleep before he and I talked."

Paul frowns. "Okay. But before he decided to take a nap, did he at least explain why he had a sudden change of heart and decided to come all the way to Italy to find you?"

"Yes, in fact." I push my hair from my face. "Apparently, Violetta posted on social media one of the pictures she took of you and me in St. Peter's Square. She even captioned the photo to indicate we were engaged. So when Stuart saw Violetta's post, he thought I was recklessly rushing into marriage with someone I had just met. He was worried about me, so he flew out here."

"He was worried about you," Paul repeats flatly. "What about you, Irene? Now that you've seen Stuart again, how do you feel about him showing up?"

"How do I feel?" I echo weakly. If only Paul understood how complicated his question is!

"Yes. How do you feel about Stuart?" Paul glances up the stairwell again. "More specifically, how do you feel about the potential for the two of you getting back together? Because, let's be honest, that's clearly what he's hoping will happen."

I continue gaping at Paul while floundering in vain to come up with a way to accurately answer his questions. How can I possibly describe to Paul the agonizing debate I've been having with myself ever since I met him a week ago? How can I convey to Paul that with every passing day I've become increasingly torn between duty and feelings? How can I make Paul understand that, in the course of just a few days, my entire understanding of love has been blown apart, leaving me scrambling to put the pieces back together? My heart is screaming one thing while my mind insists on another. My feelings belong to Paul, but my mind says I should talk with Stuart.

I groan inwardly, feeling utterly miserable. The truth is that it will be impossible to make Paul really understand this . . . because I barely understand it myself.

My silence, I know, is deafening. Paul takes a step back from me.

"Irene, I'm not going to try to persuade you or stand in your way. It's your life, and you need to decide how you want to live it. If you're not one hundred percent over Stuart, that's my cue to leave." Paul begins retreating for the door. "Thank you again for helping my grandparents. You've made more of a difference for them than you'll ever know." He opens the door, letting the intense heat and sunlight from outside fill the foyer. "I wish you the best. Thanks again."

Paul steps outside and shuts the door behind him.

***

I stop typing to check my phone for what is probably the hundredth time this hour. I sniff as more tears roll down my cheeks. A while ago, I texted Paul the final photos of the property in Florence, and I said I would email the write-ups as soon as I finished working on them. Paul hasn't replied.

I set the phone beside my laptop and look out the main room's windows. More tears fall, which I don't bother wiping away. Ever since the gut-wrenching moment when Paul left me behind this morning, I've been here in the apartment, completing the write-ups for Donato and Rita's property in Florence. Normally immensely enjoyable, the work today has been torture. Every word I type, and each photo I review, is a reminder of Paul and the amazing week we spent together. Making matters even worse is the fact that I'm also mourning the loss of Paul's family. How desperately I wish I could have told them goodbye and apologized for misleading them! It's too late now, though, and working on this project is like stabbing a dagger into my heart over and over again.

I check the time yet again. A little over two hours have gone by since Paul left. After he walked out, I remained in the foyer, consumed by an awful sense of numbness. With Paul's departure, all the passion, excitement, and hope that I had dared to feel lately—all the possibilities and dreams of what my new life might hold—left along with him. My instincts screamed that letting Paul go was a horrendous mistake, but I didn't go after him. I couldn't. Paul clearly didn't want me to. Also, I knew I had to talk with Stuart, who was waiting for me upstairs. So in my distraught and heartbroken state, I made my way back to the apartment. Stuart actually didn't have much to say about what had happened, other than he thought Paul reacted rather unprofessionally. Stuart then got another drink of water and went back to sleep.

Since that time, Stuart has continued napping, and I've done my best to keep myself occupied with work. All I can think about is Paul, though. Our last exchange mercilessly keeps replaying in my head while the memory of him walking away torments me. It feels completely wrong for us to be apart. I long to be near him. I want to see him smile. I want to hear him laugh. I want to be with Paul, yet Stuart is sleeping right down the hall . . . Stuart, my ex-boyfriend who flew all the way to Rome to find me.

More time passes as I work. After reviewing my completed write-ups for a final time, I pick up my phone and compose another text to Paul:

I finished the write-ups for Florence.
Is there an email address I could send them to, so you can have them?

I press the *send* button.

I wait. And wait.

When there's still no reply, I sigh despondently and resume peering out the window. What am I supposed to do now? No matter how much Paul despises me, I want to get the write-ups to him. Apparently, though, he has decided to cut off communication between us. I can't entirely blame him.

An idea hits me: I'll reach out to Violetta. I'll shoot her a private message on social media, giving her my phone number and email address. I'll ask for her email address in return, explaining that I want to send the write-ups to her. That way, she and Rafaele will have what I've written when they finish setting up the new website this afternoon.

Scooting my chair closer to the table, I use my laptop to get on the Internet. I log into my social media account—my first time doing so in a very long while—and I gasp aloud when the picture Violetta previously posted of Paul and me suddenly fills my screen. I stare at the photo in shock, my heart racing as I mentally flail to process the surreal sight that has met my eyes.

In the photo, I'm leaning into Paul as if it's the most natural thing in the world. Paul has his arm around me, and his smile is warm and genuine. We look so happy together. So connected. So content. Seeing us together causes another awful surge of remorse in my heart. Forcing myself to look away from the picture, I click on Violetta's account and send her a private message.

I hear the door down the hall being opened. I raise my eyes, and I watch as Stuart comes into the main room. He has brushed his hair, and he's wearing a crisp button-up shirt and jeans. I wait for a feeling of joy and excitement to fill me, like it always did whenever I saw Paul, but such a feeling never comes.

I manage something like a smile. "How did you sleep?"

Stuart takes a seat on the couch. "The bed wasn't comfortable at all. Thankfully, I was jet-lagged enough to fall asleep anyway." He peers around the room. "If that bedroom is any indication, I'm guessing staying in a place like this for a week has helped get your obsession with Italy out of your system."

I literally bite my tongue to stop myself from retorting, reminding myself that both Stuart and I need to be lenient right now. Getting up from the table, I make my way over to the couch and take a place beside him. I study Stuart's expression to get a read on what he's feeling, and I find that the look on his face is one I know well. It's the expression I've seen him adopt before countless business meetings. It's a look that tells me Stuart feels confident. Certain. Sure that he's right.

I turn away. In striking contrast to Stuart, I'm not sure at all.

Stuart rests one arm along the back of the couch and casually crosses a leg so his ankle is resting on the other knee. I know this pose of his, too. He's trying to appear approachable while maintaining an in-charge air. Apparently, one of Stuart's business meetings is about to begin, and this time, it's between us.

"So if you're ready, Irene," Stuart starts, adopting his workplace tone, "I think this would be a good time to commence with our discussion."

"All right." I face him squarely. "I—"

My phone begins ringing, causing me to jump. My heart starts flying inside my chest. Is it Paul?

I face Stuart again with an apologetic look. "Sorry. I forgot to put my phone on silent." I hastily get to my feet. "I'll go mute it."

I dash across the room and snatch up my phone from off the table. The caller ID indicates it's an international number. I'm shaking as I answer the call and put the phone to my ear.

"Hello?" I eke out.

"Irene?"

To my surprise, it's not Paul's voice I hear. It's Violetta's.

On the other side of the room, Stuart lets out a loud, exasperated sigh. He's obviously not pleased that I'm delaying our "meeting," but I don't care. I need to finish helping Donato and Rita.

I shift away from Stuart and face the window. "Hi, Violetta. Did you get my message?"

"Yes." Violetta sounds atypically subdued. "I do not think we are going to work on the website today, though."

I pause, a sense of unease rising up inside me. "What's wrong, Violetta?"

"Grandfather is sick."

Twenty Four

I slowly sit down on one of the chairs at the table. "Sick? What do you mean? What's wrong?"

"Grandfather says it is nothing to worry about." Violetta's voice is shaking. "But he does not look good. He is very pale."

"When did he get sick?" I inquire. I'm already compartmentalizing away my emotions as my mind shifts into emergency medicine mode. Right now, nothing matters but making sure Donato is all right.

"This morning, he told my grandmother he was not feeling well. He says he has nausea. That is why we are not going to work on the website today. Rafaele and I are at my grandparents' house to help while he is sick. Paulo is here, too."

"Paul is there?" I sit up taller. "He's in Pago Veiano?"

"Yes. We called him this morning to let him know about Grandfather, and Paulo got on the train right away. I thought you knew this, though." Violetta sounds puzzled. "Paulo said you were very busy with work, which is why you could not come to Pago Veiano with him."

"Oh. Right." I flinch. Everyone still thinks Paul and I are engaged, and this isn't exactly the time to disclose the truth. "What I meant was, Paul has already made it to Pago Veiano?"

"Yes. He just came from Benevento in a taxi."

No wonder Paul hasn't replied to my texts. It couldn't have been long after he left me this morning when he got the terrible call about his grandfather. Suddenly, he had far bigger and more important things to worry about.

I can't think about Paul right now, though. I need to remain focused on Donato.

"What else did your grandfather say about how he was feeling?" I ask Violetta, making sure to keep my voice calm and steady.

"He said he is tired. Also, the top of his stomach hurts."

My heart rate ticks up. "Violetta, is Paul nearby?"

"He is in Grandfather's room."

"Could you ask him to get on the phone, please?"

"Yes."

I hear what sounds like Violetta walking, followed by rustling and muffled talking. After what seems like a long time, Paul's voice hits my ear:

"Irene."

I get to my feet. "How's Donato?"

"He keeps saying it's nothing to worry about," Paul replies in a strained tone. "He insists it's just a stomach bug."

"How does he look to you?"

"He's sweaty. I don't know if it's something he ate or—"

"Paul, where's the nearest hospital?"

There's a beat before Paul replies, "Benevento."

"Your grandfather needs to go there."

"We've been wanting him to, but he keeps refusing." Paul sighs. He sounds exhausted. "So we've been trying to convince Gramps to go see the doctor in the village, at least, however he remains as stubborn as always. He keeps saying he's fine."

"Paul, your grandfather needs to go to the hospital," I repeat. "Now."

There's another pause, and then I hear Paul starting to walk fast.

"Irene, what are you thinking is going on?"

"I suspect Donato is having a heart attack."

"A heart attack?" Paul is clearly stunned. "But Gramps hasn't said anything about having chest pain."

"Sometimes heart attacks don't present with classic chest pain." I cradle my phone against my ear while I close my laptop and slip it into the computer bag. "Donato must get to the hospital. He needs an ECG, labs, and imaging. Get him to the hospital, Paul."

"I will. I'll make it happen."

Paul ends the call. I jam my cell phone into the pocket of my jeans, already calculating how long it will take me to get to Benevento. If I remember correctly, there's an afternoon train that departs from Termini, so if I leave right now, I should get to the station in time to catch it. Once I arrive in Benevento, I'll find a taxi to the hospital and—

"Irene, what are you doing?"

I let out a yelp, Stuart's question whipping me back to awareness of the world around me. I had actually forgotten Stuart was even here. I halt, already halfway out the room with my laptop bag hanging over one shoulder. I turn toward the couch and see Stuart getting to his feet.

"I'm going to Benevento." My eyes flick to the clock on the wall. "Paul is taking his grandpa to the hospital. If I leave now, I can catch the afternoon train and be there in a couple hours."

Stuart's mouth slowly falls open. His nostrils flare. "You're not seriously thinking about leaving me to go be with Paul and his family, are you?"

I raise my eyebrows. "What kind of a question is that?"

Stuart exhales and starts speaking in slow, deliberate tones. "Irene, I flew all the way over here to talk with you and make things right." He fixes a harder gaze upon me. "Are you really going to abandon me in order to go see a man who isn't even your real grandfather? Someone you hardly know?" He motions between us. "What about us?"

I stare back at him. He asks a good question—perhaps the most crucial question of all. What about Stuart and me?

Stuart comes across the room and places his hands on my shoulders. "I still don't know what happened this past week, but it's obvious you've been experiencing severe emotional distress. It's not surprising that while you were vulnerable and confused, you got swept up in a fantasy world with the people here. You convinced yourself that those people are important, but what's actually important is you and me." He brushes a hand along my cheek. "If you're ready to go anywhere, let's go home. Paul's grandfather is going to the hospital at your recommendation. He'll be in good hands. There's nothing more you can do for him. What happens to that old man from here on out—or to Paul or anyone else in that family—doesn't concern you. What matters is making things right between us."

I peer up at Stuart, processing what he said. Out of all the emotions I could be experiencing in this moment, what I begin feeling is an overpowering sense of relief. At last, the questions, confusion, and torment that have been swirling in my heart and mind disappear. Everything is suddenly crystal clear and calm. I know exactly what I want to do. I know how I want to live. I know what will bring me happiness. I know who I love.

"Stuart, I'm so glad we broke up," I say, my voice not wavering in the slightest. "I can see now that I'm not the right woman for you, and you're not the right man for me."

"What?" Stuart snatches his hands from my shoulders. "Irene, are you . . . rejecting me?"

I shake my head. "No, I'm not rejecting you. I'm simply acknowledging reality. We've never been in love. Not really." I pause, aware that I've never felt more certain about anything in my life. "We were a good team, Stuart. We were focused, supportive, and dedicated, but we weren't in love."

Stuart's eyes widen. He takes a step back, viewing me as though he has never seen me before. "Listen to yourself. You're making absolutely no sense."

"I'm making perfect sense," I reply simply. "I've always believed that love requires loyalty, dedication, and working together even when times are hard, and I still believe that's true. However, this past week, I've learned love is about even more than that. Love is passion and chemistry. Love requires excitement. Real love generates a powerful, unspoken connection between two people. Love leads to fun and laughter. Love needs spontaneity. Love means the freedom to show your emotions, express your thoughts and feelings, and be yourself. Love is . . . well, love is the most powerful, glorious thing in the world." I smile, and now it's my turn to motion between us. "You and I just don't have those things, Stuart. Our priorities are different, what we want out of life is different, and how we view love is different. I spent a long time trying to convince myself that we had a spark, but we don't. We never did."

Stuart takes another step back. His jaw clenches. "I know what this is really about. This is about that Paul guy you're infatuated with. After everything you and I have been through— after the years we've spent building our relationship—you're choosing to throw it all away for some fantasy with a guy you just met."

I calmly shake my head. "Actually, no, this isn't about Paul. This is about us, Stuart—rather, it's about realizing that you and I don't have what I'm looking for." I check the clock again. "I am going to go see Donato. He's a sweet, dear man, and though I only met him a few days ago, I care about him like he's part of my own family." I break off to work down a swallow. "As for Paul, after what happened today, I know he won't want to see me once this is over." I hike my laptop bag higher on my shoulder. "Now, if you'll please excuse me, I need to go."

Stuart is visibly fuming as he points at the door. "If you walk out of here, don't expect me to come looking for you again. Don't expect me to be willing to reconcile once you realize what a mistake it was for you to throw everything away for those strangers."

"Don't worry. I won't." I walk out of the room without looking back. "Goodbye, Stuart."

Twenty Five

The room is pin-drop silent. Crammed in Donato's hospital room with Paul and the rest of his family, I have to resist the urge to shrink back and hide from everyone's curious stares, which are all fixed solidly upon Paul and me. The moment has finally come. Paul and I are going to tell his family members the truth, and then I'll have to say goodbye to these wonderful people forever.

The last few hours have passed in an anxious, nerve-wracking blur. After leaving Stuart at the apartment this morning, I raced to Termini Station, barely managing to get there in time to buy a ticket and catch the afternoon train to Benevento. Upon arriving to Benevento, I used my language app to explain to a taxi driver that I needed a ride to the hospital. (Thankfully, the journey was much shorter than the last taxi ride I endured, so the near-death experiences were kept to a minimum.)

When I reached the hospital, I halted outside near the entrance, realizing for the first time that I hadn't even told anyone I was coming. I sent Violetta and Paul a text. A few

minutes later, Paul and Violetta stepped outside .
. . followed by an entourage of their uncles,
aunts, and cousins. Paul appeared shell-shocked
to see me, but we didn't have a chance to
exchange a word before his family members
started smothering me with hugs and kisses on
the cheek. Everyone was speaking loudly in a
mixture of Italian and English as I was
introduced to the family members I hadn't met
before. I was tugged inside. The flurry of activity
continued as everyone jammed into one elevator,
which took us to an upper floor of the hospital.
As we squeezed out of the elevator, I discerned
we had reached the waiting area of the cardiac
ICU. Luckily, a nurse who spoke excellent
English happened to be working, and she and I
were able to discuss Donato's case. Donato had
undergone an ECG upon arriving to the hospital,
was diagnosed with a heart attack, and had been
taken to the catheterization lab so the
cardiologist could attempt to open a blockage in
one of the main arteries of his heart.

Along with the rest of the family, I took a
seat on one of the vinyl-covered chairs in the
waiting area and settled in for what I knew
would be an agonizing wait. Rita tearfully kept
hugging and thanking me. She explained that
after Paul and I had spoken on the phone that
morning, Paul had disclosed that I was an
emergency medicine physician in the US, and
that I had advised for Donato to go to the
hospital. According to Rita, it was only because
of my recommendation that Donato finally
agreed to get evaluated. Through her tears of

gratitude, Rita said her husband would have died at home had it not been for me. All I could do was cry along with her—openly crying from relief that Donato had made it to the hospital in time, and privately crying from worry about whether or not he would survive his critical procedure.

At times, Paul and I exchanged looks across the waiting room, but we never had a good chance to talk. Through our silent communication, though, it was clear we mutually agreed to maintain our act of being engaged just a little bit longer, until Donato was safe.

At last, the cardiologist came to the waiting area to give the family the report: Donato's catheterization had been a success, and he was recovering in his ICU room. More tears, this time of relief and joy, were shed by all of us. Later, once Donato was deemed ready for visitors, the family was invited by his nurse to see him. I held back, intending to stay in the waiting area, but the family insisted I join them. I was deeply moved that they included me, yet I felt more guilty and more like an imposter than ever, knowing I was being included in something profoundly personal and private that I didn't truly deserve to be a part of.

Donato cried when he saw me. Taking my hands in his, he tenderly expressed his gratitude. As I gazed down into Donato's eyes, I knew I couldn't lie much longer. I exchanged another glance with Paul, and the slight nod of his head that he made in reply told me that he had reached the same conclusion: the time had come for us to tell everyone the truth.

Paul and I allowed the family a chance to relax, talk, eat, and enjoy one another's company for a while more. When I felt sure the acute roller coaster of emotions had passed for everyone, and Donato was securely out of danger, I sent Paul another look across the room. Solemn but steady, Paul stood and asked for everyone's attention. His family members fell into curious silence, waiting for Paul to go on. I went to Paul's side; though I dreaded what was coming, I wasn't going to leave Paul to explain things alone.

And now Paul and I are about to tell his family the truth.

"I have something important to tell you," Paul breaks the silence, speaking to his family in English. "Irene and I aren't engaged. We've never been engaged. We've never even dated, in fact. We met only a week ago at the airport, and it was by coincidence we met again when she rented the apartment in Rome."

In the stunned silence that follows, I can almost feel everyone working through a series of emotions: surprise, bewilderment, and uncertainty. Some of Paul's family members begin whispering; others keep staring at us with looks of total confusion.

"So there is not going to be a wedding?" Violetta sounds as though she might cry.

Francesca actually has tears in her eyes. "Irene will not be part of our family?"

Paul's stoical expression falters. He glances at me, and then he shakes his head and replies, "No, there isn't going to be a wedding."

"Why did you pretend?" Mateo asks. To his credit, he doesn't seem angry or accusatory— just puzzled.

Paul sighs and rubs the back of his neck. "Before answering that, I want to make something clear: this was entirely my idea. I bear complete and total responsibility for everything that happened."

"That's not true," I interject quietly, looking up at Paul. "I'm equally responsible. After all, I agreed to go along with the plan."

"No, Irene." Paul fixes a firm gaze upon me. "All you can be blamed for is for having the goodness of heart to agree to help my grandparents—even before you met them— when you learned they were in need." He rolls back his shoulders and resumes speaking to the others. "I asked Irene to pretend to be my fiancée because I didn't want Gramps and Grandma worrying about my love life any longer. Though they were well-intentioned, Grandpa and Grandma obviously had far more pressing matters to deal with, and the last thing I wanted was for them to carry any extra stress because of me." He uses one hand to rub his forehead, as though it's aching. Dropping his arm back to his side, he continues. "From the start, I knew pretending to be engaged was absurd, not to mention dishonest, but I decided that if I could take one worry off my grandparents' plate for a while, it would be worth it."

Paul breaks off from what he's saying to look directly at his grandparents. I follow his gaze. Donato is sitting up in bed and observing Paul and me with tears in his eyes. Rita is standing at her husband's bedside, holding Donato's hand and crying softly.

"I'm sorry," Paul tells them, his words catching. "I was going to tell you the truth once the estate crisis was over. I'm sorry I lied."

"Oh, my dear Paulo. Do not say you are sorry." Rita's voice shakes with emotion. "What you did was out of love. You were trying to help us, as you have always been so good to help us. We are lucky to have such a wonderful grandson. Thank you. We love you." She dabs her eyes with a handkerchief and then looks at me. "And you, Irene, are a kind, generous girl. We love you, too."

Emotion fills my throat, and I cannot hold back tears any longer. "And I love all of you," I reply softly. Peering around the room, I discover that most of Paul's family members are also crying as I go on. "Thank you from the bottom of my heart for being so welcoming and accepting. Your kindness has meant more to me than you'll ever know."

I look down at my hand. With a silent sigh, I slowly remove the fake engagement ring from my finger and put it in my purse. Drawing in another breath, I raise my head back to the group and say:

"Before I came to Italy, an experience at work inspired me to start trying to live more fully. Unexpectedly, this led to me breaking up with my boyfriend, Stuart. Wanting to clear my head, I impulsively boarded a plane to Rome. Needless to say, I arrived to Italy feeling lost, confused, and unsure." I shake my head and then smile warmly at the group. "Thanks to each of you, though, I've found the joy and meaning I was desperately seeking. You have let me feel like part of this amazing family, and I will cherish the memories of your kindness forever."

"Irene," Donato says quietly, "you *are* part of our family. You will always be part of our family." He breaks into an unexpected and rather impish-looking smile, and an amused gleam appears in his eyes. "You were welcomed into our family even when I knew you were not really Paulo's fiancée."

My eyebrows shoot up. "Wait . . . what?"

"What?" Paul says at the same time, staring at his grandfather with eyes that are wider than mine.

"What?" Rita echoes, turning to Donato. "You knew Paulo was not really getting married to Irene?"

"Of course." Donato chuckles. "Do you remember when Lorenzo told Paulo to kiss Irene? Paulo did not kiss Irene on the lips." He looks again at Paul, still grinning. "I know my Paulo, and I know he would kiss Irene on the lips if they were really engaged."

I blink a couple of times, and then I break into laughter. Turning to Paul, I ask, "Is your grandfather right?"

Paul is chuckling as he ruffles his hair with one hand. "Gramps is most definitely right."

Rita begins laughing, too. "Oh, my Paulo! You silly boy!"

Everyone else also erupts into laughter, the boisterous, joyful sound filling the room with warmth and happiness. I look Donato's way again, and he motions for me to come to his bedside. I approach, and when I get close, Donato takes my hand and says in almost a whisper:

"I do hope Paulo will marry you one day."

My cheeks get red, but before I can recover from my surprise enough to reply, the nurse who speaks English pokes her head into the room. Everyone quiets down and looks her way.

"I am sorry to interrupt, but visiting hours are over." The nurse pushes open the door all the way. "Only one family member is allowed to stay overnight."

"I'll stay," Paul offers. He turns to his grandmother. "You go home and get some rest. I'll make sure *Nonno* is all right."

Rita seems to hesitate. Her forehead creases with unmasked worry, and she looks to Donato.

"Yes, listen to Paulo: go home and rest," Donato tells his wife, patting her hand. "I will be fine."

"I will drive you home, *Mamma*." Francesca goes to Rita's side and shows a reassuring smile. "I will bring you back in the morning."

"We will all be back in the morning," Lorenzo adds with a grin, motioning around the large group and causing everyone to laugh once more.

The room comes alive again with activity and conversation as everyone begins wishing Donato a good night, kissing him on the cheek, blotting away their happy tears, chatting amongst themselves, and heading out the door. I don't get an opportunity to say anything else to Paul before I'm swept up in the wave of family members and pulled out into the hallway. With only Donato and Paul left in the room, the nurse steps out after the rest of us and closes the door behind her.

As the group of us starts making our way out of the treatment area, Francesca comes to my side and links her arm through mine.

"Paulo said you came all the way from *Roma* to be here, and he was very worried about you taking a train back by yourself tonight," Francesca tells me softly. "I assured him that you will be welcome to stay at my house."

I show her a sincere, appreciative smile. "Thank you for your kind offer. However, I'm going to stay here in the hospital tonight, just in case something comes up that I can somehow help with."

Francesca's brow furrows. "But where will you stay? Only one visitor is allowed."

"I'll sleep on the chairs in the waiting area." I can't help laughing. "Don't worry: it's definitely not the first time I've slept in strange places in a hospital."

Francesca's eyes brim with tears, and she gives me a hug. "Thank you."

"You're welcome," I whisper in return.

I accompany the family the rest of the way to the elevator bay, and I giggle as I watch them all cram into the one waiting elevator. I wave to the group, and everyone starts calling out jovial farewells and waving in return until the elevator doors close. And then everything gets very quiet.

I glance at the clock, shocked to discover how late it is. All at once, the physical and emotional fatigue of the day washes over me. I return to the waiting area, pick out a row of chairs that are lining the back wall, and sprawl across the chairs in a futile attempt to get comfortable. Before long, the lights in the waiting area are dimmed, marking the start of the overnight hours. For a long while, I stare at the wall. Eventually, my eyelids droop shut.

Twenty Six

My eyelids flutter open. As my vision comes into focus, the first thing I see is the vending machine on the far side of the waiting room; it's filled with drinks and candy bars I don't recognize. Blinking from the sterile glow of the overhead lights, which are now back on at their full brightness, I push myself up into a seated position and swing my legs off the chair. I twist my torso a couple of times to stretch. Yes, sleeping on hospital chairs in Italy is as uncomfortable as it is in the US.

A yawn escapes my lips as I peer around. The waiting room is empty. Except for the hum of the vending machine, the only sounds I hear are occasional overhead announcements spoken in Italian and the faint beeps of cardiac monitors coming from the treatment area. I catch a faint whiff of hospital food, which lets me know breakfast trays are being distributed to patients as the day begins.

I stand up, rub the wrinkles from my shirt, and check the time on my phone. It's a little after seven in the morning, and I'm guessing it won't be long before Donato's family members arrive. The thought causes a remorseful ache to fill my heart. I would love to see everyone, but it's for the best if I leave before they come. I've caused enough drama, and I've imposed on the family long enough. It's time to let them continue on together without me. Besides, I'm not needed here any longer. I'm confident Donato will make a complete recovery, Violetta and Rafaele have their grandparents' new website nearly finished, and most importantly, everyone knows the truth about Paul and me.

Paul.

His face fills my mind, and the ache in my heart deepens painfully. For good and for bad, the façade with Paul is over, too. I—

"Irene? What are you doing here?"

I jump when I hear his voice, and I spin around. Paul is stepping out from the treatment area, and his eyes are wide as he observes me. Paul's hair is messy, and his shirt is even more wrinkled than mine, yet he somehow looks more handsome than ever. My whole soul comes alive when I see him. However, I force myself to maintain an unaffected air. It will be better for both of us this way.

"Oh, hey." I casually motion toward the exit. "I was just leaving."

"Leaving?" Paul keeps staring at me as he draws closer. "Were you here all night?"

I nod. "I wanted to stay nearby, in case anything came up that I could help with."

Paul stops right in front of me. "You slept out here." He glances around the waiting area and runs a hand through his hair. "On these chairs. Alone."

"I promise it wasn't a big deal. I went through residency, remember?" I put on a grin. "I've spent plenty of call nights trying to get a few minutes of sleep on hospital chairs that are far less comfortable than these."

Paul exhales and focuses more intently on me. "Irene, thank you. With everything that has happened, I haven't even had a chance to say that to you yet." He breaks off to swallow. "You saved Grandpa's life."

"I'm glad I was able to help." My voice trembles with emotion. "I'm relieved he's okay."

The doors separating the waiting room from the treatment area swing open again, and Paul steps aside for a couple of nurses who appear to be going home after their overnight shift. Paul then puts his attention back on me.

"I'm heading to the cafeteria to get something to eat. Would you like to come?" Paul's lips curve up into a slight smile. "Admittedly, the cafeteria is about as glamorous as this waiting room, but at least it's a change in scenery."

I laugh. "Thanks for asking, but I'm all right." I remove my phone from my pocket. "I, um, actually have a couple time-sensitive work emails that I need to take care of."

"May I bring something back for you?"

I motion to the vending machine and force another light laugh. "Thanks, but if I get hungry, I'll just sample one of those undoubtedly nutritious items from over there."

Paul chuckles. "Okay, but please text me if you change your mind and decide you want anything." He takes a step to go, but then he stops and looks back at me. His expression grows serious. "By the way, I hope everything turned out well with Stuart. I mean that. You deserve nothing but happiness."

Paul doesn't wait for me to reply before he walks away. As soon as he's gone, the dam inside me bursts, and my feelings overflow. I stagger, putting a hand to my chest while I work to catch my breath. I keep staring in the direction that Paul went as my mind races. I could wait for Paul to return. I could tell Paul the truth about what happened with Stuart. I could explain to Paul everything I've come to understand about life and love. I could tell Paul the truth: that I love him with all my heart.

I won't tell him any of this, though. No matter how I feel, the fact remains that the relationship between Paul and me was built on a lie and formed only out of necessity. Worse than leading on his family, though, is the way that I led on Paul. I didn't mean to lead him on, of course, but it happened all the same. While Paul made his interest in me respectfully clear, I kept him in limbo as I foolishly tried sorting out things with Stuart. The uncertainty I imposed upon Paul was no better than the uncertainty that Stuart imposed on me. I can't ask Paul to trust me now, and I can't put him through any more pain. Because I love him, I have to leave him.

A ping from the elevator causes my insides to lurch. I hastily gather my things, slide to the doorway of the waiting room, and peek out into the corridor. It's empty. Taking my opportunity, I dash to the door that leads into the stairwell, slam it open, and make my way down to the ground floor. I poke my head out of the stairwell, confirming my route across the lobby is clear. I then race for the doors that lead outside. When I emerge into the sunshine, I start looking around for where to catch a taxi.

"Irene!"

I freeze when I hear Violetta's voice. Slowly, I turn around, putting on a smile when I see her coming toward me.

"Good morning, Violetta. How are you?"

"I am good. We just arrived to see grandfather." Violetta stops in front of me. She glances down at my bag. Her brow furrows. "Are you leaving?"

"Yes," I admit. "I'm leaving."

Violetta's eyes widen. "You mean, you are leaving for good?"

"I'm leaving for good. It's time."

Violetta whimpers and wraps me in a hug. "I will miss you, Irene."

"I'll miss you, too." I hold back a sob as I let her go. "Do me a favor: please don't say anything to anybody about my departure, okay? Once I'm out of the apartment, I'll text Paul to let him know he can advertise that it's available for rent again."

"Okay. I will not tell anyone." Violetta wipes away her tears. "May I ask where you are going?"

I smile gently at her. "I'm returning to Rome to pack, and then I'm taking a train to Florence. One good thing about waking up in the middle of the night in the ICU waiting room was that it gave me a chance to do a little online research. I miraculously found a vacancy in a hostel not too far outside of old-town Florence. I'll be staying there tonight and tomorrow night, and then I'll be flying home."

Violetta hangs her head. "I am so sad you are not really in love with Paulo. I was excited for you to marry him." She looks up at me again. Her expression evolves into a scowl. "Are you going to marry that Stuart man?"

"No," I reply, immediately and firmly. "I'm not in love with Stuart, and we're not back together."

"Good." Violetta crosses her arms. "Because I do not want you to marry him."

I actually laugh. "That makes two of us." I let my laughter fade away, and then I glance at the time on my phone and sigh sadly. "I have to go now. Thank you for everything."

Violetta hugs me again. "I will miss you."

"Me, too," I whisper as I watch her walk away. "Me, too."

Twenty Seven

My feet are sore, but my heart is full. While the warm evening breeze brushes my face, I lean forward against the waist-high wall at the center of the *Ponte Vecchio* and gaze out at the Arno River, reflecting on all the incredible sights I've seen here in Florence today: the Uffizi Gallery, the *Piazza della Signoria*, the Duomo with the nearby museum and baptistry, the Accademia, Pitti Palace, and the *Santa Croce* church. This jam-packed day has been overwhelmingly plentiful in culture, beauty, art, and history . . . and it has also been incredibly cathartic. Immersed in the enchantment of Florence, I've finally had a chance to catch my breath and start processing everything that has happened over this life-changing week.

The breeze starts tousling my hair, which is hanging freely past my shoulders. I sigh and continue observing how the evening's golden light is glistening upon the water. Behind me, countless tourists are passing by, browsing the shops that line the outer thirds of this famous, historic bridge. Aromas of delicious foods are wafting through the air. A street musician is playing an accordion. I close my eyes, soaking in all of it. Today has been nearly perfect.

Nearly.

I reopen my eyes, which are now tinged with tears. This day couldn't be perfect, of course, because of the unrelenting and agonizing ache in my heart. Leaving Paul yesterday—leaving the hospital without telling him goodbye or confessing that I love him—was the hardest thing I've ever done. The only other communication between us occurred yesterday afternoon after I boarded my train to Florence, when I sent Paul a brief text letting him know the apartment was available for renters once again. I didn't say anything else, but I knew that I didn't need to. I was certain Paul understood that I was leaving for good, even if he didn't understand the truth behind why.

I blink away my tears, adjust the way my purple purse is hanging across my sundress, and continue staring out at the river. Based on how low in the sky the sun is drifting, I know I should return to my hostel. However, I'm finding it impossible to walk away from this place. This view. This beauty. I don't want to let it all go. Not quite yet.

"*Buonasera, signorina,*" I hear a man behind me say in a rich voice. "That's a nice purple purse you have. May I ask where you got it?"

I go completely still. That man sounds exactly like Paul.

An instant later, it's like a lightning bolt hits me. My heart begins thundering inside my chest. My body starts tingling and trembling. Gripping the wall and hardly breathing, I slowly look over my shoulder. And I gasp.

Paul is standing only a few feet away from me.

Paul is watching me with a smile upon his lips but something intense and focused swirling in his dark eyes. Keeping his gaze locked on mine, Paul strides forward to join me at the wall. Stopping at my side, he lets his smile disappear as he shifts his attention to the water and rests his hands on top of the wall. In shock, all I can do is stare at his profile, taking in the stunning, unexpected, breathtaking sight of him: how his thick, dark hair is being rustled by the breeze; the handsome features of his chiseled, cleanly shaven face; and the way his dark shirt and jeans fit his muscular frame. It's as though this is some sort of glorious dream, yet I know it's real. Paul is here. He's here with me.

I finally recover from my shock enough to find my voice. "How in the world did you . . ." I trail off, still too overcome to finish my own sentence.

Paul draws in a slow breath, his eyes still surveying the river. "This morning, Violetta told me that you were planning to visit Florence before you returned home." He pauses, and then he turns my way. "I have no idea how many hostels there are in and around Florence, but I've probably visited every single one of them today, trying to find you."

I stare at him. A spark of hope that I've been too scared to let myself believe in suddenly catches fire in my heart. My pulse rises even more. I feel breathless. Is this really true? Am I understanding Paul correctly? Is this actually happening?

Gazing at Paul through the new tears that are brimming in my eyes, all I can clumsily utter in response is, "Why didn't you just send me a text?"

Paul is studying me closely. "If I had sent you a text, would you have responded?"

I hesitate. "No," I admit, a tear escaping down my cheek. I look away. "I desperately would have wanted to respond to you, but I wouldn't have."

Paul reaches out a hand and gently brushes my cheek, wiping away my tear. His touch sends shockwaves through me, causing my body to awaken with desire. My eyes leap back to his.

"Why did you leave Benevento the way that you did?" Paul's fingers brush my cheek once more, this time in a more lingering way, before he lowers his arm back to his side. "Why didn't you say goodbye?"

I sigh remorsefully. "You had already been put through so much because of me, and I didn't want to cause you any more confusion or pain. So I decided it would be easier if I left quietly."

Paul inhales and exhales. He then takes a step closer to me, his eyes suddenly aflame. "Nothing was going to make your departure easy,

Irene. Nothing could ever make it easy to be apart from you. Because I love you."

His words soak in, and then my heart leaps and starts beating wildly. My eyes get wide. "You . . . you do?" I whisper as an incredible sense of total ecstasy consumes me. "You love me?"

Paul breaks into a captivating smile. "Yes, Irene, I love you. I started falling in love with you the moment when you fought with me about that outlet at the airport." He searches my face while he slowly—tenderly and cautiously—takes my hands in his. "This morning, Violetta also told me that you had said you weren't in love with Stuart. That was when I allowed myself to hope. That was when I knew I had to find you. I needed to know if I had a chance." His thumbs caress the backs of my hands, sending exhilarating sparks up my arms. "Surely, though, you must have known—you must have sensed—how desperately in love with you I am."

I stare into Paul's eyes, drowning in his soulful gaze, never wanting to look away. I have to keep telling myself this isn't a dream. This is real. This is real life. This is *my* life.

"I hoped you loved me, and yet I feared you loved me." My words catch with emotion. "I don't fear anymore, though. I realize now how I want to live my life. I understand what it truly means to be in love. Most importantly, I've discovered *who* I love, and it's you, Paul. I love you. "

Paul falls completely still, and then, while he continues holding my hands as his eyes search the depths of mine, he steps even nearer to me. Our bodies are nearly touching now, and the heat of his closeness unleashes more unbridled desire within me. Tingling sensations are rippling down my spine, and my breaths are growing shallow as the magnetic pull between Paul and me becomes overpowering.

I see Paul's respirations quicken. My heart starts pounding with anticipation. Paul releases my hands and encircles his arms around my waist. He suddenly draws me in against him, leans down, and passionately begins kissing me. Elation unlike anything I've ever felt before fills my soul as our lips intertwine. Wrapping my arms around Paul's neck, I return his fervent kisses, sharing with him all the feelings that have been building up inside me since the moment we met.

When our kiss is done, Paul keeps holding me in his strong, secure embrace as he tips back his head to see right into my eyes. "Irene, we have a chance to move forward together and start living the life we want to live. Will you have me?"

I'm crying with pure joy as I break into a smile. "Yes, Paul. I will have you. I want nothing more than to have you at my side."

Unable to resist, I stand on tiptoe, grab Paul's shirt, and pull him down so my lips press against his once more. Paul moans with desire and holds me against him even more tightly, kissing me fearlessly in return.

I collapse fully into Paul's arms, letting him hold me. Just then, the street musician begins playing another song on the accordion, and the romantic melody encircles Paul and me as if the music is meant just for us.

Paul adjusts his hold around my waist, and he takes me by the right hand. "Would you care to dance, Irene Thatcher?"

I gaze up at him, relishing the sight of Paul's dark eyes shining in the lamplight. "There's nothing I would rather do, Paulo Conti."

With beautiful music filling the air, and the gorgeous hues of sunset illuminating the sky, Paul and I start swaying together to the music. I rest my head against his chest, certain Paul and I will hear a perfect melody playing for us throughout the rest of our lives.

Epilogue

"Okay, I want to go back to my favorite part of the story: you set off an emergency alarm in the apartment? In the middle of the night?" Adrienne starts laughing quietly, like she has been doing throughout dinner. "While you were taking a shower?"

"Yep." I resume laughing along with her. "Once I got over the horror of thinking I had woken up everyone in the building, I was convinced I would die with embarrassment when Paul burst in to make sure I was okay. Things only got worse when I realized I wasn't wearing anything but a towel."

Adrienne laughs harder, quickly using her napkin to cover her mouth and muffle the sound. I exchange a playful glance with Paul, who's seated beside me and has his arm draped casually over the back of my chair.

"I certainly didn't mind," Paul says to me in a low voice, his tone making my insides quiver and my cheeks blush.

I turn back to Adrienne, who's seated across the restaurant table from Paul and me. Earlier this evening, Adrienne was understandably stunned into speechlessness when she saw me walking into the restaurant while holding hands with Paul. Once Adrienne recovered from her shock, I explained to her that she and I had a lot to catch up on, and I had figured it was better to do so in person. After Adrienne and Paul were introduced, and the waiter led us to our table, Paul and I began telling her our story. When Paul and I finished our tale, Adrienne surprised me by stating she was glad I had ended things with Stuart. In a thoughtful, insightful way, Adrienne admitted she had never thought Stuart was good enough for me. I couldn't have agreed with her more.

Though it has only been a week since Paul and I returned from Rome, our time together has been nothing short of magical, and my life has already changed for the better in more ways than I can count. For the first time, I'm doing things I want to do—things I wouldn't have taken time to do previously—and in the process, I'm discovering the wonder of things like stargazing and curling up by the fire with a book. Each day, I'm gaining a deeper appreciation of the importance of embracing life's opportunities and moments, because those are what life is really all about. Of course, more than anything, with Paul at my side, life has become far more rich and fulfilling than I could have ever dreamed of. For the first time, I'm experiencing what it's like to truly be in love and to be loved in return.

Adrienne picks up the dessert menu that the waiter just placed on the table. "So are we going to top off this fabulous meal with dessert?"

"Absolutely," I say.

Adrienne grins at Paul and me. "Let me guess: gelato?"

Paul chuckles. "Sounds great."

"I agree." I smile up at the waiter. "I'll have three scoops, please."

The waiter next takes Adrienne and Paul's orders, and then he collects the menu and saunters away. We're soon served, and I dive into my dessert without regret, savoring every bite.

After our meal is over, the three of us leave the restaurant, and Paul and I walk Adrienne to her car. Adrienne gives me a hug and whispers in my ear:

"I totally approve. I'm so happy for you, Irene."

"Thank you," I whisper in return.

Adrienne gets in her car and drives away, giving us a wave before she disappears from view down road. Paul and I then make our way over to his car, and he opens the door for me. I slide inside. Paul gets into the driver's seat, and just as he shoves the keys into the ignition, his phone starts to buzz. Paul pulls his phone from his pocket, and when he views the screen, he smiles.

I'm watching him curiously. "What is it?"

"Take a look at this." Paul's smile broadens as he turns his phone toward me.

I lean in closer. To my delight, I see that Paul has just received a text from his father,

Alonzo. The text includes a group photo of Donato and Rita, Alonzo and Paul's mother, and Paul's numerous extended family members. They're all standing outside the rental apartment in Venice, and they all look happy and, thankfully, healthy.

"That's so wonderful!" I exclaim.

"It wouldn't have happened, if it weren't for you." Paul puts away his phone and kisses me.

I stroke his cheek. "I think your grandparents' extremely intelligent, helpful, resourceful grandson may have also played a role in the success of the venture."

Paul kisses me again. "I actually have more good news. I was going to wait to share it with you, but this suddenly seems like the perfect time."

"Really?" I sit up. "Yes, please tell me."

"Both the Venice and Florence apartments, as well as the rentals in Rome, are already reserved through the end of the year."

"Already?" I clasp my hands to my chest. "That's wonderful! I . . ." I pause, peering at Paul more closely. "So what's that mischievous gleam in your eyes all about?"

Paul takes my hands in his. "Well, I happen to know the guy who reserved the rental property in Florence for Christmas."

I do a double take and then break into an amazed smile. "You mean . . . ?"

Paul gazes right into my eyes. "What do you say to Christmas in Florence?"

"Yes. Absolutely. One hundred percent yes."

Paul kisses me once more. "I love you."

"I love you, too," I sigh dreamily.

We share a long, exhilarating look before Paul starts driving out of the parking lot. I'm still smiling as I watch out the window, blissfully lost in thought. Once upon a time, I assumed I knew what life was all about, but Paul has helped me realize it's so much more. I cannot wait to see where our life together will lead.

Acknowledgements

"It takes a village," it's often said, and in the case of this novel, the phrase couldn't be more true. A few years ago, my husband and I took a trip to Italy, and a last-minute change of itinerary found us in the little village of Pago Veiano, the home of his ancestors. Words cannot describe the welcome, love, and generosity his distant relatives showed us. I am forever blessed and grateful that they let me feel like part of the family. As soon as I got home from that trip, I penned this story in their honor. I owe endless thanks to Susan, Giuseppe, Giuseppina, Nicolangelo, Chiara, Michele, Angela, Martina, Carmela, Luigi, Donata, Donato, Rita, and Mauro - all who so graciously helped us arrange and enjoy our amazing visit.

Thank you, Madeline for a two-hour phone call about a back-cover blurb and just about everything else. You are the best.

To my readers, once again I thank you from the bottom of my heart. Thank you for letting me share my stories with you.

My endless thanks to my stalwart proofreaders and ARC readers.

To Pip, thanks for showing us you're actually just a big softie who loves scratches behind the ears.

Thank you, Nick, for being my best friend, my travel companion, and as always, my best spur-of-the-moment story advisor. I love you.

About the Author

TJ Amberson hails from the Pacific Northwest, where she lives with her husband, the most wonderful guy and best on-demand story advisor ever. When she's not writing, TJ might be found enjoying a hot chocolate, pretending to know how to garden, riding her bike, video editing, or playing the piano. She loves to travel. She adores all things cozy and holiday-themed. And she thinks there's no such thing as too much seasonal décor.

With a love of several genres, TJ Amberson writes sweet (clean) romance and romantic comedies with happily-ever-afters, and clean fantasy stories for teens and advanced tween readers.

www.tjamberson.com

Facebook: authortjamberson
Instagram: tjamberson
YouTube: realtjproductions
Pinterest: tjamberson

Made in United States
North Haven, CT
23 June 2022

20551739R00186